Dancing on
Tisha B'Av

Stonewall Inn Editions

Buddies by Ethan Mordden
Joseph and the Old Man by Christopher Davis
Blackbird by Larry Duplechan
Gay Priest by Malcolm Boyd
Privates by Gene Horowitz
Taking Care of Mrs. Carroll by Paul Monette
Conversations with My Elders by Boze Hadleigh
Epidemic of Courage by Lon Nungesser
One Last Waltz by Ethan Mordden
Gay Spirit by Mark Thompson, ed.
As If After Sex by Joseph Torchia
The Mayor of Castro Street by Randy Shilts
Nocturnes for the King of Naples by Edmund White
Alienated Affections by Seymour Kleinberg
Sunday's Child by Edward Phillips
God of Ecstasy by Arthur Evans
Valley of the Shadow by Christopher Davis
Love Alone by Paul Monette
The Boys and Their Baby by Larry Wolff
On Being Gay by Brian McNaught
Parisian Lives by Samuel M. Steward
Living the Spirit by Will Roscoe, ed.
Everybody Loves You by Ethan Mordden
Untold Decades by Robert Patrick
Gay and Lesbian Poetry in Our Time by Carl Morse
 and Joan Larkin, eds.
Reports from the holocaust by Larry Kramer
Personal Dispatches by Joan Preston, ed.
Tangled Up in Blue by Larry Duplechan
How to Go to the Movies by Quentin Crisp
Just Say No by Larry Kramer
The Prospect of Detachment by Lindsley Cameron
The Body and Its Dangers and Other Stories by Allen Barnett
Dancing on Tisha B'Av by Lev Raphael
Arena of Masculinity by Brian Pronger

Stonewall Inn Mysteries

Death Takes the Stage by Donald Ward
Sherlock Holmes and the Mysterious Friend of Oscar Wilde
 by Russell A. Brown
A Simple Suburban Murder by Mark Richard Zubro
A Body to Dye For by Grant Michaels
Why Isn't Becky Twitchell Dead? by Mark Richard Zubro

Dancing on Tisha B'Av

Lev Raphael

St. Martin's Press/New York

(Credits continued on page 232.)

DANCING ON TISHA B'AV. Copyright © 1990 by Lev Raphael. All rights reserved. Printed in the United States of America. No part of this book may be used or reproduced in any manner whatsoever without written permission except in the case of brief quotations embodied in critical articles or reviews. For information, address St. Martin's Press, 175 Fifth Avenue, New York, N.Y. 10010.

Library of Congress Cataloging-in-Publication Data

Raphael, Lev.
    Dancing on Tisha b'Av / Lev Raphael.
      p.   cm.
    ISBN 0-312-06326-1 (pbk.)
    1. Gay men—Fiction. 2. Jews—Fiction. I. Title.
    [PS3568.A5988D3 1991]

91-21613
CIP

First U.S. Paperback Edition: November 1991
10 9 8 7 6 5 4 3 2 1

For Andrew,
who knows that "one must be serious about something,
if one wants to have any amusement in life."

Contents

" 'To speak it in words is to see the possibility emerge.' "

Players
Don DeLillo

Dancing on Tisha B'Av

Brenda was already used to the men, sitting across the chest-high wooden *mehitzah* that separated them from the women, saying they needed one more "person" to make the *minyan* of ten, while she and sometimes as many as six other women might be there. Like now, suspended in summer boredom, their conversation as heavy with heat as the sluggish flies whispering past in the small gray-walled shul on the musty ground floor of the Jewish Center. Sometimes they all waited half an hour before continuing with services, for a man, any man, to be tenth. It amused her that even the dimmest specimens counted when she didn't: shabby unshowered men who shouted rather than sang, and read Hebrew as if each line were the horizon blurred by heat; yawning men whose great round gasps for air seemed their profoundest prayers; men who sneeringly hissed game scores (and had to be hushed) to show how immune they were to the ark, to anything Jewish and sacred.

Sometimes, on the other side, her brother Nat corrected them and said, "Man. You mean another man." And she smiled at his embarrassment for her.

Though raised Conservative, she had come to like the Orthodox service. Here the purpose was prayer, not socializing, showing off Judaic knowledge, filling the shul, or even getting away from the kids for a morning. People sometimes joked, but the service itself was serious. At the faculty-dominated shuls in their university town, the persistent chitchat and laughter were like the desperate assertion of rationality and control in the face of what was mysterious—as if to let go, to be silent and feel, would be an admission of nakedness and shame.

"Too many Ph.D.s" was Nat's comment, and she, a graduate student in history, had felt accused. A junior, Nat had been attending the Orthodox services for two years, and his commitment was as fierce and sullen as the clutch of a baby's hand on a stolen toy.

Nat went out now to practice his Torah portion in another room. Thin, with the twitching walk of a jerky marionette, and that pale and narrow face, he seemed a genetic rebuke to their handsome family, a warning that all gifts were uncertain. As a boy, he'd been aloof, watchful, building castles out of blocks and bricks, pretending to be powerful, a knight. He never cried, never apologized. Spanking him was pointless, scolding absurd. The little mean eyes just shut inside, his face grew stupid and closed.

"*Red tsu a vant!*" their father would shout in Yiddish—"Talk to a wall!"—uneasily admiring the stubborn boy. The stocky pharmacist would peer down at Nat, hands clenched, as if wishing they were equals and could fight.

Nat was sullen and silent until he went into theater in high school, stunning Brenda with his intensity as Tom in *The Glass Menagerie*. He had felt, to her, more maimed by life than the girl playing Laura. Onstage, his walk, his thin face were larger, more compelling; his *authority* was beautiful. It had been the same here at State the few times he did a show.

What did their parents think?

Their mother said, "He takes makeup very well, it doesn't look like him."

His father, when he didn't fall asleep in the darkened auditorium, smirked, "Sure . . . *here* he can act—so what? Try Broadway!"

They were just as supportive of Nat's slow move to Orthodoxy, his father shaking his head. "What I gave him isn't enough—he has to go to *fremdeh menshen*, strangers, to be a Jew." And their mother wondered if Nat would be allowed to touch any woman he wasn't married to, and was he going to Israel to throw stones at cars that drove on Saturday?

How much this all affected Nat, Brenda didn't know. He had

always refused to acknowledge successes as well as failure, living, she thought, in stubborn exile, unreachable, untouched.

Nat had learned to tie his shoes too early, was too neat and alphabetical in his approach to life. It was as if saying "First things first" and making points in conversation by clutching successive fingers could order and control the world. He read Torah in a dry triumphant chant as if the letters piled around him in tribute. He was a vegetarian and drank only mineral water and herb teas. He ran seven miles a day, even in the winter. He loved men.

Brenda had known this, known something, for too long. When she was sixteen and Nat eleven, she found a folder in his pile of *Life, Car & Driver,* and *Reader's Digest,* crammed with pages sliced from magazines, all ads. They were men whose exquisite eyes and hands and hair, whose tough hard bodies shot one hopeless accusation after another: You are not beautiful—you never will be. Nat had distilled this terrible poison from harmless magazines.

It was that year Brenda found an open notebook on his desk in which he'd written out pages of new names for himself, first and last, a parade of loathing.

And worse, because she was worried, she saw too much. She noticed that her mother's closet door would often be closed when her mother—who always left it open—was out for an afternoon and Nat had been alone. It was their stale family joke: her mother and closets, cabinets, drawers.

"Yes," her father would growl. "Let everything in the bread box see what's happening in the kitchen they shouldn't get lonely."

At first, she thought that Nat was just snooping in that rich confusion, as she had done years before. But then, allowing herself no vision of what she suspected, Brenda set little traps for him: a purse hung just so, a dress belt folded under. And she learned that Nat did something with Mom's clothes: put them on? pretended he was beautiful, like her? What did plucking earrings from the shiny madness in her mother's jewel box *mean* to him?

Before these discoveries, Nat had been annoying to her, or unimportant, or sometimes, unexpectedly cute. Suddenly, he was dangerous, unknown. In the next years, she'd wait for Nat's oddities to burst from the neutral box of his silence like trick paper snakes, but he was only more sullen, blighting family dinners like the suspicion of a pitiless disease. Her father gave up cursing and her mother shrugged, as if Nat were a strange country she'd never been able to find on a globe. When her mother did talk about Nat, she had the brisk bored sound of a librarian stating facts that anyone could check.

"He doesn't have wet dreams," her mother announced, folding laundry in the basement. "I've checked his sheets, Bren."

Brenda, nineteen then, tried to think of something adequate to her surprise.

And when Nat was in high school: "Bren, why doesn't he date more? I think he's afraid of sex. Your father said he blushed when they talked about condoms."

"Wait till eleven," a man on the other side was saying now. "We always wait."

"Forget it." That was Nat. "I called this week and no one's in town." He listed all his calls.

She knew that Nat was right; the Orthodox *minyan* drew on a very small group of Jews, and strangers rarely joined them.

The women behind her stirred the pages of their prayer books as if scanning merchandise in a dull catalog. They were mostly the bleak girlfriends of men who ran the *minyan*, wearing artless, dowdy plain clothes and talking after services about movies or food. She imagined they would welcome marriage and the children who would release them from regular attendance. She thought of them as The Widows, because though in their mid-twenties, they already seemed isolated, like survivors of historic loss.

Around her, the heat, spread by a weak ceiling fan, settled like a film of soot or car exhaust; her light dress, sandals, and short hair didn't help her feel cool.

"Brenda, you look very nice today."

Clark, the law student who looked like Al Pacino and thought he was Bruce Springsteen, hung over the *mehitzah*. He was from Bloomfield Hills, and always talked to her with the smugness she remembered in adolescent cliques, as if his good looks and hers bound them in undeniable complicity.

Before she could say anything, Nat was back at the door, bleating, *"Gut shabbos!"*

At the chipped bookcase with the prayer books and Bibles stood a tall tanned man who looked thirty to her, blue-eyed, with thick close-trimmed mustache and beard that seemed very black above the tan summer suit and white shirt. He slipped a prayer shawl from the wooden stand, covered his head with it as he said the blessing, and found a seat up near the front of the men's side, shaking hands, nodding. After finding out the man's Hebrew name (for when he'd be called up), Nat marched to the lectern.

It was a blessing to be the tenth man, she thought, as services continued with unexpected excitement. They sang and chanted like forty people, not fourteen. When there wasn't a *minyan* and the Torah had to stay in its plainly curtained ark, she felt a fierce longing to see it borne around the shul to be touched with prayer books, prayer shawl fringes, or kissed like a bride as some of the men did.

When the stranger, Moshe Leib ben Shimon haLevi, Mark, was called to the Torah for the second blessing, he loomed over the lectern like a dark memorial in a way that dried her throat; his back seemed broad and forbidding. But his voice was sweet, smooth, rising and falling with the self-indulgent sadness of a Russian folk song. He sight-read the first portion without a mistake. They were all impressed.

Nat, always well prepared, read badly today. He made mistakes even she could catch, and it was painful watching him struggle with easy words. The silver pointer in his hand usually paced serenely along each squarish path of Hebrew, but now it was as listless as an uninspired divining rod. She looked away from him, from her Bible. Nat would probably tell people after services that he was tired, and because he never read poorly, no one would doubt him. She hoped.

What did people say about him? Could they tell?

"He should date more": his mother's verdict. Mrs. Klein often mentioned friends' daughters to Nat at holiday dinners as if genially passing a liqueur, but to Brenda she had recently said, "Is he gay?"

"No!"

"You're sure—?"

"*Mom.*"

Her father had said nothing directly or indirectly to Brenda; if it concerned him that Nat had hardly dated, he probably classed that with Nat's habitual stubbornness. Besides, she imagined her father sneering, "With that *punim*, that face, who would want him?"

For Brenda, Nat was Coronado discovering the Seven Cities of El Dorado everywhere—in the pumping bare thighs of bikers on campus, the ripe curves of jeans-tight asses, the heavy twin swells of runners' chests under cool molding cotton—flash after flash of heaven-sent gold in hundreds of men around town. But he was a Coronado without armor, without guides, troops, provisions, maps, or even a commission. He had only his hunger.

She never spoke about this with Nat, never asked about dates or parties, had no idea what his life was like. Nat lived in his dorm and she in her apartment in town, with the huge ecstatically land-scaped campus between them. They had lunch sometimes, she phoned him, they met at services and occasionally drove home to Southfield together, but she seldom mentioned that her brother was "up at school."

She was ashamed.

In her freshman year, back at the University of Wisconsin in Madison, on her coed floor, there had been a lovely dark-haired boy named Tom who did up his single room with Japanese fans, silk scarves, and other gentle souvenirs of summers abroad. Cool, quiet, musical, literate, he was the eye of a storm: doors banged, voices hushed and growled, or cracked with laughter, and the jocks on their floor simmered like guard dogs on maddening chains. One morning, a camping ax was found buried in Tom's door, the handle chalked, for clarity, "Faggot Die." Tom moved off campus, and that was what she feared—violence in the night, a scandal.

Having drifted away during the Torah reading, she didn't reen-ter the service, but stood and sat with everyone and prayed aloud mechanically as if she were in an educational filmstrip, each action large and stiff. Mark, the stranger, had asked to do the last part of the service, and his Hebrew was fluent in the thick summer air.

On the way out after the last hymn, Mark wished her *Shabbat Shalom.*

"You read well," she said as they milled at the table set with kiddush wine and cakes in the little social hall.

And then Nat was there, grinning, his pale face spattered with excitement. After blessing the wine, Nat pulled Mark aside to talk about the next week's Torah portion.

Helen, Clark's cousin, bore down on Brenda. With her thin

ugly legs and heavy shifting hips and rear, she resembled a pack
mule struggling up a hill.

"*Gut shabbos*," Helen murmured, round face doleful, as if she
was passing on unpleasant gossip. "Isn't he terrific?"

"Mark?"

"Uh-huh. What a *spa.*"

"Spa . . ."

"Sure, he works out . . . look at his chest, those shoulders.
Yum."

Brenda watched them; Mark with the cool, one-dimensional
beauty of a brass rubbing, Nat grasping at him with a sickly smile.
She ate a dry piece of pound cake.

There were at least a thousand Jewish students on campus, but
hardly any came to the Orthodox *minyan*, which was a mix of
graduate students, one or two shabby faculty members, and several
university staffers. Mark's arrival was exciting, Brenda knew, because
he could take some of the burden of leading services from Clark
and Nat and the others who sometimes felt like prisoners of their
obligations. An assistant to the registrar, Mark spoke little about
himself, but seemed to have for Nat the impact of an analyst whose
silence and concern at last permit an entrance to oneself. Nat told
Brenda that he talked about his acting, his Russian and French
classes, his desire to enter the foreign service, about everything. He
was like a child dragging pretty treasures from pockets, under the
bed, from drawers, to entertain, attract, possess a fascinating friend.

Brenda saw in Nat, for the first time, a resemblance to their
mother. Generally, Mrs. Klein was like an antiques dealer displaying
a find—herself—with chic reverence. She was slim, wide-eyed,
fashionable even in a bathrobe, especially in a bathrobe whose rough
folds set her off like a pretty girl's plain best friend. But sometimes
their mother emerged from this haze of self-absorption to talk with
merciless charm to strangers or her children's "little friends." She
asked them endless unimportant questions until they found themselves like flood victims forced onto the roof of their self-possession,
praying for the waters to subside.

Brenda saw Nat talking with that intensity to Mark one Sunday
afternoon two weeks after that first Shabbat, at a restaurant in town,

saw him through the wide front window, face twisted and alive, fingers plucking at a sugar packet. Mark sat deeply back from him, sky-blue tennis shirt open at a dense-haired throat, heavy fine arms crossed, a smile, some kind of smile nestled in the mustache and the beard. Mark was not just passively beautiful, she realized as she hurried on to buy her *Times* at the chain bookstore down the block, not a man to merely watch, admire, but warm, receptive, inviting. It was the lush curves of shoulders, chest, the gleaming hair and beard, the hard-lined nose and high cheekbones, the paintable mouth.

Not her type at all, too dramatic, too intense. The men she dated were at most "cute," and their ideas about Third World debt or German reunification gave them more color than the way they walked or dressed or were.

"They don't scare you," Nat had concluded, and it was too obvious for her to deny.

Mark and Nat started running together at the high school track near her apartment, like a boy and his puppy eager to show off how fast it moved. Mark's legs were hairy and dark, strong admonitions to the pale, weak.

They'd stop at her place afterward for water, to towel off, talking about the weather and their wind, old injuries. Mark spoke even then as if emerging from a past that wasn't his but something he had learned, borrowed details of a spy. He sat on the floor, back against her gray-green sofa bed, legs out, relaxed, holding the tumbler to his face and neck. Nat looked wild and flustered, as if he couldn't decide whether to yell or leap or cry.

In late July, when the whole state settled into a heat wave that seemed as inexorable as lava sweeping down a barren slope, Nat made an announcement to her one Friday afternoon.

"Mark has the use of a place on the lake, near Saugatuck, and he invited me to go next Saturday night after Shabbat and spend a day or two at the beach." Nat's face was so surly that she saw him as a boy again, daring their parents with his refusal to eat beans, or wash his hair, or turn from the television.

"Does he know you're in love with him?"

Nat gave her a liar's grin, stalling. "What?"

She looked down at her cool plate of deviled eggs, potato salad, tabouli, as if the food were an exhibit in a museum case, proof of customs stranger than one's own.

"What?"

She felt guilty now, tight-eyed. "If he's not gay, he's being very cruel."

Watching Nat lean away as if the sprigged tablecloth were dangerous somehow, she understood how strong soft people really were—they could retreat across vast plains of silence, disappear.

"I wrote him a poem," Nat brought out heavily, a pauper facing his last, most precious coin. And when he turned away, she jerked up from her chair to crouch by her brother, hold him, and ease the ugliness of tears.

Mark called after Nat was gone, to invite himself over that evening. From Nat, she'd learned that he and Mark had spent many nights together since the first Shabbat in June, at Mark's apartment near the university and then the one he moved to in a nearby town.

Mark wore white jeans, Top-Siders, and a white Lacoste, as if to show her he was normal, American, no threat. But sitting in her small cramped living room, he looked like a model posed in an unlikely spot to throw his beauty into high relief.

They drank coffee.

"I was married," Mark offered. "Nat didn't say? In New York. We split up two years ago; I moved to Philadelphia, then here." He nodded like an old man in a rocker whose every motion confirms a memory.

"Children?"

"We couldn't."

She wished, in the quiet, for a clock that chimed, a noisy refrigerator, dogs outside, something to ease the tension in her neck and hands. She imagined her parents there: Dad scornful, incensed; Mom peering at Mark with distaste, curious, purring, "But he's handsome, don't you think?" Closing her eyes, Brenda saw the ax saying "Faggot Die" like the afterimage of a too-bright bulb.

Nat had pursued Mark, she knew, even if Nat didn't, so there was no blame for her to spatter on the canvas of Mark's silence.

"What about AIDS?" she asked.

"I've been tested. I'm okay. And Nat was a virgin."

"How about people seeing you at the lake, or in town?"

"It's not a secret for me being gay."

"But Nat's only twenty-one." She rose to bring the coffeepot to them. "It could destroy him."

Mark shrugged.

She asked about the house on Lake Michigan two hours away, and Mark described the drive there, the beach. While he spoke, a thought crossed her mind with brazen clarity: even though she felt warmer to Nat after his crying confession, she didn't love him, still, and feared what people would say about *her* more than what might happen to Nat. I'm like Mom, she thought. Cold.

The weekend was fabulous, Nat raved, returning with color, some new clothes, and a haircut that made him subtly more attractive.

"He wants to take me to Paris next year!" Nat crowed.

"On *his* salary?"

"He has friends there."

Friends, she thought.

At services, Nat sat next to Mark, the fringes of their prayer shawls touching, perhaps, beneath their chairs. Nat had coolly talked about Mark's divorce to most people there, had reported it with enough vagueness and somber gaps to make it seem a tragedy of some kind, a wound too open to discuss. "That's why he came to Michigan," Nat would conclude, delighted with his subterfuge. He could've been a child pretending there were dragons in the dark that only *he* could slay.

"Mark doesn't like me talking like that," Nat smirked.

Did *she?* Did she like any of it? When she wasn't plowing through the book list for her last comprehensive in September, she wondered what she felt. Mark was apparently kind to Nat, and luckily not one of those bitchy homosexuals whose standards were as vigilant and high as satellites, but he was real, and puzzling.

"What do you see in Nat?" she asked one noon in town, where she'd come across Mark waiting to cross a street to campus. He frowned and she felt exposed, her lack of understanding, her contempt as clear to him as diamonds on blue velvet.

"He's very shy," Mark said. "I like to make him smile."

She remembered Nat years ago, little, awash in bedclothes, small eyes tight with disapproval as their mother brought tea, sat on the edge of the bed holding the saucer in one hand, bringing

the cup to his lips and back in a steady hypnotic beat, meanwhile
telling him a complicated silly story to get him to smile.

Mark and Nat started spending less time with her after she
asked Mark that question, as if she, a bumbling parent, had mortified
a group of teens by trying to be sincere. Mark was busy helping Nat
prepare for Tisha B'Av, the late summer Ninth of Av fast, teaching
him Lamentations. She didn't like the fast memorializing the Temple's destruction by the Romans, which reading Josephus's *Jewish
Wars* had made more awful to her. The slaughter, the terrible thirst,
starvation, and ruin were all too real for her, too historic, harbingers
of camps and numbered arms. At least Mark and Nat, leading the
services, would have something to do to keep them from falling
into the past—or so she felt.

Her parents were even less sympathetic to Tisha B'Av; they
liked the more decorative holidays, like Passover and Chanukah,
and suffered through the High Holy Days as if paying stiffly for their
pleasure later in the year.

Less than a week before Tisha B'Av, Helen's grocery cart pulled
up next to hers at one of the mammoth vegetable counters in the
town's largest market.

"Is your brother a fag?" Helen shot, and the two women feeling
tomatoes nearby glared up at them. "Because I saw him coming
out of Bangles downtown last Saturday, and honey, he was drunk.
Mark, too—what a waste!"

Rigid, Brenda imagined a dump truck dropping tons of potatoes
on Helen, sealing her forever.

Helen grinned, looking like a grotesque carnival target. With
more strength than she knew was in her legs and arms, Brenda
moved her cart away and down the aisle, then left, as if the metal
burned, and hurried out to her car. Getting in, she thought of flight,
retreat; no one would ever find her, hear from her again. But starting
the Chevette seemed to drain the panic through her hand into the
key and she drove out along the interstate to Mark's apartment
complex ten minutes away.

"You moron! Why'd you go there!"

"I wanted to dance," he said, sitting down, untouched by her
distress. "So did Nat. I love dancing with him. He's beautiful then,
the way he moves, his eyes—"

Brenda flushed. She had only seen Nat dance at wedding

receptions, and then he had seemed to her stiff, embarrassed, dancing only because he had to.

"I hate it, I hate thinking about the two of you together. I don't understand what it means."

"Do you have to?" asked Mark.

"Don't be so cool."

"I'm thirty-five," he said. "What should I be?"

She felt inflamed by her father's angry pounding voice, but didn't know the words to destroy Mark.

"Well," Mark said, "how about a drink?"

"Yes," she said. "I will."

He joined her on the beige pillow-backed sofa that was as neutral and expensive-looking as everything there—prints, cushions, lamps.

"You know it doesn't bother me now," Mark began. "But for years I thought God would get me, like Aaron's sons, when they offer up 'strange fire' and get zapped? My best friend all through school, from way back, was gay, too—in college he told his rabbi about us and got sent to Israel."

"Did it help?"

"Well, he got married."

"Was he like Nat?"

"No one's like Nat."

She asked for another drink.

Nat showed up just then and she tried to tell him about Helen. Nat said he didn't care, and they went off to the best Szechuan restaurant in the county for a lavish dinner. Later, they drank at a bar like witnesses of an accident, desperate to blur the vision of that crash, the blood and smoke. Nat wouldn't discuss what had happened; each time she tried to bring it up, he looked away.

Two days later, Brenda came to Shabbat services late, right before the Torah reading, and everyone was up, jabbering, flushed. Clark stood at the lectern, his back to the ark, as pale as Nat and Mark, who faced him from the narrow aisle between the men's chairs and the *mehitzah*.

"Get out," Clark was saying. "I won't let you touch that Torah. My *grandfather* donated it."

"You're crazy," Mark said.

"You're *sick*."

Brenda wavered at the door, disgusted by the ugly atmosphere of children squashing worms to make them writhe, exploding frogs with firecrackers.

"Come on," Mark said, slipping off his prayer shawl, jamming it into the gold-embroidered red velvet bag. Mark smiled relief when he saw her, squeezed her hand. White-faced, Nat followed, and Brenda was surprised that he didn't forget on the way out to touch the mezuzah on the doorpost and bring the fingers back to his lips. No one speaking, they drove away in Mark's Volvo to his apartment, as if speeding on the road could strip away that scene.

Upstairs, Mark dumped his blazer on a chair, wrenched off his tie to sit with an arm around Nat, who was still pale and silent. Mark said, "I didn't think it would happen. They need us, it's our *minyan*, too."

"Technically," Brenda said, "it's not my *minyan*." But no one smiled.

"We'll move," Nat finally said. "We'll go to New York!"

Mark smoothed Nat's stringy hair with such gentleness that Brenda felt unexpectedly released. Their closeness warmed her like a Vermeer, rich with circumstantial life.

Tisha B'Av was the next night and they made plans to attend at one of the faculty shuls. Leaving, she surprised herself by kissing both of them.

Nat didn't call her that night and she hardly slept, awash with a sort of amazement that the children they had been had grown to see such ugliness. She longed in her restless bed for escape, for some wild romantic lover, a Czech perhaps, a refugee musician who'd fled in '68, whose loss was larger than her own, a nation's freedom instead of a woman's pride. He would have an accent, she decided sleepily, imagining herself in a sleek black dress, and have a mustache a bit like Mark's. . . .

Mark was alone when he came over Sunday evening.

"Nat isn't coming. He went out."

"Out?"

"Bangles. To get drunk. To dance. He's furious." Mark smoothed down his gray silk tie, looking much too calm.

"He's dancing on Tisha B'Av?" She sat at the dinette table, more confused now than ever.

Mark pressed his hands to the back of his neck, massaging, stretching. "He had this dream last night, that he was swimming far from shore and there were sharks. He woke us both up. Shouting. He couldn't get away."

Brenda could feel her dress sticking to her back despite the air conditioning. "What if he sleeps with someone? He'll get herpes, he'll get AIDS!"

Mark eyed her steadily. "Maybe he'll just dance."

She followed Mark out to his car, and on the drive to the faculty shul, Brenda knew she was feeling the wrong things. She should be understanding, compassionate now, not think that Nat was doing something ugly and vindictive, desecrating the fast day that *he* believed was solemn and holy. She should be *happy* for him, happy that he knew who he was, what he wanted, could feel his feelings, had found Mark—all of that.

She could hear her father snapping out the contemptuous Yiddish phrase for when two things had absolutely no connection: *Ahbi geret. Says who?*

As they pulled into the temple's parking lot, Mark asked, "You okay?"

She wasn't.

What she wanted now was to slip out of the past months as if they were only a rented hot and gaudy costume she could finally return.

What she wanted more than anything on this burning night of Tisha B'Av was to forget.

The Tanteh

Those rare times the Tanteh talked about the War, we all shifted nervously at the table, unable to change the subject or know how to respond, captured like a circle of unwilling believers in the occult, whose medium has sunk into a trance. What she said would be like a violent telegram: "Once I stood in mud and rain. Two days. Naked." Or: "The day we were liberated, the Elbe was flowing with bodies." When she stopped, we went on eating, passing dishes, cutting, spooning, the surge of mealtime sweeping us away from her wasteland.

Ours was a large formal dining room in a dark rent-controlled Upper West Side apartment, with sliding doors stale from seventy-five years of paint, glass-doored china cupboards set into the wall, plaster stars and arabesques bubbling the high ceiling. The Tanteh made that room more natural and fitting than any of us could, because she was a woman of bearing. Straight-backed and hard like an old upright piano, she was gray-haired, gray-eyed, and handsome as much for being seventy and firm as anything else. We called my mother's Great Aunt Rose "the Tanteh," as if she, the only close European relative of ours who had survived not only the Nazis, but Russians, Ukrainians, would always live and speak in capitals. She had come to stay with us five years after her husband, a rich dentist, had died; I was twelve then and my sister, Melanie, had moved to California to join an architectural design firm. The Tanteh filled Melanie's large empty room with books in six or seven languages, the strange gold-stamped spines leering at me from ceiling-high shelves, like eager gypsies. Many books were by writers behind the

Iron Curtain, cries of outrage, cries for help, she said, or cunning little parables that mocked and buzzed.

I envied her, but it was more than just the books; it was everything I dimly understood her to represent: Europe, sophistication, travel, a larger, more glamorous world. For other Jews, I suppose their old-country relatives summon up a personalized *Fiddler*, a glowing cartoon, but the Tanteh was so resolutely un-Jewish—and her parents before her—that I couldn't imagine her haggling in a market, whistling a mournful Yiddish tune, attending a Zionist meeting, doing anything ordinary and Jewish that mass death had made seem otherworldly. Rather, I saw her as one of those lustrous women in Thirties movies, forcefully in love, her stabbing words like brisk steps taken in a walk to mend her health, stalking her sleek young man (Francis Lederer, perhaps), with a large leather bag clutched under one arm and a cigarette waiting to be lit. The Tanteh smoked with spiteful grace, one arm close in and parallel to her waist, palm up, supporting the elbow of the arm that leaned out slightly from her body, as smoke twined up from her Sobranie Gold.

I thought I loved her.

Dad, an accountant, found her affected. No one in *his* family spoke with an English accent or read more than a weekly magazine. He glanced at her books suspiciously and never commented when she talked about school. After moving in with us, the Tanteh had decided to take classes in French literature and criticism at Columbia, and the comments on her papers amazed me. I had never leapt from all those cute little French tales of kids getting into trouble and making puns to the world of Great Books, so the Tanteh's familiarity with writers I found impossible in English (when I tried) awed me. She seemed to glide through that alien world like a dangerous debutante cutting across a dance floor with all the decision of great and untried beauty.

When the Tanteh mentioned a paper or a class, Mother looked away, perhaps paying the Tanteh back for her criticism of the Jewish things we did, like lighting candles on Friday night, keeping kosher (at home), observing a number of holidays.

Once, soon after she moved in, the Tanteh had peered at Mother as she covered her eyes and blessed the candles in their tall brass stands.

"What are you looking at?" she asked the Tanteh, finished.

The Tanteh shrugged with all the distance of an anthropologist unwilling to influence the primitive life he was studying.

Mother slid the lace covering from her head and said with great dignity, "I light candles because I am a Jew, so was my mother, and yours."

The Tanteh nodded, wickedly slim in gray silk and pearls.

"I believe in God," Mother said, heading for the kitchen.

"They prayed," the Tanteh called after her. "And still they died."

I knew who "they" meant—all the lost Jews who spoke to us in pictures, films, and books, so terribly nameless in their millions.

"But some believed," Mother retorted, bearing the steaming blue tureen to the table.

The Tanteh shrugged. "Whatever you say."

Dad came in from the bathroom, smoothing back his hair, scrubbed face as shiny as the challah waiting for his knife.

The Tanteh avoided our Passover Seders and candle-lighting at Chanukah, happily sweeping off to a concert, party, or film that would spare her the affront. The rustle of her cape and her lush scent—White Shoulders, I believe—would mockingly crowd the air and we would all want her there with us: Dad because he said she was our responsibility, Mother because she was family, and me because somehow, with the cosmic vanity of adolescence, I hoped the Tanteh would "convert." I hoped our vague but steady faith would warm her, heal the past I knew so little.

But she appeared content in her world of books, chatting about editions, critics, translations, conferences (I'd hear her on the phone sometimes—flashes of English bursting from sentences in other languages). We rarely met her friends; she entertained them in restaurants, as one did in Europe, and she often seemed less to be living with us than visiting until a more suitable arrangement presented itself. Did she miss her large home on Long Island, or the furniture she'd donated to Jewish charities? I didn't know; the Tanteh was as private about the recent past as about the War.

When she had trouble with a paper, she'd call me to her curtained room and hold out a page wrenched from her old typewriter.

"Is it good?" she'd ask, which meant, Was it English? It was, usually, but always with a trace of another language, like the remains of a figure incompletely painted out on a canvas. She knew Russian, German, French, Hungarian, and Czech, so who could say *what* was stirring in her mind as she resolutely typed?

If I told her it was good, she'd lean back, slim, stern, and explain the paper in a lecture that could last half an hour. Her talk was bright and blinding, and if I did comment, she nodded regally.

My parents were glad I talked to her. She was so foreign and disapproving; at dinner, the table could often seem impoverished by her air of acquaintance with finer meals, more elegant company—though not for me, of course. It was precisely her detachment I adored. She was the perfect figure of romance for a teenager—someone I saw a great deal but knew mostly through my imagination. My visions could not be blurred by facts: her occasional ugly limp, due to arthritis, her rumbling stomach, her spotty wrinkled hands, from which she'd long since removed all jewelry to make them less noticeable, her gray hairs in the bathroom sink. When she contradicted Mother or Dad about, say, politics, they deferred to her history while I enjoyed the pageantry of grimaces and frowns. Because she was the Tanteh, we were more ourselves, too, the Americans, possibly. Or the Ungrateful. It's hard to say. The Tanteh was so much a presence in our large shabby apartment with its leprous windows and gouged parquet floors that maybe we were simply an audience, or even less: a background.

It was the Tanteh, and her talking to me in a pungent voice smothered by years of smoking, who brought me out of the blindness of youth. She was the first person I observed wholeheartedly, and with greed.

"You're so American," she sometimes said, and the word always came from her with surprise, as if she wondered how such a creature could be related to *her*. That thrilling reproach filled my mind with fireworks of speculation, great bursting cascades. *She* was not American, and the difference was no mere attribute of geography or time; it was more, mysterious.

The older I got, the more I found myself watching her, learning her: the hand extended to the hollow of her neck, fingers gentle there, the matchbooks she often twirled and tormented when bored. In senior year of high school, when an English teacher asked us to do a character sketch of the most unusual person we knew, I chose the Tanteh.

My teachers had always said that my writing had "flair," but now I realized I had something more: a treasure. The Tanteh was mine, someone to write about, rich with possibility. I was important; I imagined writing a book someday that would gleam down from her shelves. I brought together the years of reports, skits, and sketches and put all my writing in a box under my bed. I had a history.

I wrote a little story about her, about having dinner with her, her classes, her books and ankle-length mink coat, everything, her contempt for my parents, but what I concentrated on was when she would blurt out parts of the past. How I felt helpless then, trapped, assaulted by each unbearable word that I could not really understand. Writing, I realized how the Tanteh crushed us with what had happened to her, and how I hated it, hated her, even, just a little. My teacher said the story had energy and pushed me to submit it to our yearbook. His praise was so nagging that I finally took it to the small yearbook office seething with posters, photos, clippings, and files, to a thin, bleary-eyed girl who accepted it from me impatiently, as if I was late.

I was excited and triumphant without knowing if it would be printed, as if those few pages were brighter and more alive than the Tanteh would ever be. The story was my child and seemed perfect.

Three months later, bound in a heavy red and black cover, crammed with class pictures and poetry, the yearbook frightened me. Mine was the only piece of fiction—relevant, I guess, because the class was 90 percent Jewish—and it said too much, revealed too much about *me* and how I felt. I had mistaken simple observation for creation, the amateur writer's ugliest confusion. There was no distance, no shaping, no disguise. It was too raw.

I was ashamed.

"So where's the yearbook already?" Dad asked me the week it came out.

Mother smiled expectantly and I muttered about a printer's delay.

I imagined falling at the Tanteh's slim small feet, her walls of books a judgment of my crime, begging her to understand, to feel for me forgiveness, mercy, love. I saw the Tanteh accepting me for the sake of literature; we would cry, be close. She'd become my muse and guide.

It wasn't like that at all. Before I could figure out how to prepare them all, a friend's mother brought a copy over, beaming, a little jealous: "My Marcy *also* gave in a story, but she wasn't so *lucky* as you."

The Tanteh waited for me one Thursday afternoon, in my room, the desk chair turned to the open door, smoke wreathing the curtain rod, her eyes cold. We were alone.

"How could you?"

"It was just an assignment—"

"Why do you want to hurt me?"

"No, I *love* you." But I didn't know if I believed it.

She rose with a quivering face and I expected her to advance on me with her cigarette and burn my desperate tongue.

"*That's* love?"

I fled the room, grabbing my jacket from the bench in the foyer. I missed dinner that night, staying out to see a James Bond movie twice, hiding in the shadows and the light of the balconied, gold-ceilinged Depression-era theater. When fatigue brought me home, there was more: the Tanteh had gone to stay with a friend for the night.

"How could you write it?" Dad asked, holding up the yearbook as if it were the photograph of a desecrated synagogue or grave. We sat at the dining room table like survivors of some dreadful break in customary time, the cool mahogany reflecting our hands. "What's wrong with you?"

I shook my head. If he'd accused or threatened me, I could've yelled something about art, I guess, but he was only disappointed, hurt.

Mother, sitting in the Tanteh's place, clasped her hands. "I've never seen her like that."

The Tanteh's cold rage was alien, none of us had seen her "like that," seen beneath the languages, the pearls—except when she suddenly spoke about the War in those terrible few lines.

I wasn't close to my sister, Melanie, who was fifteen years older, but I called her that night, hoping she would take my side. What was my side, though?

I pictured her sitting out in her lush English-style garden, complete with gazebo, oak benches, elegant, expensive shrubs.

She was curt. "Don't do it again, kiddo. And you'd better apologize *fast.*"

"The Tanteh can't sleep," my mother told me. "She keeps dreaming about you, that she's trying to climb out of a cesspool, hanging on the edge, and you're a Nazi, stomping on her hands." My mother was pale, wide-eyed, as if the dream were true. She shook her head. "Why couldn't you leave her alone?"

A week later, the Tanteh decided not to finish her semester at Columbia, and to visit friends in Brussels. She was quickly packed and gone. The days before her flight were bitter; she stopped eating with us entirely and wouldn't talk about what had happened, about not sleeping anymore, but playing the radio in her room softly through the night, reading, reading.

I feared more disaster like a child, some nighttime curse that would tumble down my walls or smother me in books, her books. But the Tanteh said and did nothing. Hers was the cruelty of silence.

She wrote to my parents from Brussels, then Paris, Marseilles, Madrid, Rome, Venice, Vienna. The postcards, even the stamps, dazzled me. She was triumphantly the woman of Europe, distant and immense, but colored by my shame now. I shot off several wild letters of apology she might have received and even read; I never found out.

The Tanteh died in Prague on the eve of Yom Kippur and was buried there by a distant cousin of her husband.

"It's a saint's death to die then," my mother said, hushed, surprised, repeating a Jewish superstition I'd never heard before.

Did the Tanteh go to get away from me? I believed that at first. I imagined her feeling humiliated by my words, powerless, exposed, forced to plunge into the volcano of her past, which we knew only in its rumbles and flashes of fire or steam. I must have seemed perverse to her, a snake of disapproval and contempt, spying on her soul, or thinking I had.

"Another month," she told us once at dinner. "The Allies would have found nothing. No one. Cholera," she explained. "Dysentery." If her camp had been liberated in May of 1945 and not

April, she would not have lived. Spring was more to her than weather or a song.

Did she go to find her past? Why was she in Prague—to see if her home still stood and who lived there?

In synagogue on Yom Kippur with my parents, I cried for the first time, not even knowing that she was dead, beating my heart as I recited the collective prayer of guilt—the *Ashamnu*: "We abuse, we betray, we are cruel. We destroy, we embitter, we falsify. . . ."

I had to atone for writing about her, but she wouldn't let me, and begging God's forgiveness did not seem like enough. My father squeezed my arm through the prayer shawl, whose fringes I knew were supposed to remind me not to follow the desires of my heart. What had I done?

A postcard from Prague came to me two weeks later, well after we had heard the Tanteh was dead. I don't know why or how it was delayed.

"You had no right to steal from me," it said. "My life is not an *assignment*."

I remembered overhearing her on the phone one time, years before. "Americans are like vampires," she said, then switched to French: "*Dégoûtants*." Disgusting. She went on in English: "They feed on everyone's disasters because it makes them feel happy and safe. *Pauvres petits*."

And I heard all the times she had marveled at me: "You're so American."

War Stories

*"I have heard too much, I have been told too much;
I have had to listen to too much, too long."*

Absalom, Absalom!

Marc's father had an odd, stubborn way of standing: His hands were inevitably in his pockets and all of him seemed to lean forward, as if he'd placed himself in your path and the next move was up to *you*. In his father's presence, Marc often felt as if he had to excuse himself; one look of those narrow dark eyes would put him so much on the defensive that even a hello could come out apologetically. Ten minutes alone with his father could exhaust Marc. Luckily, his father rarely spoke to him.

His mother never stopped. She read several newspapers and weekly magazines and was endlessly fascinated by politics; she talked about her neighbors and friends; she talked about his school and what it was like for her as a girl. And she could talk about the War so calmly, no, not even calmly, because her expression at such times wasn't peaceful, but blank. She seemed then to have no connection with the experiences she related in a stifling monotone. Marc would suddenly see how old she'd become; see not that broad, grinning, sweet face on the other side of a large birthday cake years ago, but a face that belonged to a survivor. The face of a woman who had been forced to stand in the snow for many days, without clothes; the face of a woman who had fled four hundred kilometers on foot through forest, only to be captured by pistol-whipping soldiers. Her hair was starting to fall out, so that the skin showed pink above her forehead through the teased graying mound. Her eyes seemed to have wept flesh they were so pouchy, and her hands were blunter, wider.

Marc hated being outside her in that way and feeling the ruin;

each line in the sagging flesh held him, glared at him, hurt him. He had an image of his mother—glowing in a white summer dress that was splashed with big yellow flowers, leaning across the table over that cake and helping him blow out the three candles, then sweeping masses of thick red hair off her forehead, bracelets jangling, laughing and saying, "You're three! You're three!"—that was destroyed whenever she told him a War story.

The distance between them would grow intolerable as she forced word after word on him, until he thought something had to break. But nothing did. He never screamed, never said anything, just nodded, helpless, listening to what he had no real way of understanding. Oh, the words themselves made sense—but slowly strung together, the pictures they created crushed Marc. How was he to deal with the unimaginable? His mother could talk about the War with her friends because they had been through it and were able to discuss dates and camps and trains and punishments and bombings. They had lived with the unbelievable for years, had fought off searing moments when a man—"Over there, on the corner . . . see? The one with the head tilted."—looked like a commandant at Treblinka, or a guard with a chair leg at Matthausen, or even an uncle, a cousin, a beloved friend whose ashes went into no urn.

If Marc's father never talked much, and then only about commonplaces, at least he never mentioned the War. If anyone did, he would announce, "I'm walking out of this room," and did so, leaving a chorus of knowing nods. And then the nodders would discuss Ljuba, who was still seeing an analyst, and Ann, who never used the glittering copper pots that hung in her kitchen, and, in fact, lived in the basement of her immaculate white-on-white house, and all the others who were more visibly battered than the rest. Many sighs, many shrugs, many "What can you do's?" in Yiddish, Russian, Rumanian, Czech. Those times when his father left the room filled Marc with a longing to follow and touch his arm, to make his father understand that he didn't want the gap of comprehension that was between them.

Marc had decided that it was because his mother was unable to share her stories with his father that she told them to him. In a way, he felt touched, but what about *his* needs? Yes, she loved him. Yes, she'd taken him wherever he wanted to go, baked him cookies or marble cake when he was sad. Yes, she'd helped him with his homework and advised, consoled, and berated him when he most needed all three; but was listening to her War stories the price he had to pay for his mother's love?

When he was younger, all that he'd heard were marvelous descriptions of the first snow in Riga and the special crunching sound snow in America didn't seem to have. Dark sleighs laden with heavy worn blankets had gone hurtling down those streets, filling the snow-thickened air with the faint jingling of their horses' bells (a sound he imagined was like that of his mother's bracelets). Gradually, the visions of her home had changed and there were troops on those streets, first Soviet and then Nazi, and bombs falling on the Jewish cemetery during a funeral, and then the ghetto and then the camps. So imperceptibly had the shadow of the War fallen over her stories that it was as if Marc himself had relived her life, slowly becoming aware of being trapped in the horror and unable to stop it or escape.

Once, while putting on her coat, Rushka, one of his mother's friends, sang very softly, as if the words couldn't bear hearing themselves: *"Es brennt, briderlech, es brennt. . . ."* "There's a fire, little brothers, there's a fire. . . ." It was a pre-War line of warning that for Marc didn't come so close. It had nothing of the brutal clarity of his mother's stories.

Marc had no idea what his father did with his part of the War. He had gathered something about his father standing in front of a fascist firing squad as the RAF bombed wherever it was, but Marc knew little else. He had no sense at all of his father's past, and sometimes he wondered if his mother wasn't incorporating his father's experiences into her own stories. Had his father perhaps told her everything and forbidden her to repeat a word?

When Marc was sixteen, his mother had been at the very beginning of a story, in the kitchen, standing at the stove and stirring a pot of soup. She broke off when the front door opened and his father walked in early. He nodded, put his meter, coin changer, and call sheets on the table. No one said anything. As his father fingered the meter and his mother stared into the pot, it occurred to Marc that there was a gap between his parents, too: the War, which should have bound them in understanding, divided them. After that, Marc had trouble seeing his situation in black and white;

there were flashes of color, wild and upsetting. It had been so easy, resenting his mother and fearing his father. The two feelings began to switch back and forth now with a will of their own, and for all their intensity, lacked true definition.

His father talked mostly about the people who got into his cab, and then only to his mother. She would sit at the table, her face tight, hands folded like a petulant schoolgirl's. She didn't like his driving a cab, even though he owned it. Marc was unwilling to probe those feelings of hers, but he had figured out that she thought it was undignified. One night when his father was two hours late for dinner, his mother muttered something about "sleigh drivers" and "lower-class."

He envied his father's freedom and couldn't imagine seeing and talking to so many people in one day. His father looked wonderfully scrubbed and tall, leaning over the wheel of his Checker cab, wearing the perpetual white shirt, his dark hair brushed back off a wide forehead, handlebar mustache looking thick and dark against the pale freckled skin. In a wildly confident moment, Marc had once ventured asking his father if he could sit up front for a whole day to see what it was like.

"What're you . . . a *baby?*" His father spaced the words carefully, as he always did when angry. Those cool dismissive questions of his would stalk Marc, mostly at night, pouncing just as he was falling asleep. Strap marks would at least have faded.

Soon after, Marc started having his dream. He'd been frightened, hearing his mother and her friends talk about this one's husband and that one's sister screaming in the night and seeking some magic from analysts. A plump dark little woman who always made a point of asking how Marc was doing in school, and *listening*, once told his mother, "Analysts are fine for these Americans—what do they know about real problems?"

The light—that was the beginning of the dream. His eyes would open and Marc would find himself in a large feather bed piled high with white quilts. They seemed to shine; everywhere there was a clean white glow. No rats, no lice, no dirt, no death, no people. It's over, he would think, I'm safe. And just then, the whiteness would rip apart and images would come stabbing through the glow: a graying rabbi on his knees, his beard on fire; an overturned sleigh, the blankets bloodied; a grinning, monocled doctor with a scalpel. On and on they came as the blankets turned into a putrid fog that smothered him.

He never told his mother about the dream because somehow it didn't seem to be *his*. He'd wake up afterward, not frightened, not caught up, not even out of breath, but instantly aware that he was in bed, at home—and disappointed. He was almost ashamed of the dream because he felt it was a distillation of his mother's stories, and things he'd seen on TV or read about, though he couldn't pinpoint the details. Marc hated not being able to respond from the depths of himself. For all it mattered, he could have been dreaming of a car accident. Why was this dream so obvious and what was it trying to tell him? Was it simply that the horror he felt was too oppressive to let him settle into peace at night?

His father was usually home around six and they watched the news over dinner, a tradition that began in fourth grade when Marc had to do public-events reports. The reports stopped the next year, but dinner went on being served at six, maybe because then they could talk about the news and not have to talk to each other. The older he got, the more Marc welcomed the TV's distraction; the tension at table was so strong. Eating at a friend's house was a treat; at home, Marc worried whether his father thought he ate too fast, too slowly, too noisily. His father hardly said anything personal to him, and that made Marc feel his standards were impossibly high. He came to suspect his mother's easy approbation; it was as if she was still speaking the young mother's dialect of indiscriminate praise for her infant: everything he did was "Wonderful!"

On an evening a week before his seventeenth birthday, Marc lay stretched on the couch in the living room, reading the *Times*. His mother was in the kitchen with a crossword puzzle. He didn't see how she had the patience to work on them; he gave up after being stumped a few times, but she plunged on, intent, muttering, steadily darkening each white square. When the doorbell rang, Marc assumed it was a neighbor. He sat up and heard his mother ask a sharp question out in the foyer. His father entered, headed for the wall unit, opened the liquor cabinet, and took out a bottle of vodka someone had given them last New Year's, and a shot glass. Marc had never seen him drink except on holidays.

His father turned, shook his head and crossed to the couch. His cheeks were beet red, as if someone had slapped him. Back straight, his father set the bottle and glass down on the large square table on top of the Chagall book, opened the bottle, very slowly poured a shot, and downed it as if he wanted to feel pain. He had another shot in the same exalted, self-absorbed way.

Marc's mother stood at the door, hands thrust into her apron pockets. His father signaled and Marc poured another drink for him. He had never done that before.

"I was at Kennedy Airport," his father began softly. "And a woman, my age, nice-looking, got in. She gave an address and something . . . something in her voice made me look at her good. '*Foon vanent koomt a Yeed?*' I asked her. '*Foon Litteh.*' Lithuania—"

"Stop it!" Marc's mother leaned forward, rigid, her face pale. "Stop! You'll make yourself sick!"

"And then the woman stared, saw my picture and name tag hanging on the dash. 'Wolf Landau?' she said to me. 'But I'm you're Betsia!' "

"She was *Betsia*, my mother's a cousin. They told me she died at Ponar, everyone said. She's been here, in America, for years. She thought I was dead—she never could find me after the War over there. She gave up."

"But where is she now?"

"Not far—Kew Gardens. She's coming soon with her husband, and two sons."

Marc reached for the vodka and then looked at his father, who nodded, gestured for him to drink. He had a *family*. It was no longer true that all his parent's relatives had died in the War. . . . They were no longer so alone.

His father sat stiff and silent, hands on his knees, and stared out into the room, trembling. Marc could almost feel it. He reached out and touched his father's arm. His father started to sob. Marc's mother rushed forward and Marc leaped up, grabbing her arms to hold her back. She pulled away, bracelets jangling.

"Let him cry," Marc said. "*Let* him."

Remind Me to Smile

"I'm not perfect, but I'm perfect for you."

Grace Jones

Stefan kept saying that it was none of our business. He meant *my* business; Stefan doesn't dish. But I wondered about my new office mate, anyway. Bob Shields, hired to teach Renaissance Poetry and Drama for a year, talked about Ann-Margaret too much. It was Bob's little joke, how he'd always had the hots for her, seen all her movies, wanted to give blood when she fell in Vegas—off that thirty-foot platform?—and when Bob was "free" (between marriages), *she* wasn't. And of course he thought she was the best thing ever to happen to Tennessee Williams when she did *Streetcar* on television. I suppose it's like being fourteen and saying, "Boy, if I had *her*" (fill in your own blank) and all your friends leer and shift their legs apart to give themselves some room. But a man in his thirties, a professor (okay, temporary) at a Big Ten school? It just didn't sound right— it was a cover: the two marriages were a cover.

"Who cares?" Stefan asked.

"Material," I said. "It could be material for your writing. All literature begins as gossip."

"That's just something you'd tell your freshman and when they'd write it down, you'd laugh."

He was right.

My specialty is contemporary American fiction, but I mostly teach freshman composition, in the same department as Stefan. In class I generally end up hectoring students about their writing, which is so dismal and characterless that I could be reading generic papers: High School Graduation, College Life's New Responsibilities, My First Job, My First Love, My Best Friend, Spring Break in Florida.

Sometimes, though, I connect and help kids see their writing differently, help them discover how to grow, how to find and develop their own voice. I know, I sound like one of those "Reach out and touch someone" ads, but that's how I feel when it works. Stefan had finally come to like teaching—well, he was the new writer-in-residence at State, so it was about time!—but he didn't like me rhapsodizing about my good days.

And Stefan did not want to hear me speculate about Bob Shields, or anyone. He may observe people more than I do, but he keeps what he sees for his writing, which one critic has called "volcanic." And I'll tell you, prose isn't Stefan's only volcano.

I pushed. "Why doesn't Bob come out?"

"It's not a good time for that."

Well, Stefan stopped me there. Besides AIDS, three arrests had been made on campus recently, for sexual misconduct in a men's room at the Union. Important university staffers. Their case had been lurching from one grim headline to another all over the Midwest, generating ugly letters in all the local papers. People wrote about the Devil and sin, filth, sickness, evil and all the rest, as if the defendants were Jews in the Dark Ages.

"Well," I went on. "Why doesn't he come out to *me*?"

"Maybe he doesn't like you."

"Toad."

"Or maybe you're so busy being gay you didn't notice."

"Snake."

I had tried *luring* Bob out, partly because he pissed me off pretending to be straight. I'm not in favor of everyone coming out; I think lots of people aren't ready, and I'm not a "professional gay," as Stefan calls them—you know, people who make that their lives?

The other reason Bob got to me was the obvious one: he was quite humpy. One of those tall, dark, reedy Thirties matinee idol types—you want to find him a gold cigarette case just to see him take out a Dunhill, tap it once, twice, a gentleman's tap, and stick it into those knife-blade lips. I left some novels by James Purdy, Andrew Holleran, and Edmund White on my desk, even an issue of *Christopher Street*, but he didn't bite.

By which I mean, he didn't pretend not to notice, but what he said was so casual, it couldn't seem false. Like Tina Turner sings, I just wanted a little reaction.

Just enough to tip the scales.

But Stefan, he didn't want to hear any more about Bob that evening. "I'll be in the study," he said, and I lit up. When Stefan became successful, selling stories and then a novel, I discovered that I *love* being a votary of Literature, screening his calls, brewing his coffee, copyediting, fixing yummy snacks. It's not just a game, I mean, he *is* a terrific writer. He's developed this weird poetry in his stories that sneaks up on you like the things you think you see out of the corner of your eyes at night when you're tired. He's not just good by accident—he works hard. And I help.

Being successful, being the new writer-in-residence, there was no way he could avoid the faculty parties, though he would've sent me by myself if possible. And I would've been happy to eat, drink, and chat for the two of us. I like the parties, like complaining about students as if we in the English department were survivors of some great cataclysmic flood that had swept away all of Western civilization, except for us. Am I exaggerating? Not after four or five drinks.

The first term party that fall was at the chairwoman's, as usual. I didn't like her. Dr. Bold had a pinched, angry, pale face that made you feel even a "Good morning" was an imposition. She had only a vestigial sense of humor, and ran department meetings with all the grace and charm of a reluctant mortician. Someone told me that she was taking a correspondence course in Improving Your Interpersonal Relationships. The Remedial Level.

Her house was beautiful, though, bare shiny birch inside and out, a kind of intellectual train station: enormous cathedral ceiling and spotlighted Matisse drawing.

Bob was standing there at the unlit fireplace, drinking, holding his glass loose-wristed, elbow on the heavy oak mantel like someone on *Masterpiece Theater*. Don't ask me why he had so much attitude. He was surveying the crowd buzzing about the latest budget cuts, the latest bits of adultery, the latest publications. I pointed him out to Stefan, who hadn't met him yet, and then I drifted into the stone-walled kitchen that was as big and dreary as something out of *The Name of the Rose*, if you've seen the movie. I chatted up Dr. Bold's husband, Jorge, a plump and humpy Brazilian ex-lifeguard who should have been gay if he wasn't, while he fussed with an elaborate tray: the Siege of Troy in *pâté forestier* bas-relief, I think.

I was surprised that Bob and Stefan really got talking, though I thought Stefan might be trying to figure him out. I didn't join them by the fireplace, or later seated halfway up the broad uncarpeted stairs, or even on the patio near the end of the party when everyone was drunk and tired of having had the same fun they tended to have at every department party.

That's what I had.

"I think I should tell you something," Stefan said when we were getting ready to leave. "It's about Bob."

I wasn't really listening; I just followed Stefan out to our Saab, annoyed that he had apparently found Bob so interesting, and all night, too. It was cool, clear in the sky, just a threat of winter edging the air.

"I know Bob." Stefan sounded stiff, tentative, like someone on a soap opera coming out of amnesia.

"Bob? You know him? How?"

"Let's go home." He started the car and we drove away down the maple-lined street.

In one breath, I said, *"Don't* tell me I have to sit down for this because I *am* sitting down and I'm not drinking *anything* more tonight I feel like a *mop."*

Stefan said, "Wait," but he didn't look at me or take my hand or smile. He insisted on making a fire when we got home, even though it wasn't really cold enough.

"Atmosphere? This must really be bad."

Stefan pushed in some more kindling, lit it, and turned to me, still squatting. "No, it's humorous, in a way."

"Okay," I said. "Remind me to smile at the funny parts."

I sat in the leather armchair, put my feet up on the ottoman. Stefan sat near the fire, which was catching quickly, and this is what he told me.

The first year Stefan was at Columbia, Bob had been sitting in on a writing workshop, to decide about applying to the program. And he and Stefan went out for drinks after an especially degrading class where the professor bashed the stories like piñatas. Oh, and there was a girl, too, Maggie; there had to be, someone sweet and pretty and half in love with both of them, and confused, too (of course), since they were both gay.

"It was safe," Stefan said. "For all three of us." Movies, parties, dinners, shows, and bookstores, always bookstores—around Columbia, along Fifth Avenue, in the Village. They were happy, self-conscious refugees, fleeing what they thought were the wilds of sex and complication into something purer: friendship. They wound up trapped by their flight. At least Stefan did.

"We were driving," he said. "Up Broadway from Columbus Circle, from a movie. Maggie was sick; she didn't go. It was late, very late. Bob put in a Bowie tape, *Aladdin Sane*, and up past Seventy-second it started raining. All these red reflections, taillights everywhere, red lights clear uptown. And we stopped, and Bowie's singing 'Gee it's hot, let's go to bed.' And I kissed him. Bob said, 'You're not what I'm looking for.' "

And the weeks of hiding what he felt from himself and Maggie and Bob were over for Stefan; he was lost. They screwed, of course, but only when Bob wanted to. Mostly, Bob said no—like Cleopatra, he was Queen of Denial.

It dragged on for months, with Maggie struggling to make Stefan give Bob up or convince Bob to love Stefan—someone had to be happy if she wasn't. "Then I met you," Stefan finished.

"What's that mean? You met me?"

Stefan hugged himself, eyes down.

"I was the Red Cross after the hurricane? Blankets and hot soup? Great."

I wished then that he'd told me all this at the party. I could've gotten drunk and stretched out in front of Bob's car and shouted, "Why don't you finish the job?" or pushed him into a bathroom and drowned him in the tub, or shoved his face into the Cuisinart.

"All those times I talked about Bob in my office, didn't you know who it was?"

Stefan frowned. "I tried changing the subject." Then he added, "When I heard he was one of the applicants, I said some good things about him. I think it helped."

I'd always been suspicious of revelation scenes in books because the truth has seemed sneakier to me, less aggressive. Maybe that's because I'd never really come out dramatically, preferring to reveal myself in stages, hints, suggestions. Now, when people say, "I have something to tell you," my first thought is to head quickly and quietly for the nearest exit.

That night, by the fire with Stefan, I was not just feeling

threatened and betrayed, but scared by something new. I'd often worried about death and losing him that way, but though I got sarcastic if I saw him talking to a "talented" student of the male persuasion, I did not ever doubt my importance in the life we had created.

"You *helped* him get the position? You must be crazy," I said. "No—don't tell me, you thought it would be wrong not to."

Stefan nodded.

"Shit, Stefan! Join the Peace Corps if you want to help people so fucking much! Try Bangladesh!"

"Let's go to bed." Stefan rose and came to my chair. I was too surprised to feel I could let go; I said I would stay up for a bit, with the fire.

"Wake me when you come to bed." Stefan leaned down to kiss me good night. Was I supposed to huffily pull away, or let him kiss me, or what? The whole situation seemed ludicrous, a cliché: The Confession Scene. The Astonished Lover. Maybe Stefan was embarrassed by that, too.

I saw myself sneaking into the English department at night and throwing Bob's books out the window onto the lawn. Or I could send him anonymous threatening missives, fly over campus with a broomstick spouting smoky letters that spelled SURRENDER STEFAN.

See? The whole mess was partly like a stupid joke to me. I couldn't believe it.

I remembered how I first fell in love with Stefan's voice when we met at a party in Morningside Heights. He'd introduced himself, sounding as silky as a radio announcer for a classical station murmuring to you at night (and he looked like Bruce Jenner, only taller). He warned me right off that he was getting over a disastrous relationship he didn't want to talk about. It was so unexpected, I laughed.

We took the subway down to his studio apartment on Hudson Street, and what I remember of the ride was the Hispanic guy hanging from the strap next to me, his shirt open, revealing the fattest, darkest nipples I had ever seen on man or woman. We fucked kind of wildly that night—it was exciting and it hurt—and then we both passed out. In the morning, we looked as haggard as just-released hostages. What was special the next day, what was remarkable was feeling as if we had slipped into somebody else's comfortable and comforting life.

Stefan told me then that his parents had started pushing him to give up "this writing thing" and get a real job. They thought he was wasting money on the degree. Stefan was depressed and wondered if they might be right—after all, he hadn't been able to publish anything yet. I told him that the power of parental doubts and prophecies of doom is often in inverse proportion to their accuracy, but he just shrugged.

He was even talking about dragging all his stories out of their file cabinets and burning them, just to be free, clarified, to start over—or something.

"Oh, bullshit," I said. "That's just a scene from a cheap movie."

And he smiled.

"Are you any good? Well then, just keep writing and shut up."

It wasn't a memorable line, but it helped.

There were no lights on while I thought about our past, just the wavering fire I did nothing to keep going. Watching it, I began to feel like Isabel Archer in *The Portrait of a Lady* when she finally realizes what her husband is like.

I grabbed a pen and the *TV Guide* from the coffee table, and in the margins of yet another article on *Dallas*, I wrote a list of my options.

1. I could eat everything in the kitchen.
2. I could drink until I passed out.
3. I could drive around aimlessly all night and come back bleary-eyed to haunt and rebuke Stefan.
4. I could call Bob and curse him out.
5. I could kill myself.
6. I could eat everything in *Bob*'s kitchen.
7. I could write a nasty autobiography, *Stefan, Queerest*, go on Phil Donahue and wow America.
8. I could cry.

I stopped there and put the *TV Guide* down to face the possibility of great pain.

* * *

In the morning, Stefan told me he'd invited Bob to dinner.

"Here?" I must have sounded like one of those commercials with a housewife shocked by termites. Roaches! Rats!

We were having breakfast, Stefan dressed for class, me in my bathrobe. I felt vulnerable, unprepared.

Stefan said, "He's had a pretty rough time."

"That's what you talked about last night?" I poured myself more coffee.

Stefan nodded. "There's a lot to tell. Married twice, divorced, he's got a little girl and his first wife won custody, he can't see her at all, he can't land a tenure track position anywhere, just these one-year, two-year shots, hasn't published. . . ."

"We're aiding the needy, is that it? Couldn't I just send him some typing paper? A little check, perhaps?"

"It's different imagining him here, and seeing him." Stefan was staring off behind me.

"So it's not over?"

"He's here."

It was a stupid question, I admit that. How could it be over, it'd just begun for me last night.

"Why is he coming to dinner? Why did you get him the job?"

"I need to find out what I feel." Now he looked straight at me, serious, solemn even.

"Oh shit."

"Listen, people can stop for you, but that doesn't mean they end. I have to know."

"But Bob was years ago. And I love you!" It came out angry and inconsequential, an unimportant claim.

"Then you want me to understand this." Stefan sounded reasonable and warm. "If I'm not honest, what'll happen to my writing?"

"Wonderful! Now I'm destroying your career! Go to class!"

Well, of course Bob was coming to dinner. I wasn't just up against him, it was Stefan, too, and Stefan's mysterious feelings. After all I'd done for him, been his one-man ticker-tape parade, he didn't know what he felt! I was trapped; I had to be patient, wait this out, help Stefan decide whether he still wanted Bob or not—

and what that meant. Can you see Mary Queen of Scots telling the executioner, "Let me help you sharpen the blade"?

I cleaned the house all day in a fury; it would puzzle Mrs. McCormick when she came on Wednesday. Then I cleared out the leaves that had started to collect in the gutters, raked what little had fallen in the yard, got a pile of leaves burning in the driveway, washed my car, and even contemplated reseeding a weedy patch under the kitchen window, but I gave up by the afternoon and settled for doing wash and grading all the papers I could concentrate on.

What made me maddest about the thing with Bob was Stefan framing the whole problem ethically. He was on solid ground, laying everything out like someone setting tiles into a mosaic with a sure, responsible hand. He hadn't gone off to fuck Bob, or driven away to be by himself while I stewed and mourned, or manipulated me into blowing up so that he could feel blameless, cool.

He was keeping me *informed*. It would be like having a crisis break on CNN news: I could follow it through each microscopic permutation, all day if I wanted. All night.

I planned revenge. Dinner that Saturday would be extravagant, eight courses of Byzantine splendor: truffles on a Tambourine, Pheasant in an Hourglass. But then I thought, *no way!* I'd make Tater Tots and franks, just to show Bob that I wasn't threatened and that Stefan didn't care what we ate because our love transcended food.

I saw Bob a few times in our office that week and everything I'd admired in him now aroused my contempt, especially when he said he was "looking forward" to dinner! I almost said, "Why don't you bring Ann-Margaret if she's not busy?" But there wasn't much point in either of us acting like Alexis. Not now. Not yet.

I started thinking about dessert. I make an excellent and attractive cheesecake; the colors and textures always look wonderful up on the glass-topped silver cake dish my mother gave us on our first anniversary. I bought a bottle of Baron Philippe Sauternes to go with it, solid but not flashy. Salad would be easy; Stefan loves Brie, so I would make a marinated tomato and Brie salad. The blend of olive oil, garlic, fresh parsley, and basil is almost hypnotic. Braised leeks with a pink peppercorn mayonnaise would be lovely

after that, but what about the entrée? I picked through our shelves
of cookbooks for something new or reliable, I couldn't decide, and
Stefan seemed anxious when I hadn't made up my mind by Saturday
morning.

"Listen," I said. "You're exploring your feelings; I'm exploring
the menu."

"Let me help."

"Okay. Buy some flowers—tea roses, white; alstromeria, purple. Clean the bathrooms, wash the guest towels, set the table with
my mother's china. Trim your sideburns."

He didn't have sideburns, but he got to work.

I finally chose pasta shells stuffed with escargots, prosciutto,
spinach, cream, Parmesan, white wine, garlic, and Pernod. The
Pernod decided me—it's so Hemingway in Paris, so slutty and
tough. I shopped for an hour and returned with bags of goodies, to
find Stefan lying on the bed, a hand over his eyes, the window
shades down.

"You sick?"

"Maybe this dinner is a mistake." He sounded like a medium
unsure whether she's contacted the other side or not.

"Stefan, if I'm a condemned man, I want my last meal to be
a good one."

"Bob, having Bob over."

I asked him to open his eyes: "It's like talking to a tomb effigy."
He didn't. "I'm ashamed of myself."

I wanted to shout, "Good! You should be!" But I just went to
unpack the groceries.

Now, I'm a good cook if I know what I'm doing, if I've made
the dish before. Otherwise, I get easily panicked, and that whole
afternoon I kept rushing to the stove, to the sink or the refrigerator,
shouting, "Oh my God! I forgot—"

Stefan would peer in, ask what was wrong as I nervously stirred,
poured, mixed, and I'd snap out a sullen "Leave me alone!" or
"Shut up!" After an hour of that, he said, "I'm not going to invite
people over if this is what happens."

"How many ex-lovers did you have in mind? Let's do a buffet
next time!"

"This would be easier if you weren't so upset."

I was taking shots of Pernod every time Stefan made me mad,

or when I even thought about why I was preparing dinner. Each shot I snapped back was like hurling a dart at his face on a wall poster. I began to stop caring how the escargots would turn out; at least the salad and cheesecake were fine. I would just have to keep myself from taking up the baguette and swatting someone.

Stefan stayed out of the kitchen, but he radiated tension and disapproval the way only quiet people can.

Showering, I imagined myself on the Riverwalk in San Antonio, or dancing in Key West rain, or walking the beach at Newport, with those mammoth houses gazing out to sea like the ugly, touching monoliths on Easter Island. They were all places Stefan and I had discovered together.

Since some people would call this "a gay story," now's the time for me to dry myself off in the mirror and admire my rock-hard chest and washboard stomach, bragging about how going to the gym changed my life. No way. Running, weights, aerobics, I can't stand any of it now for more than a few months at a time. Then I stop, my clothes start getting tighter, and Stefan begins watching me intently, as if his silence could force me into an aria of confession: Yes! I gained ten pounds!

The point is that I hadn't been heaving and grunting for months, and while I didn't look awful, I sure wasn't any slim-jim —and I needed a haircut. Getting dressed, I thought of the *I Love Lucy Show*—if she were faced with her husband's old flame, she'd dress to kill, to *annihilate*, or dress like a hillbilly, blacking out some teeth, to embarrass Ricky.

"You have a comic vision of life," Stefan said to me once, in bed, after chasing me around the house while I went "Mee-meeep" like the Road Runner.

"Is that okay?" I asked when he didn't go on. "Do you still like me?" Stefan rolled me onto my stomach and began kissing the crack of my ass. "Lick once for yes," I said, "and twice for no."

"What're you wearing?" I asked Stefan an hour before Bob was due.

"Socks, underwear, shoes, pants. A shirt. Oh, a belt, too."

I didn't smile.

"That was like a joke," he said.

"*Like* a joke, but not an actual joke."

"You win."

"Good, then let's call Bob and cancel."

Stefan ended up wearing the red and blue Alexander Julian outfit—slacks, sweater, shirt—I'd bought him a week before, and he looked too good, too big and inviting, like an athlete turned model.

Stefan hugged me in the kitchen in the large abstract way that sometimes bothers me because it feels like it has little to do with me. It was not the way I wanted to be held with Bob coming in a few minutes, I wanted one of those hugs that fills the world, I wanted everything.

When Bob knocked and Stefan went out to the front door, I downed another shot of the Pernod, which was starting to taste vile. I was like a fat little kid stuffing doughnuts into his tear-lined face, thinking, "That'll show everybody," choking on hurt and rage.

Bob had brought a bunch of tiger lilies.

Cheerfully, I said in what I thought was an Irish accent, "He's laid out in the other room and don't he look marvelous?"

Bob smiled.

Great start, I thought, going off for a vase.

Then I followed them through Stefan's perfunctory house tour, deploring Bob's somber blue suit, white shirt, and red tie. He looked like a camera-conscious young Senator, handsome, slick, as artificial as floral air spray.

"This is great," Bob said as we settled down for caviar.

"Compared to what?" I asked.

Bob smiled again, glancing at Stefan for a sign of complicity, but Stefan just sat back in the blue and gold wing chair, eyes wide, as if expecting those feelings of his to show up at the door. Bob and I were on the stiff and shiny camelback sofa; I squeezed some lemon onto my caviar-heavy Carr's biscuit and asked, "So where will you go at the end of the year?"

Bob took that in, sipped his Southern Comfort. I bit into my cracker with all the verve, I thought, of Margo Channing and her celery stalk. I went on. "*Since* your appointment's over in June, I mean." I chomped away while Bob proceeded to mention people he knew who knew people at Stony Brook, Boston University, Florida International—unimpressive connections.

"What about you?" Bob asked Stefan.

"It's tenure track for both of us, of course," I said. "But Stefan's doing so well, and Ecco Press is bringing out his new collection next year, so we might get better offers. We're talking about some-place warm, where we can tan on the way to class." Well, I had started, and I went on and on through dinner about every one of Stefan's publications, quoting reviews, letters from fans and other writers who'd seen his work in *Triquarterly, Paris Review, Vanity Fair.* It was all true. He'd been called remarkable, stirring, and even brilliant: "one of the brilliant young writers remaking American fiction." I was cheating there, because almost every other writer reviewed nowadays gets called brilliant by *somebody*, if only in *People.*

Stefan and Bob ate quietly while I rhapsodized about Stefan's work, pointing out at least twice that he'd become successful *after* we met, not before. I was as inexorable as a brace of competing grandparents launching their grandchildren's grades and school re-ports, accomplishments, and personal qualities like a fleet of hot-air balloons. I was dizzied by my own praise, the Pernod, and the half bottle of Puligny-Montrachet I had downed. They didn't get a chance to talk about the past.

Stefan said almost nothing. What could he say? I'd practically renamed several campus buildings in his honor, established a Stefan Valenstine scholarship fund, given him a Pulitzer, an American Book Award, and a Congressional Medal of Honor. Bob nodded, smiled, said "Wow" or "Neat" or "Really?" when I gave him the chance.

With dessert, I launched into something new: Stefan and me, how happy and productive we were together. I guessed that Bob didn't have any kind of lover and I was as cruel as those rebels in the Sudan preventing emergency flights of food into starving enemy-held villages.

"We have a very full life," I said, after talking about our trips to Greece, Sweden, the Riviera, Tuscany, and our yearly visits to the Shakespeare Festival in Stratford, Ontario, each summer. "We're thinking of adopting."

Stefan stared at me and put down his fork. Nothing dramatic, no explosion, just that. I thought, It's over, I've gone too far, and Bob's won. I could see that Bob thought so, too. He looked like a jackal on one of those nature specials, about to dart between two squabbling lions to snatch a piece of the felled zebra.

"It's getting late," Bob said. It was ten. I managed to ask if anyone wanted more coffee.

"I'm fine." Bob thanked us both and rose from the table like a crown prince waiting for the inevitable news from the king's sickroom, gracious, thoughtful, posed. "Dinner was wonderful," he said. "That cheesecake! You're a very good cook."

That was my consolation prize, I suppose.

Bob shook my hand when he left and I turned back to the dining room. Surveying the littered table, I wondered where I would go now and what Stefan would say.

He headed for the kitchen, opened the dishwasher.

When I brought in the first dishes from the table, Stefan said, "You acted like a jerk tonight." I piled the dishes on the counter near the sink. "A real jerk."

"Was dinner okay?"

He turned. "I've never seen you like this."

"I've never been under the gun! You set the whole thing up like—" But I couldn't finish. I continued ferrying dishes in from the dining room as if each plate passing between us marked the end of our connection. When I pictured myself hurling them all onto the floor, I started crying, sat heavily at the kitchen table, wanting him to leave now, to not drag it out anymore.

Stefan knelt by my chair. Here it comes, I thought.

"What's your opinion of Bob?" He asked.

"Bob?" I reached for a napkin to blow my nose. "Bob? My opinion? Are we voting?! Who breaks the tie?"

Stefan shook his head, that beautiful head full of unexplored feelings. "You know that Bowie line you like? About looking into somebody's eyes, 'they were blue but nobody home'?"

"Bob's eyes are brown."

Stefan pulled a chair close, sat with our knees touching. "Listen—"

"You said I was a jerk."

"Wait—you were *real*. Okay, a real jerk. But Bob's just the *idea* of a person. Hollywood, you know, perfect stage set, you walk behind it, bare boards propping it up. And he was always like that. Nobody home."

"And I'm a jerk."

He took my hands with the gravity of a nineteenth-century

suitor. "Bob can't love, he's too busy watching, seeing what kind of impression he makes. Not like you. I had to *see* it." He shook his head. "*I* was the jerk. I'm sorry."

"I'm going to set his file cabinet on fire. Monday morning, I swear."

Stefan hugged me, a real hug, personal, alive.

"So what happens now?" I asked.

"We clean up, we finish the Sauternes, we make love, we live happily ever after. How's that?"

I convinced him the dishes and the wine could wait.

So. When I thought I was alienating Stefan with my desperate monologue at dinner, he was delighted, intrigued. He enjoyed me; I was "various," he said later, even wonderful, and I showed Bob up as colorless, vapid, void.

This is really a very old story: The Triumph of Love. What's new, I suppose, is the principals—three men—and what didn't happen between me and Bob. In the old days, if you had a rival, you wanted to draw and quarter him, drink wine out of his skull. Nowadays, you defuse him. You pull out the plug.

Which *I* managed to do. Even in the dark.

A New Light

With the traffic noise outside the office window as loud and familiar as New York's, I sat wondering how I'd gotten into sparring about Yiddish, in Chicago yet, and at a Jewish newspaper! The senior writer whose office I'd been sharing for a month, had found me during lunch reading a many-paged letter from my parents. Even though he was supposed to be training me, Leon Grossbart generally sneered at whatever was on my desk. I had been hired to write features; he covered the Middle East. But this time he stopped and peered down.

"Yiddish?"

Thin, pretty-faced, precise and critical, Leon had the air of suffering the constant violation of his standards. My parents would have simply called him a *Yekkeh*—uncomplimentary slang for German Jew.

"It's not even a language," Leon said that October afternoon. "Hebrew is. And Russian, German. But Yiddish—it's just a mess." He shrugged.

"Have you ever *studied* Yiddish?" My wood swivel chair felt more uncomfortable than usual. "Or read Peretz? Sholem Aleichem?"

"Folk artists, not writers."

All I could say was, "You don't know what you're talking about." But I knew that he was just parroting generations of arguments that Yiddish was a "jargon," an ugly bastard child of the Diaspora. It was a point of view that had strangely survived the Holocaust and even all the romantic outbursts of enthusiasm for

Yiddish across the country that you often heard about: a club, a newsletter, a college minor.

And then Martha, Leon's girlfriend, appeared at the door for him—a large, lavishly freckled, tawny-haired woman with the grace and vigor of an athlete—and he was gone with a satisfied nod.

The crowded high-ceilinged office seemed to cheer Leon's exit, the file cabinets hulking around me like "I told you so" cousins. I was new to Chicago and to writing full time, so having a letter from home was a special treat. Until then, I'd done free-lancing for Jewish newspapers and magazines, and this was my first real job. The money was terrific, more than I would have made starting out as the journalism professor my parents had hoped I'd become ("We sent you to Columbia to scribble?"). But I kept explaining there was plenty of time for me to teach if I wanted to—I was only twenty-six. My parents were proud of me in their blundering way: I was doing something good for the Jews, making a living, and if I didn't always date Jewish girls, well surely that would change over time, given the world I worked in.

I can't claim a relationship with my parents that's especially enviable, but their letters and phone calls had always pleased me because Yiddish was what I'd spoken as a child, and still spoke to them at home. I had learned French in high school, but it was a transplant that never really took. Despite my teachers' propaganda and a blaze of posters, films, and travel anecdotes, I found French not beautiful but simply foreign. Perhaps because French meant exams and drilling, while Yiddish was my mother reading rhyming children's books to me, or my worn copy of Peretz's collected stories, or my father sarcastically murmuring about people we passed on the street.

I had gone to a Workman's Circle Sunday school for years, regularly leafed through *The Forward*, and was more startled by an English word in my parents' Yiddish than the reverse. They spoke English well enough when they had to—and with little accent— but it always sounded hard, unyielding, a language of necessity. I felt closest to them speaking or reading Yiddish.

Leon's arrogance offended me so much, I was still angry that evening when I went back to the bright office to review some notes I'd forgotten to take home. The *Jewish Journal*'s offices were in a converted loft and much brighter and cleaner than I'd expected—

not at all gritty or decayed. It was beautifully carpeted and a bit too methodically mauve and gray (like a motel, almost). Even rushing to make our weekly deadline, panic and frustration seemed muffled there. Employing over twenty people, and despite all the files and computers, the *Journal* was more like the home of a subdued Jewish charity than *The Front Page*.

I was doing a short series on women who were having bas mitzvahs. They fell into two groups, young "converts" (from all kinds of things) who wanted the ceremony to mark a new stage in their Jewish lives, and women in their late forties and fifties, many with their children gone to college, who had always felt left out and inferior at services and had decided to end their sense of exclusion. I envied their seriousness. I had done a bar mitzvah to please my parents, to get enough money in gifts for a stereo and to start saving for college. I had memorized all the Hebrew—and sung it quite nicely—with no interest in understanding what it meant. Afterward, like all my friends, I stopped going to services, having run my mock-spiritual marathon. The women I'd been interviewing were infinitely more thoughtful than I was or could have been at thirteen.

The first one, Mrs. Rudner, a tiny woman adrift on an enormous white and gold couch, had been reserved, almost suspicious, until I took a chance on her accent and switched to Yiddish. We chatted for two valuable hours, once she could stop marveling at how well I spoke. Now, though, reviewing my notes, I was struggling. I'd written some in very sloppy Yiddish which kept colliding on the page (going right to left) with phrases and sentences in English. I thought of Henry Higgins singing "And the Hebrews learn it backwards, which is absolutely frightening."

Leon's bare shiny desk grinned in the fluorescent light. I settled in to decipher what I'd written, gradually losing myself in the work, eased by the big old building piled around me in the cool evening. I heard the distant slide and groan of the janitor's cart, jangling keys, and slamming doors. At ten o'clock, there were footsteps out in the receptionists' area.

Martha burst in, red-cheeked, squinting, a ring of keys in her left hand.

"Leon's not here," I said.

She stared at me, hands vague at her sides. And she surprised me by saying "Good." I watched her cross to his desk, sit on it, her strong back to me, wild hair a tumult of light. She was very striking in jeans and gray turtleneck, jean jacket.

"I thought he'd be here," she brought out after a moment, as if wondering why she'd said "Good" before. When she turned her beautiful full face to me, the white light slashed at her wide cheeks and made her look a little like Marlene Dietrich. I studied the grayish eyes, long eyebrows, nose and mouth. I had seen her only a few times, and never like this.

"Do you have a mezuzah?" she asked.

"What?"

"At home, on your doorpost? You are Jewish, right?"

I told her that no, I didn't have a mezuzah.

"Leon didn't want me to have one because *he* doesn't." Martha stood, pulled a chair over, and sat loosely in it like a dancer after a grueling class, gracefully exhausted. "Leon said it would happen, someone would rip it off. I hate when he's right."

"Someone stole it?"

Martha shrugged. "It's gone. Just two little holes where the nails were. He said it would happen."

I didn't add that's why I had never had one for any apartment I lived in outside New York. I'd imagined it destroyed and a swastika smearing my door in jagged black paint.

"He doesn't want me to be Jewish," she went on, hands clasped thoughtfully, eyes pained. "He doesn't like that I'm a secretary at Hadassah. It's too Jewish for him."

Then why was he working here? I wondered. But I just shuffled together my notes and suggested a drink, without imagining she would say no. I was that sure of myself.

We strolled out to the closest bar, a little place plastered with Toulouse-Lautrec posters. Sitting with Martha was exhilarating because she was so beautiful, with a face I found not perfect but fine, shaded and unexpected. For the first time, I felt I could be deeply at home in Chicago.

"When I saw it," she said, "I wanted to scream. Run up and down the hallway, pound on doors, find who did it."

"You felt powerless."

"I felt Jewish. I felt someone violated me as a Jew."

"Was it just kids, maybe?"

"No, I hammered it in too well." She grimaced. "It makes me sick thinking of someone touching it, throwing it out somewhere."

Martha's father, she told me, was not Jewish and her mother was "only by birth," but in college Martha had dated a guy who later went to the Jewish Theological Seminary.

"It started being important to me," she explained. Leaning back, gorgeous with anecdote, hands commandingly still on the table, she went on: "Once in this introductory psychology class, the professor said something like, Freud's view of man as basically evil was from Jewish tradition. Well, what did I know about Freud or anything, but it sounded funny, so I asked Ron, who I was dating. Next class, I told the professor that Jewish tradition emphasized man's free will, the choice between good and evil. He just stared."

"What happened?"

"He asked if this was a new development in Jewish thought. I said no, just the mainstream of Judaism for over two thousand years. One girl in class told me later she wanted to applaud." Martha smiled. "I started reading a lot, books Ron gave me, history, fiction; I felt pretty dumb. I wanted to know where my mom came from."

We left without having mentioned Leon. I walked her to the blue Volvo parked in the lot near our building. I took Martha's hand to wish her good night and drove north to Evanston to think about another man's woman.

My parents would've called that *grub*—Yiddish for coarse, dirty.

I sat up late in my rigorously modern apartment with its glaring white walls, motel-like sliding windows, a place of pure and boring lines unlike my parents' West Side New York apartment with its archways, moldings, and deep windows. I was as intrigued by Martha as by her story—and I wondered why Leon was hostile to her *being* Jewish. Drinking a beer, I wondered how else she was discovering herself to be a Jew.

I wondered how I could help.

That was Monday. Thursday, Leon went off to a four-day Zionist conference in St. Louis, and the next day, which I had off, Martha called me at home.

"Alan, would you come shopping with me?"

I said yes and dressed, without having asked why, what for.

All that week, Leon had been annoyingly polite, as if he felt he'd bested me in our discussion of Yiddish, so when Martha arrived at my apartment building, I stepped into her car with a keen sense of annoyance. She wore red that day, looking cool and deliberate. As we drove to Skokie, I felt we were escaping in the provocative sunshine that urged action, movement, life.

"I want to go to Tamaroff's, the Jewish bookstore. I've never been there."

I assumed Leon wouldn't go with her.

On the short drive over, we had the half-furtive preliminary conversation I'd had before, sharing our romantic pasts, or highlights from them, anyway, in a mature casual fashion: emotional historians. I told her about the Rumanian girl in college I'd almost married; she told me about her affair with an English professor. The details—my poor comprehension of Balkan history and her labored villanelles—weren't of real consequence.

As we drove through the flat modern suburb replete with shuls, Jewish community centers, kosher food stores, bakeries, and delis, I felt almost lazy, suspended in the present.

Tamaroff's was a small store in a shabby mall, crammed with glass shelves full of menorahs, kiddush cups, spice boxes, candlesticks, kosher wines filling one corner and books spreading in every direction on shelf after shelf: popular Jewish novels, books on the Holocaust and Jewish holidays, scripture, and then higher up, great gleaming-backed Hebrew volumes that seemed too beautiful to touch. There were bumper stickers, song albums, holiday cards, kids' T-shirts, cases of *tallis* bags, and rows of glass-fronted drawers jammed with yarmulkes, phylacteries, and things I couldn't make out. It was a flood for me; I gawked along with Martha, who reached and pointed and stared and held as if she had been released from some prison. Even I, who'd grown up in Manhattan, had never felt such richness before—perhaps because I was with Martha. I wanted everything, and I wanted to share it with her.

I bought a heavy black and gold scroll-type mezuzah whose weight said something wonderful to me. The gold letters spelling *Shaddai*, Almighty, were hypnotic.

I saw Martha choose a plainer mezuzah, two low brass candlesticks, and a wooden board with *Shabbat* carved into it. The bearded man at the counter asked if she was getting married. She laughed.

In the car, she opened her bag and handed me a blue velvet yarmulke.

"I want us to have *Shabbos* dinner tonight," she said.

"It's beautiful." I had not worn one in years, since a cousin's wedding. I tried it on as if expecting to be seared with a vision.

"You're gorgeous, Al."

I took it off.

But driving back, I enjoyed her approval. I had my father's looks—we were tall, wide-shouldered men with broad, strong features, curly dark hair, blue eyes—and growing up I had resented being his copy. I struggled to blur the resemblance, first with a mustache and then a desperate little beard, but for a few years now I'd felt more relaxed; after all, no one in our family was exactly a "raving beauty," as my mother would say. Martha's compliment delighted me.

As if her gift had freed us, we talked about Leon.

"He hates being Jewish." she said. "He had it shoved at him all his life."

"By his parents?"

"Oh yeah. I was lucky, I guess, but Leon's parents made him go to Hebrew school and have a bar mitzvah."

"That's not so terrible."

"His father *beat* him if he didn't study. All his friends had to be Jewish, he couldn't bring anyone else home. It was kind of crazy, so he hates it and he hates Jews, most of them. You like being Jewish, don't you?"

I told her how important Yiddish was to me, though talking to Mrs. Rudner I'd wished I was more fluent. I told her that in college I had drifted away from going to services, not because they were meaningless, but because I found too much meaning: obligation, history, challenge, belief. I struggled against a way of life even though I sometimes fantasized about living in Israel or going to a yeshivah to *immerse* myself in Jewishness.

Martha was quiet for a time, eyes ahead, but her fine hand rested more easily on the wheel, I thought, and her shoulders were lowered, relaxed by my words, perhaps. In that car, the vague deep longing to find some authentic way to be Jewish came back to me with the intensity of regret.

"Have you ever read Lawrence Kushner?" she asked.

"I've heard of him."

"He's mystical, he says somewhere about holiness, 'Entrances are everywhere and all the time. You don't have to become something other than yourself, because you're already there.'"

My parents would definitely have called Leon a *mudneh mensh*—a strange unpleasant fellow—I thought the following Monday afternoon in our office. He smiled stiffly when I said hello.

"Did you like Skokie?" he asked, settling at his desk.

I turned, hoping I didn't look guilty. "I didn't really see it."

"Well, Tamaroff's, then."

I nodded.

He glanced aside. "Martha's always magnetic on the run."

"On the run?"

He leaned back in his chair, smug-eyed. "I'm sure you think her interest in Judaism is exciting. It is. All her interests are exciting. For a few months. What a devoted jogger she was! Read the magazines, learned the language, changed her diet. And that red sweatband, wow. Yoga? Three kinds. Biofeedback. Adopt an Asian child. Save the baby seals. Disco. Tanning. She tries everything—it's like having your own *People* magazine. She probably thinks you'll make a Jew out of her. I bet you had a lovely *Shabbos*. . . . I saw the candlesticks." Leon sat rigid, cynical, unblinking. "You probably imagined having a child with her."

I flushed, trapped by his guess.

Leon nodded triumphantly while my shamed silence rose around us like a flood. "What'll you do, Alan, when Martha decides to go to Mass? She's half Irish, you know."

"But her mother's Jewish—"

"So she's all Jew? Martha isn't all anything. She couldn't be. I know."

I wanted to pull a wall down on him or strike and strike at that knowing, vicious face—but my rage made me feel doubly helpless, like a small boy cornered by his father.

"Why do you stay with her?" I managed.

This seemed to amuse him. "I can see right through her, no surprises. That helps."

Leon went off for a meeting with the managing editor, and I jammed stuff into a folder and left early, calling "I don't feel good" to the frowning receptionist as I fled. I was sure that Leon's malice was practiced, that he'd outfaced other men before about Martha.

At home, lying in the tub, lost in steam, I fought Leon's slurs. Perhaps Martha had other enthusiasms, but *Shabbos* had been too real, too beautiful. When she lit the candles, simply, unpretentiously, I sensed in her a *Yiddisheh neshomeh*, a Jewish spirit. When I salted the challah, that rite connecting us to the incense in the Temple, I felt that we were two pilgrims emerging from different deserts. Was it wrong to picture introducing her to my parents, teaching her Yiddish, reading to her from Peretz, to enjoy being Jewish with her, to feel romantic that evening?

I worked at home until Martha called to say she was coming over, and then I felt nervous, suspicious. Maybe Leon was right about her. . . . But then I thought of the women I'd been interviewing, all so dedicated and serious, and how proud their families and rabbis were. I wondered how many women were struggling like Martha to be Jewish in some way that made sense to them.

I expected Martha to be harassed or crying when she showed up, but we rarely get to play out the scenes we imagine. She was warm, relaxed. We sat on the couch with some wine and watched the sky darken, the city light up. She spoke calmly; we held hands.

"Leon was so nasty when he found the candlesticks. He asked if he should buy me a head kerchief and lumpy shoes and throw out my makeup. He started humming things from *Fiddler on the Roof*! But it didn't touch me, he was just spinning his wheels."

"Where did you meet him?"

She grimaced. "Two years ago in a bar."

Then I told her what Leon had said.

"But it's true, Alan. I *have* done lots of things and got bored. This isn't the same, though; that's why Leon's fighting it. You're different." She laughed. "When we went out last week, I thought, God, he is so *normal*." After a silence, she asked, apparently thinking of Leon, "Did your folks beat you?"

"No."

"My father did, sometimes, when I was little, but I used to scream so loud, he couldn't stand it. Do Jews beat their kids?"

"You're not supposed to. You can only hit a child if he's refusing to do a mitzvah."

"I know what that is: a good deed."

"Right. But that leaves out kids who're too small to understand what the mitzvah means, and you can't hit a kid old enough to hit you back, you'd be causing him to sin."

"Is there more?"

I grinned. "You can only hit a kid with something that breaks easy."

"Which leaves out hands."

"Right. Basically, you can only use a reed."

"A what?"

"A dried reed."

"How do you know all that?"

"A friend in high school asked his rabbi, after his mother slapped him around for something."

"She must have been mad when he told her."

"She was ashamed."

"You know so much," Martha said, shaking her head. "No, you *do*." There was a flattering hunger in her eyes that filled me with enthusiasm. Years ago, I had been a Jew, had prayed, with my family, with friends, or alone, but never with anyone like Martha, never anyone for whom being Jewish was so much a problem, so promising and so alien. Cause a new light to shine upon Zion, I thought, *Or hadash al tsion ta-ir. Shabbos* melodies began to stir in me.

"Would you take me to services someday? Would you teach me?" She was as open as a child sharing a secret.

I wanted to tell her about my series, maybe introduce her to some of the women. She could have a bas mitzvah, too, and I could help her study.

"What about Leon?" I asked.

"Forget him."

"We share an office. He's supposed to be training me."

She shrugged. "Train him back."

"But what about Leon?"

Now Martha rose. "He doesn't *own* me," she murmured.

She went off to the bathroom and I surrendered to memory: seeing my father cry one Yom Kippur as he beat his heart; practicing the Torah blessings with my mother; the Passover seders; the Chanukah *gelt*; fasting on Tisha B'Av. The simplicity of Martha's hunger for the unknown, the guessed at, had opened me to my old longings for a commitment that filled as well as bound. I wanted to reenter that world of possibility, with *her*, and when she came back to hug me, I realized that we were *already there*.

Sanctuary

"We like it best here on the porch," Louise Bedford was telling him while she fixed gin and tonics, her smooth white hands gentle, encouraging, as if the ice were a cranky child she was coaxing to bed.

"It's very pretty." Victor glanced around the wide, deep, shaded porch where a flotilla of unmatched wicker chairs drifted around the large worn couch. The pre–World War I brick house, like the others on the thick-treed, ostentatiously quiet street, murmured serenity to him, but he couldn't relax.

"Yes, it *is* pretty," his adviser's wife replied after a moment, as if she had been hoping for a more original adjective. Louise Bedford handed him the drink, seeming to mark with it the privilege of knowing her. It wasn't exactly arrogance in the cool blue-eyed glance, the thin smile, but what Victor thought of as assurance, Eastern Assurance. She was from Vermont, he knew, vaguely related to the Kennedys, dressed and walked like a tennis player, spoke with a slur of geographies, her words occasionally curling with a French or an English accent. Mrs. Bedford had gone to school "abroad," he'd heard from other graduate students at Madison, and wore her studies and travel like perfume. She also had "money of her own."

"I'm so glad Bedford brought you out here. He says you have potential."

Was *that* why Bedford had invited him? Victor hardly knew his adviser, and had taken only one of Bedford's classes—a James seminar. Bedford was one of the country's most important James scholars, having published two acclaimed books on James's late novels, a biography of Alice James, edited many collections of essays on James, and even written a book analyzing Edith Wharton's literary debt to James.

But Bedford didn't look Jamesian. John Bedford was a large, bearded, informal man whose broad chest, hearty good mornings, and pump-handle handshakes were like cloudy swoops of skywriting compared to the other English professors' copperplate. Bedford's corduroy jackets, chinos and loafers, the ravaged leather briefcase, all seemed talismanic, prizes in a contest Bedford was sure he'd won. Bedford had mentioned once at a department party that he'd grown up in Sheboygan, a tailor's son, dreaming of the University of Wisconsin, of being a teacher there or someplace like it. "I couldn't imagine a more fulfilling way to live."

Though last term Bedford had praised Victor's paper on *Washington Square*, the weekend invitation was a big surprise. On the ride out of town, an hour south, Victor, very nervous, had little to say and even less chance to say it. Bedford, large and wooly in black turtleneck and leather jacket, asked big booming questions without waiting for answers, laughed indulgently at his own jokes, and somehow made Victor feel like a poor relative on a yearly outing.

Now Louise said, "There'll be others coming, you know. Harry and Genevieve and Jack."

"Jack Porter?"

"J.P., yes. We grew up together." Louise Bedford thoughtfully sipped from her glass.

Bitterly beautiful, middle-aged Porter—their department's writer-in-residence—had written seven novels that seemed to Victor to have had as much literary impact as the erratically piled student papers seething in every spare corner of the graduate assistants' offices.

"He should've been a fashion model," Victor once heard someone spit at a party, annoyed no doubt by Porter's Baume & Mercier watch, Gucci loafers, and Evan Picone separates. Porter's father had been an executive with IBM, and that was the money he really lived on.

"What's he like?" Victor flushed, trying to think of something to make the question sound less childish, but Louise seemed to take it seriously, and sat with her head back, eyes narrowed.

"Demanding, I think."

"I haven't read his work."

Louise looked surprised, as if Porter's books were too personal to discuss.

"Where's my drink?" Bedford stomped out to join them, voice as hard as the slam of the screen door. "J.P.'s driving up after dinner—just called." Bedford grabbed at the silver ice bucket.

"After," Louise echoed, and the word sounded like code to Victor, who watched them as they discussed their dinner, trying to catch some intimate emanation, a spark of their fire, but they seemed more like partners than lovers or husband and wife. Partners, as cool together as the five-bedroom house washed in yellows, gray, and rose, the luminescent *vision* of a house. Bedford and his wife of twenty years made sense in this setting, composed well, Victor thought, wondering briefly what James might have made of the couple.

"Do you know Harry?" Louise asked him, languorously crossing her long tanned legs, smoothing the white skirt. Bedford gulped his drink, leaning back in a frazzled wicker chair, sloshing his ice around.

"I took his Iris Murdoch seminar."

"God," Bedford muttered, looking down into his glass as if repulsed. "What the hell for?"

"Will you write on James for your master's?" Louise went on, dim, distant, as if playing with the words of a dreamy torch song.

Before Victor could answer, a gray BMW pulled into the wide driveway behind Bedford's Renault. Harry and Genevieve Fisher issued from the car all smiles and quips and road talk, chattering up the stairs to kiss and hug and nod and squabble over seats and drinks. Sitting opposite Bedford at the bar cart, they gossiped about a new instructor; Bedford fueled the talk with ice, liquor, and lemon shards.

Victor listened only to the interplay of voices, now and then stirring uneasily as if under the weight of all the trees that marked how fine a street this was—like pretty chorus soldiers in a comic opera, ludicrous and stiff. He watched the Fishers.

Harry and Genevieve both taught Modern British, were small, thin, prissy-looking in steel-framed glasses, and given to tweeds. They smoked Dunhills, spoke in vaguely English accents though they were from Brooklyn, and each had seen *Brideshead Revisited* on PBS four times. Their plain fifty-year-old faces were pinched and unattractive; despite having been married since high school, the Fishers had the neglected look of spinsters.

"J.P.'s joining us later," Louise dropped, breaking off the discussion, which had inexorably plunged through the thickets of speculation into a clearing of slander. "Dinner in an hour?" Mrs. Bedford stood as if to shoo them inside.

"He's bringing Rose," Bedford said to his wife as they entered the house. Victor followed. Upstairs in the small, scented, pleasant guest room he unpacked his bag on the yellow and gray striped quilt. Everything matched perfectly in this room—curtains, rug, book spines.

"Rose," he said aloud, surprised. She had also entered the master's program last September, but from the first day of orientation she had seemed as aloof as a fairy-tale princess hiding among her people to prove a theory or foil a plot. On their first and only date, Rose picked him up at the graduate dorm in a black Cutlass Sierra whose interior was like an exotic creamy dessert. She wore sandals and a lime green T-shirt dress forced outward by her heavy breasts. Victor had fantasized about Rose in their research class, but the rich fact of her presence—her loose thick black hair, blue eyes, the tan that was so even it seemed ordered from a catalogue—burned away even the possibility of thought.

Dinner at a Mexican restaurant was unexceptional, as was talk about classes. Things went wrong when she asked what his father did.

He blushed. "He's a piano tuner."

And she smiled as if wanting to say "How sweet."

"Yours?" he asked.

"Investments."

Victor asked about Penn, her undergraduate school, and Rose told him about the nose jobs. Forty percent of Penn's students were Jewish, and most, she said, had at least one nose job.

"One?"

"Well, you have to get it right," she said.

Rose talked about her friends' cars, vacations, and clothes with disdain, and after dinner, as they walked on campus, he thought she sounded like the New Yorkers who complain about crime, noise, crowds, strikes, and garbage as if each outrage proved them superior, was a gleaming medal to be hung on a brave and noble chest.

There was nothing between them. Back at the dorm, he stripped, pulled on running shorts and his Nikes, went out to run off his disappointment. He had known rich girls like Rose at high school, who even at sixteen treated the unimportant boys like coffee shops you'd only enter to get change of a quarter.

He did ten miles.

After a dinner of cream of asparagus soup, spinach and artichoke hearts salad, angel hair pasta al pesto, a raspberry sorbet, vol-au-vent, rum torte, chocolates, apples and Brie, three wines he'd never heard of, and a heated discussion of Flannery O'Connor in which Victor just listened, they drifted into the luxurious pale living room for coffee and Courvoisier. Bedford made a small fire with not one wasted motion.

"This is *incredible*," Victor blurted, unable to moderate his praise any longer.

Bedford grinned and Louise thanked him, gracious, pleased.

There followed an argument about department politics Victor was too mellow to follow, which Genevieve Fisher interrupted by describing a Fassbinder retrospective she'd seen in New York. Bedford roared: "German bullshit!"

"You always were a perceptive critic," Louise purred.

Harry Fisher laughed, his small tight mouth gobbling open. Bedford shook his head, Louise insinuated herself more deeply into her ecru chair, Genevieve yawned.

Victor didn't hear a car drive up, but suddenly the doorbell stroked the air like a patient clock.

Bedford ambled out. "You're late!"

Jack Porter said something indistinguishable and glided into the room, battered and delicate, like an older actress bravely playing the ingenue. Rose followed in black boots and dress, her hair piled at either side of her head. She looked like a Doric column, Victor thought.

"You all know Rose Klein?" Porter asked, his broad green-eyed face luminous, reserved.

There were nods, smiles, and Rose came to sit by Victor, patted his hand with a silky "So, how've you been?"

* * *

After the others had drunk their way to bed, he and Rose sat on
the porch with nothing more than a distant hum of traffic and the
night blur of crickets and birds. The air smelled uncertain to Victor.
Rose was excited, firing smiles at him, her eyes delighted, wide.

"We ate at Benvolio's—our first real date." She stretched her
shoulders as if massaged by the memory.

Rose was treating him like a confidant and it was subtly de-
meaning.

"What's he like?"

Rose paused as if dazzled. "*Honey . . .*" was all she said.

Rose had been there only a semester and was already involved
with their writer-in-residence. It struck him as cunning.

"Where'd you meet?"

"A party. I've read all his books."

"Nobody's read all his books."

Rose grinned and he felt outside the closed little world she
seemed so free in. She'd called Bedford "John" and joked with the
Fishers as if they were family friends.

"I've read some twice," Rose dropped.

"Do you like any?"

"I like *him*."

Was it the *idea* of Porter she found fascinating, the figure,
show, the position? Porter seemed faded to Victor, with no real
talent or magnetism—and no future.

"Jealous?" Rose teased.

"What?"

"I don't mind." She laughed, a full, sexual, drunken laugh
from her throat, her breasts, and then strolled upstairs.

Victor sat on the porch, flushed. Going to bed would be an
admission of something like defeat, so he made another drink,
feeling that tonight his flight from New York was over, that the
energy of escape had bled away into the sharp April air and he was
alone.

He had left New York to get away from his parents' silent
nagging. As if acting on the instructions of a team of psychologists,
they had left him resoundingly to himself for years, turning everything back with "What do *you* think? What do *you* want?" and

always behind this great display of freedom he suspected plans and expectations they would never discuss. In their heavy silence, he read despair: "Your sister's an alcoholic, your brother drives a truck and lives in a trailer park . . . don't let us down." It was too much to live with, and so he had fled—but to what? He had no real friends in the program, no one he wanted to see or talk to more often than once a week over drinks or between classes to complain. Nothing had really touched him here. He felt trapped in one of those ridiculous acts lounge hypnotists make people perform to amuse a dinner and drinks crowd; he could have been miming breakfast or grunting like a pig, for all it mattered.

Louise Bedford was pouring coffee for Porter when Victor, in jeans and black T-shirt, entered the large white kitchen the next morning. They glanced up from a litter of saucers, spoons, marmalade, and brioches. Both wore robes: Louise's, long, pale blue, tightly belted; Porter's, thick, brown, monogrammed, ending at his thin hairy calves. Louise smiled, pointed to a seat for Victor.

Porter continued the story Victor had evidently interrupted: "Then last week she came to class with pink hair and announced she'd taken a new name. Ready? Cremora du Bois. Instead of a story, she brought in a Betamax and a five-minute tape of herself shouting 'You mama sucks! Your mama sucks!' The class loved it. Visigoths! They said it was 'intense' and 'total.' I told her she was still talentless, despite the pink hair. She called me a fascist." Porter wiped a crumb from his hand.

Regal, uninterested, Louise asked Victor if he'd slept well.

"Very."

She smiled and he stirred sugar into his coffee, embarrassed now to be dressed so early.

"What're we doing today?" he asked after a silence.

"Doing?" Louise looked at Porter and they smiled. "Well . . . I suppose someone could go for a drive if you like, and there's a sort of nature museum in—"

The Fishers breezed in, wearing matching pajamas and kimono-style robes, pouncing on breakfast, noisy, bitchy. Victor slipped off to the study with its deep gold rug, honey-colored shelves displaying James first editions, everywhere the gleam of brass in fittings, picture frames, on the large desk bristling with leather accessories. He took the largest chair and plunged into a recent copy of *The Massachusetts Review.*

From the kitchen came a steadily increasing morning clamor that was seductive but private. He wondered again why Bedford had bothered inviting him.

"Are you pouting?" Rose asked at the door, elegant in a Chinese-collared green silk robe, her hair loose and inviting. She padded in, barefoot, and sat on the edge of the desk as if it was the best place, the *only* place in the room.

"You're pretty lucky," she said.

"How?"

"Being here . . . Bedford doesn't like most graduate students, because they try to suck up."

"He likes me?"

Rose frowned. "Why else would he invite you? Morbid curiosity?"

Victor thought of a line in Bedford's comments on his seminar paper: "You have the makings of a highly original critic." Could it be true?

"And it doesn't hurt that you're Jewish, I guess," Rose was saying.

"Bedford's *Jewish?*"

"Sure—at least his parents were." Rose made it sound like a childhood injury Bedford had overcome. "Let's eat."

At the kitchen table, he watched Bedford and thought there was, in fact, a resemblance to a cousin of his, Larry. But would he have guessed without Rose telling him?

There were no Jews in the master's program and only a few Jewish professors in the English department. Victor had been glad that his last name, Green, was neutral enough, and that as a blond he couldn't be pegged right away (most people here thought he was Scandinavian). He was sick of having to defend Israel, sick of hearing about the Holocaust, other people's history and pain. It had nothing to do with him, and here in Wisconsin he had been hoping to leave all of it back home.

Later in the morning, Victor went back to the kitchen, where Louise Bedford was making strudel while Genevieve lurked at the pan-ridden table. They glanced his way, curious, as if he might at last explain himself competently, with charm and even intelligence, but all he could say was "Where's Rose?"

It was clearly a disappointment, but Bedford's wife took it well. "She's off with J.P."

He nodded.

Bedford and Harry squatted in the living room playing Scrabble in German. Victor watched the ugly-looking words creep across the board, quiet, content not to be in the way. Bedford grunted as if each tile were heavier than the last, and he and Harry talked about Goethe's *Elective Affinities*.

When the exhausting game was done, Bedford went to lie down and Harry Fisher lit a cigarette and sat near Victor on the yellow and rose couch.

"You did good work in my class," he said.

"Thanks."

"And in Bedford's, I hear. But do you really think James is for you? Do you read much Bellow? Or Philip Roth?"

"No."

"Think about it."

"Darling?" Genevieve Fisher called from the kitchen. "Come tell Louise why we hate Velázquez; I can never get it right."

Fisher smiled and sailed from the room.

After another magnificent dinner, they all separated that evening. Porter wanted to write in the study; the Bedfords walked over to a neighbor's for drinks; Harry and Genevieve perched in the living room listening to a compact disc of *Daphnis and Chloé* on Bedford's Bang & Olufsen system.

Rose called it "Daffy and Cloying" out on the porch, where she lolled in a red and gold dress and gold slippers, her hair caught to one side with ribbons and beads. Large, theatrical, perfumed, sultry-voiced, she talked about her "travels"—England, Brazil, New Zealand.

Porter cut her off, emerging from the house with an awkwardly held legal pad, pages dropping and flapping: "You have to hear this." Rose followed inside.

Victor sat by himself, drinking, trying to enjoy the cool evening, the Ravel floating from the living room, punctuated by the Fisher's ecstatic little sighs. He felt stung by the image of Rose steeped in remembrance, and awed by the beautiful house. It seemed then that he had so little in his life. His family never called or wrote; he got in touch only when he wanted something. All his college friends had married or moved or both, already shooting off into their futures. None of his dates in the program had been anything more than a waste of time so far.

Everyone here had something to be or believe in. What did he have? Louise Bedford had mentioned his "potential" as if it were a spot on some map, definite, historic—but what did it mean? Could he ever have a life as rich and satisfying as Bedford's?

The street had gone dark around him when the Bedfords walked up to the house. Louise's voice broke on him first, sharp and strained. Her arm was firmly in her husband's and almost seemed to be steering him along. Bedford pulled away and lumbered to the stairs, sat at their foot.

"John."

"Go to bed."

Louise Bedford nodded at Victor as she passed coolly up the stairs into the house.

"You drunk?" Bedford asked without turning. "Good. Lou hates it. Scares her shiksa ass." Bedford grunted. "It's a great ass. Aerobics."

Victor eased down the stair to sit near him, amazed that Bedford, *the* John Bedford, was talking to him so freely.

Bedford rambled on a little about the book he was finishing for Oxford, a biography of Henry James's eccentric friend Howard Sturgis. "I can't bring myself to wrap it up."

"Why not?"

"The reviewers. They can sink you."

Victor couldn't believe that someone so famous was worried about book reviewers having it in for him!

"I hate this life," Bedford suddenly growled. "Nothing but books. We never had a kid, couldn't. Well, I couldn't. Low count. And little Fisher has seven. Seven! I wouldn't adopt even though Lou would. I wanted *my* kid, *mine*. You know, when I was a kid, five maybe, my old man used to slap me just when he thought I was looking at him funny. So I was gonna have a kid I'd treat right. I planned it all out. Cornell, Yale, then a job, sharp wife, tenure,

my boy. Take him to school with me, show him my office. He'd
be so proud. . . .

"Never happened," Bedford snapped. "So all I'll leave behind
is some books. This house, Louise, going to conferences, being
important, it's all bullshit, it doesn't mean shit to me." He reared
on Victor. "Listen, are you sure you want to stay in school? You
don't look happy here. Get out while you can, get a *real* job, have
children, don't end up like me."

" 'Live, live all you can,' " Victor quoted, " 'It's a mistake
not to.' "

Bedford stared at him. *"What?!"*

A little embarrassed he had to explain it to *Bedford*, Victor
said, "That's what Strether tells Chad in *The Ambassadors*."

"You think this is some fuckin' scene in a *book*? What is *wrong*
with you?" He leaned closer, grabbed Victor's shoulders as if to
shake him apart, but pulled back just as suddenly.

"Forget it," he said, heaving himself up and stumbling to the
door. "Forget what I said."

Bedford plunged off inside, and Victor sat there for a long time.

Caravans

My father never won at cards—not for long, anyway. While my mother would pile and twitch her nickels and dimes with fingers that almost grinned, and Sam and Pauline, their neighbors and best friends, lost or won with exclamations and applause, Dad would grow more and more sullen, his round blue-eyed face somehow flattened, lifeless, as if more than change was draining from his heavy dark hands. Gradually, the phrase he muttered as if challenging each poker round to prove him wrong would come.

"I'm cursed," he'd say, watching Pauline flutter a full house and gobble up a kitty. She was as unlike my mother as any woman her age I knew: honestly blond, full-bodied, embarrassingly rosy-looking next to her husband, Sam, a thin and simple man all shrugs and "How d'ya like that's?" They were all four in the garment industry, which had been doing "bad" for as many years as I'd been listening. That's where they all had met, after the War—not in some Displaced Persons camp, not in a sealed train or on a forced march, but in New York City. It disappointed me that they couldn't trace their friendship back across the ocean; it made the past even darker. Sam and Pauline had never said a word to my parents about what they'd lived through; my mother swore to that. I could understand *wanting* to keep silent, but not actually succeeding.

Mom spoke sparingly about fleeing Warsaw in 1939 to Tashkent, deep in the Soviet Union, where her parents and sister starved to death, but she did answer my questions, and with remarkable poise, I thought.

Dad only referred to the past, *that* past, when the cards, or his lack of skill, betrayed him. "I'm cursed," he'd bring out. "I shouldn't have lived."

I would be reading on my bed those Thursday nights, with the door open, and even though the hallway from the front of our Inwood apartment to the bedrooms and bath was quite long, you could hear most of what people said in the dining room, which was where they played. When my father's flat awful words caught my ear, stamping out the crack and slide of cards, the tinny click of silver coins on the blue plastic tablecloth, I'd put my book down, transfixed. It was ugly and intimate, but the game went on.

Mom told him to stop. Pauline good-naturedly recounted previous hands that had amazed her; Sam would talk about work. Nothing helped. Once Dad had spoken the word *cursed*, he couldn't stop the descent. His life was also "empty," "nothing," "dead"— and because he mostly spoke in Yiddish (*"leydig," "gornisht," "toyt"*), the judgment seemed more solemn and severe. In English, he would've sounded melodramatic.

Once Pauline tried a different approach: "You have a wonderful wife. And such a fine son."

"Hah!" he said. "He dresses like a girl! A *feygeleh*." That was Yiddish for faggot: little birdie.

"No . . ." Pauline hissed, always ready to defend me. "He just wants to look like his friends."

"*Piristaneh*," Mom said, Russian for "Stop it." Russian was the language in which she argued and pleaded, as if she was a diplomat required to mark the formality of his interactions.

I cringed at *feygeleh*, as I always did when Dad made fun of my long hair and bandannas, my bell-bottoms, fringed belts, tapestry vests, my sandals and beads. It was not what I wanted *anyone* to think of me. But for my father, the anger in that word was only a moment's diversion from being cursed that one night.

Hand after losing hand, the same miserable talk of his "dark fate," his "cursed luck." It was so terrible, I wanted to laugh, to burst in on them and discover the joke. But he meant it. And even after the break—in which the table was overwhelmed with honey cake, strudel, cheesecake, tea, coffee, slivovitz, and even later when the cards were put away near eleven o'clock and platters of fruit glistened in the light of our cut-glass chandelier—Dad would look battered, as if each card were a day he longed to forget.

I'd help clean up while Pauline remarked on how handsome I was becoming and Sam made his one joke, meant to get me over my by-now-legendary shyness with girls, I guess: "Got any girl-friends?"

"Three," I'd say. "That's one extra for you."

Pauline would shake her head, say "He's so fresh," and I'd be off the hook again.

When they left for their apartment a floor below, Dad would go to bed, sometimes after taking a bath so hot and long, orchids could've sprung up from the tiles. So Mom said. She was the one who could joke best. Once, in junior high, when the girl I'd finally asked to go steady with me told me she was going with my best friend (who'd encouraged me to ask!), I sat through dinner without a word until Mom wondered what was wrong.

"I wish I was dead," I muttered.

"Then you don't want dessert?"

We cracked up, while Dad just frowned.

Mom and I would often sit those Thursday nights in the kitchen with WQXR playing softly from the little black plastic radio perched on the fridge like a bird on a hippo. My mother, a slim pale woman with deep-set narrow green eyes, had a dreamy kind of elegance, as if when she lit her after-dinner cigarette or slipped a purse under her arm before going out, she was in a gentler, more refined world. There was something ineffably touching and distant about her: she was as beautiful as a summer garden seen from a speeding train. Her soft voice, for me, lit up pictures of dark paneled rooms, tiled kitchen stoves, thick velvet curtains, tea from a samovar: scenes from a Turgenev novel. I admired her; my friends thought she was "neat," liked her accent, the vaguely foreign coil of dark red hair, the lightness of her attentions. Unlike most mothers, she never fussed; food was offered easily, questions were casual. She had never once said my hair was too long, even when it was almost down to my shoulders (I would eventually cut it short when I went out for the track team); she didn't complain about my tie-dyed shirts and jeans, or make fun of any of the music I played: The Doors, Jefferson

Airplane, The Who. And she didn't even complain about Dad, except indirectly.

"They're tired of it," she sighed one Thursday, handing me a dish to dry. "It's not very interesting to listen to him."

"Why does he always lose?"

"Not always. But he plays wild, he can't bluff."

I wondered that night why, after more than twenty years, Sam and Pauline hadn't given up, but the question came to me in bed and I forgot it while I slept. I suppose they were used to him, used to the long after-dinner walks, the summers together in the Catskills or on the beach at Rockaway, the factory, the political discussions, the union banquets, all of it, every link that brought them back and back to the dining room table—the arena in which, once a month, my father fought and struggled, only to fall like a gladiator trapped in a net that readies him for the sword thrust. How could they listen to him, though, when sometimes I wanted to storm in there and slap him so hard I shook just imagining it? I was ashamed of feeling that, but the fantasy of stopping him was so powerful, I couldn't control it. Perhaps what enraged me was that I had so little sense of who my father had been as a boy in Warsaw, his dreams, his schooling, his crazy cousins (I figured everyone had a few of those), that to have the door to all that wrenched open and slammed with each bitter "cursed" was too much.

One time, Dad had given me some facts to fill the void. We may have been Jewish, but except for the Yiddish books and newspaper and the mezuzah on our doorpost that was painted over, left by a previous tenant, you couldn't tell. Besides sending out some New Year's cards, we celebrated no holidays by anything more than a special meal, and I hadn't even been circumcised like all my Jewish friends. When I was eleven, I asked my Dad to tell me why, *really*. Over the years, he'd said things about "health reasons," but that didn't make any sense, or not anymore.

"Because that's how they *knew*, that's how they could tell!" he spat. "My Polish was the best, and my German—! I had blue eyes, blue like the sky, but you couldn't hide *that*."

"This is America," I ventured, and he nodded, contemptuous, knowing, his tragedy crushing my unthinking optimism.

Likewise, when later that year I mentioned wanting a bar mitzvah because my friends who went to Hebrew school were studying for theirs—though I had no real idea what was involved or what it meant—he mocked me.

"You want presents? Bonds?"

I blushed.

"You don't need all that *chazerai*, it's *bubbeh mysehs*, nonsense, junk. There's no God, no Torah; it's only lies. All I learned in *cheyder*, those hours chanting and sweating to be close to God, what did they get me? Tell me that."

"I don't know."

He scowled and turned away from me.

I couldn't really argue, because I wanted a bar mitzvah as I'd wanted a G.I. Joe doll in fourth grade, to join the Boy Scouts in fifth, to collect *Man from U.N.C.L.E.* books in sixth—so that I'd be as much like other kids as possible.

Sometimes I envied my friends their loud or sarcastic or even violent fathers, because basically mine worked, ate, slept in front of the television, read his newspaper, and played cards once a month. We could have been boarders renting rooms in the same house; he was that much a stranger. What he thought of me came like news bulletins through my mother: "Your father's very proud of you," she might say, discussing my grades or any other achievement. To me he said nothing. At fifteen, I could bristle so easily at any comment Mom made about what I was doing or thinking of—perhaps because I was desperate both for approval *and* to see myself as a rebel—but Dad's relayed comments had as much impact on me as a list of state capitals.

I couldn't reach him. When I asked Mom why he wouldn't talk about the War, she would smile gently, as if I had blundered so horribly, kindness was the only possible response.

It was in my junior year of high school that Pauline mentioned one afternoon she knew a very nice girl. This was a change from her joking.

"That's nice," I said. She and my mother had just come in from shopping and all the kitchen cupboards were open, waiting to be filled.

"For you it's nice. She's a beautiful girl."

I assumed Pauline meant "inside." I shrugged.

"Call her, she lives not far, in Washington Heights. I know

the father." To my mother, she added in Yiddish, "Her mother's
dead." Pauline went on: "She goes to Bronx Science *and* she's very
musical."

I groaned.

"Her name's Bonnie. Bonnie Rosenthal."

"She went to P.S. Ninety-eight!" I vaguely remembered a
pretty, dark-haired girl good at math.

"See?" Pauline beamed as if pleased to correct a cosmic error.

Mom didn't comment when Pauline left; she never said anything about my dating so little, never pried.

Now, I wasn't shy with girls because I was embarrassed about
my looks or anything. I had no zits, and even though I wasn't tall,
being on the volleyball team had given me a good body, but when
I went out—bowling, to movies, for pizza—it was with other guys
or in a mixed group in which I felt relaxed, mostly because we'd
known each other since first grade. My few dates had been incon-
clusive, maybe because I'd seen the girls so often in class, in the
stands at track meets, on the bus, that dating seemed artificial. I
kept thinking that I knew them too well to find them attractive.

I felt under a lot of pressure from Pauline and my mom, and
I *was* kind of intrigued by meeting someone "new," so I called
Bonnie. After a few slow minutes, we laughed about Pauline a little;
Bonnie thought she was "sweet." Bonnie's voice was rich, but it
was what she said next that hooked me: "My Dad and Pauline went
to school together."

"In Cracow?"

"Sure."

"Your Dad was in a camp?"

Bonnie listed several names that for me were like great searing
brands on my map of Europe. I wanted to meet her right then. I
told her about my parents and we arranged to have pizza the next
afternoon after classes.

I went to bed in a strange state. All my Jewish friends were
second- or third-generation Americans, and even though many had
lost family in the War, it was distant relatives who were only names
or photographs. The barrenness of my connections—we had a
cousin in Michigan and a great-uncle in San Francisco—had always
seemed a private humiliation. I never discussed what I knew of my

parents' War years except with other kids' parents, who asked out of a kind of horrified politeness.

Talking to Bonnie was like Robinson Crusoe discovering footprints on his island: I was not alone.

Bonnie was half Italian and looked it—dark eyes, skin, and hair, figure as full as her creamy voice—and I was surprised I could talk to such a beautiful girl so freely. She looked gorgeous in purple elephant bells and a purple and white collarless knit shirt—and we laughed because we had the same fringed suede belt. "You're like me," she said, "a *clean* hippie."

In the noisy, crowded pizza place (she shook lots of red pepper onto her slices) about halfway between our two apartment buildings, I discovered as I described it to her the pain and frustration my father's distance caused me. Bonnie listened the way I imagined a doctor would, her fine face open, receptive. And then she talked about her father's books, a whole room of them, in four languages, all on the concentration camps.

"He never left," she marveled. "He's there every day. You know when you talk to him."

"Someone's staring at us," I said, pointing.

Bonnie looked up at the door and frowned. "That's my brother! He probably wanted to get a look at you." She shook her head. "He's been following me around all my life." Then she grinned. "Well, all *his* life." Sighing, she waved him over.

Daniel came to sit with us. Fifteen, he was as slim as his sister was buxom, but just as dark and even more striking, with that poignant look you somehow see only in photographs of young immigrants (Greeks, Italians, Jews) around the turn of the century—curly black hair squashed down by a huge cap, eyes incredibly open. His hair was almost as long as mine had been before I cut it.

Bonnie offered him some pizza, but he just sat there, hands in the pockets of his tie-dyed jeans, eyeing me. I felt awkward and exposed.

"Don't you have homework?" Bonnie asked him.

"That's why I came. I need help with physics tonight."

"Okay, I'll help you. Later."

And then he nodded at us both, and left.

I wasn't sure what to say.

"He's very serious," Bonnie threw off.

I was puzzled by how much cooler Daniel was than Bonnie, and it bothered me that I was even thinking about him.

On the way out, Bonnie threw the poverty of my Jewish upbringing into high relief after something I said sparked a cascade of questions.

"You've never been to temple? You don't keep kosher at home? No youth group? No Passover? No menorah for Chanukah!"

Her astonishment almost frightened me. I realized more clearly than ever that I was a Jew in name alone, vicariously, through friends at whose holiday celebrations (the few I'd attended) I'd felt stupid and ashamed. I knew so little and was afraid to ask questions that would expose me; I think people assumed I knew more than I did because I understood my parents' Yiddish. I felt Jewish in the vaguest sort of way: My neighborhood was, my teachers and friends were, mostly—so it was a backdrop, one-dimensional, something I tried to know better only when a friend made a reference that meant nothing to me. I did that rarely, because I still cringed for having confused Tisha B'Av, which memorializes the Roman destruction of the Temple in Jerusalem, and Tu bi-Shevat, the Israeli Arbor Day.

We walked down Broadway together, to Bonnie's house, and she asked some more questions before falling into silence.

"I'm sorry," I finally said.

She laughed, taking my hand. She pulled me to the curb and we sat on the huge fender of a white Chrysler New Yorker, a car big enough for a dozen of us, parked right outside a candy store. Traffic was getting heavy, but it felt relaxing just to sit out there.

"I wasn't criticizing," she said. "It's just . . . well, I'm not saying we're super religious or anything, but we go to services and other stuff and Mom always lit the candles on Friday night. I've done it since she died." I remembered Pauline's sad aside to my mother about Bonnie, "*Di mama iz geshtorbn.*" "She never actually converted, but boy, I swear she knew lots and she liked passing it on to me."

I walked her back to her building, and we met Daniel again, bringing his bike out for a ride in Fort Tryon Park. He didn't seem to like me at all.

Pauline was thrilled when I told her that Bonnie had invited me to *Shabbos* dinner the next Friday.

"She's a beauty, hah? A real *krasavitzah*, right? And musical."

I don't know where Pauline got that from. Bonnie just liked watching Leonard Bernstein on television, but that didn't matter to me. Daniel was the family's musician; he played piano, and Pauline hadn't mentioned him to me, though in Yiddish she murmured to my mother that Daniel was "strange." I wondered what that meant.

After the amazing openness of our first talk, we didn't draw back on the phone, perhaps because we felt safe, knowing something about each other that was intensely personal but transcended both of us. Of course I knew there were other children of survivors, but I'd never met one, and even though I was aware of books on the Holocaust, I'd never seen so many as in Mr. Rosenthal's little study a week later. His books made me want to learn more, to fit the fragments of my parents' lives into something larger.

Meeting Mr. Rosenthal, I felt an isolation far more chilling than my father's, perhaps because it was covered by such graciousness. A professor of Russian at Hunter College, he was a tall, white-haired, frayed-looking man whose gentle voice and handshake were like something awkward and strange out of an old newsreel: the way people *used* to act. "I don't lend books," Bonnie's father told me, but he said he would give me a list of some I could find in paperback—books that would tell me about my parents' world and how it died.

The Rosenthals' apartment—on tree-lined upper Ft. Washington Avenue in a six-story building a lot like ours with an equally pretentious name, The Woodmere—was very large and dark, I thought, and almost too clean. The crystal gleamed like a warning, and I felt unnerved by the white curtains and table linen, the white velvet cloth covering the challah, and by the skullcap Mr. Rosenthal lent me.

Bonnie wore a dark blue skirt and white blouse and when she brought in the tall brass candlesticks and set them on the sideboard, she seemed much older. Her father wore a dark suit and Daniel had his hair pulled back into a ponytail. He looked older, too.

Bonnie covered her head with a piece of lace, sang the blessing after lighting the candles, repeating it slowly in English for me, I guess: "Blessed art Thou, Lord our God, King of the Universe, who hast sanctified us with thy commandments and commanded us to light the Sabbath lights."

"Why are there two candles?" I asked.

"Because in the Bible it says 'to observe the Sabbath and keep it holy' and also it says 'to remember. . . .' " Mr. Rosenthal motioned me to sit.

"I like lighting candles because it's ancient," Bonnie said. "It goes back thousands of years."

I couldn't imagine anyone lighting oil lamps or whatever in the desert, but watching the small wavering shadows that night, I realized Dad's mother had probably lit candles, too (Mom's parents had been socialists). I felt closer to him, suddenly, surprisingly.

"Does it have to be a woman?" I asked.

Mr. Rosenthal shrugged. "Traditionally—"

Bonnie was smiling, as if she had followed my thoughts. "Men can light them."

Daniel nodded. "I do it, sometimes."

I had long hoped to find my father by knowing more about him, discovering facts, but maybe the truth of the man I didn't know would be clearer if I searched for him through our shared Jewish past, the tradition he had completely abandoned and refused to pass on to me. I felt dizzy, then, and more ignorant than ever.

Bonnie said, "I'll teach you the blessing, if you want."

"And you can come to temple with us tomorrow," Daniel chimed in. "Right?"

Mr. Rosenthal said, "Enough. Don't push him, Danny." It sounded like a familiar admonition in that family, because they all smiled, but I thought I might enjoy sitting with them at services, imagining Daniel explaining something in the prayer book to me.

Mr. Rosenthal raised the silver kiddush cup, brimming with wine, and we went on with dinner.

We talked without stop; that is, Bonnie and Daniel did, about their trips to Israel, their youth groups. Daniel seemed almost to be competing with his sister to be more interesting—but since I was an only child, I found that fascinating to watch. And I was glad that he wasn't cold to me anymore. Almost like a little kid pulling at your shirt, he kept grinning at me, trying to top his sister's stories. His eyes were wide and bright.

I felt drunk with *yiddishkeit*, Jewishness, as if I were in a Jewish Disneyland; they all knew so much about history, tradition, customs, religion, books, and legends. I felt the way I imagined Hindus were supposed to feel when they bathed in the Ganges—purified and whole.

They were so relaxed, so beautiful and kind to me.

"*Gotenyu!*" Mr. Rosenthal said when Bonnie brought me a third cup of coffee. "It's so late there won't be any buses."

"I can walk home. It's not far."

Bonnie frowned. "It isn't so safe anymore."

"I can call my folks for a ride."

Mr. Rosenthal shook his head. "You will stay with us."

"Sure," Daniel said. "I've got a double bed, or you could use my sleeping bag. Whichever."

After I called my parents, we talked some more in the quiet living room dominated by the Krakauer baby grand that Daniel's mother had taught him to play. But the thought of sleep had made me tired, and a little anxious. Bonnie bustled around getting me towels, linens, and a pillow, and in a chorus of good nights I found myself alone with Daniel in his bedroom beyond the kitchen, converted from the original maid's room and pantry.

His walls were painted a glossy dark blue and lined with Velvet Underground posters, as loud in that silent apartment as a car radio heard in a discordant flash on some still summer night.

"So," Daniel said, "bed or sleeping bag? The bed's really more comfortable."

I nodded as he stripped off his clothes, dropping them on his desk. He padded out to the little maid's bathroom.

He came back and slipped into bed. I turned away as I undressed, because I thought he was watching me, with the same disturbing look he'd had at the pizza place.

"You're not circumcised," he said. "Because your parents are survivors?"

I nodded.

Then he said good night and rolled closer to the wall, clicking off the bed lamp. When I was finished washing up, I hit the wall switch, turning off the overhead fixture with four bulbs just like the one in my room, and moved slowly to the bed across the darkened floor.

I got in, adjusted my pillow, and made sure there was as much space between us as possible. I lay there listening to him breathe, wondering how long it would take me to fall asleep. I was still high from the dinner, and it also felt kind of strange not to be alone at night. Before I could even close my eyes, Daniel said softly, "Let's jerk off."

He took my left hand—how did he know I wouldn't pull it away?—and wrapped it around his thin long penis, which felt very cool to me even as it stiffened, surged in my fingers. My whole body suddenly seemed to be pounding like sledgehammers in a quarry. His right hand felt for me, pulled at my foreskin, slowly sliding it open and closed.

"Wow," he said. "It's so different."

We worked at each other, like pistons of a strange and timeless machine. Occasionally, I brought back my hand to spit on it when he said, "It's dry." He smelled of Jade East and Johnson's baby powder, fresh and a little silly, but as our thighs pressed together and he began stroking my chest, I gave way completely.

This was what I had never allowed myself, even in fantasy, the touch, the closeness of another man. In a flash, I thought of all the different times friends, guys on the track team, had suggested messing around, or been on the verge of it, and how I'd always changed the subject, or just pretended I didn't hear them. I had always known what to fear, and avoided it. That's why Dad's taunt of *feygeleh* had been so devastating. I hadn't known how to yell back without proving I was. Mortified, afraid, I'd said nothing.

Now all that was gone, and I felt like I'd thrown myself from a skyscraper window. The plunge was exhilarating, mad, inexorable.

I fell into his arms as he pulled me on top of him, jerking us off together, our dicks sliding against and across each other. He said that no one could hear us, but I'd already forgotten Bonnie and Mr. Rosenthal at the other end of the apartment.

Daniel groaned, kissing at my neck, my cheeks, my chin. I could feel the sharp spasms in his hairless belly and legs.

I rolled him over, pulled his tight cheeks apart, thrusting my head down to furiously lick and probe as if he were a woman. His ass smelled so strongly of soap, I had this sudden image of us in a shower, sliding foamy bars of Ivory over each other's backs and arms, the lather dripping down to our balls. I stuck my tongue even deeper into him and his legs widened.

"Wait—"

But I was inside him, riding, hammering away despite his whispered "Slowdown*please*. . . ."

I clung to him like a storm battering a tiny coastal town, tearing up shutters and fences, downing trees and flooding homes, and quickly collapsed in an orgasm like thunder th..*i* shook and seared me.

When I could pull out and away, Daniel breathed in deeply a few times. He stroked my lips, played with my hair, pushing it off my forehead and back. "I'd like to see you run," he said.

I felt sweaty and sick, unused to the fishy smell of someone else's semen, which was drying on my stomach and chest.

"When I first saw you," Daniel whispered, "I thought, He's the one. I can do *everything* with him."

"What?"

"This isn't like messing around with some other kid. Because I love you. It's different if you love somebody."

"But you don't know me!"

Daniel chuckled. "I think I know a lot."

I stumbled from the bed out to the little bathroom and washed myself at the sink, making the water almost painfully hot.

I remembered the Stonewall riots I had read about in the *Times* that year, read in a fog of incomprehension and excitement, and how my parents had said, "It's sick, like the Nazis." I was sure they meant the police, and their harassment, the beatings, the oppression. But then my father said, "Men with men. It's like the Nazis, disgusting." And I had left the room so they wouldn't see my reddened face. "They did that, you know," he said. *"Parshiveh Baheymehs.* Filthy beasts."

I thought of all the times my father had called me *feygeleh,* not really meaning it. What would he say now that it was true? How would I ever be able to reach him? What I had just done with Daniel, what I wanted to keep doing, again, always, would make him despise me. And worse, despise himself even more, and his "cursed" luck. While all his friends would have doctors and lawyers and show off wedding pictures and all the rest, I would force him outside that circle of simple continuity.

I was sitting on the edge of the tub, head down, when Daniel knocked and slipped in. He crouched at my side.

"It's not so bad," he said, lightly. "Hey . . ."

And when he held my head up to kiss me, I felt like a straggling desert caravan, savaged by bandits, swept up in a sandstorm, that had suddenly emerged near an oasis—still devastated, but humbled by relief.

Cossacks

Like the first and second violinists of some glorious defunct orchestra, Sam Levine's parents, refugees from pre-War Poland, had a dim estimation of almost every expression of American Jewish life. Example: They winced every time they heard someone pronounce *rebbe*, the Yiddish for rabbi, as rebby and not rebbeh, as you were supposed to, as they did, because they spoke a pure and refined Vilno Yiddish. But that treasure they had saved from German thoroughness seemed like the chestful of Czarist rubles Sam's father said *his* father had brought from Moscow to Vilno in 1917, convinced that the Czar would restore order. A colorful relic, interesting, perhaps, but valuable only as history. And Vilno itself, that Jerusalem of Poland in which their families had flourished for three hundred years, the name did not provoke awe or even respect here in America. It was like Atlantis, mythical, sunken, lost.

Because of their criticism of anything Jewish and American, Sam decided not to tell his parents right away that he wasn't going to move back to his dorm at Case Western Reserve, but off campus, to the Hillel co-op. He just moved, and wrote them a week later, and by then he knew he would have to say as little as possible about what the co-op was really like. He could describe the two-story Tudor house ringed with maples and elms, the beautifully furnished room he had, the small wood-paneled shul with its ark set into the wall, the large modern kosher kitchen downstairs, the cozy lecture rooms and lounge. All that would be okay, would get a neutral response, as almost anything else about his school life in Ohio. Sam had come to feel less like their son, or even a relative, than a cause they supported with regular and generous checks in exchange for newsletter reports and—possibly—a sense of purposeful commitment to something outside their daily life. For he, too, was American, and so, unreal to them in a way, or at least insignificant.

But he could never tell them about Rabbi McGee, the Hillel director, who looked like a chubby Richard Dreyfuss. A rabbi whose father was Irish? Only in America, Sam could hear them sneer, *typical*.

And what would they think of the co-op members, like Fred, the six foot two blond, blue-eyed Viking whose swimming, weights, tennis, and lacrosse gave him the bulk and curves of a magnificent Fifties Chevrolet? Fred was supposedly majoring in advertising, but almost always talked about vitamins, diet, cramps, marathons, equipment. Sam's parents would have called Fred goyish and vulgar, *prost*, in Yiddish.

That first day, Fred came into Sam's room sweating, toweling his red and heaving chest, and offered him the use of his weights next door, "any time." Did Sam work out? Swim? Sam admitted that he was from L.A., where staying in touch with the latest film, book, song, clothes, club, and expression was his kind of workout. But he mentioned running, which his girlfriend Mandy and he had taken up in high school as soon as brunch spots had begun filling up with sweatbands and mesh tops on Sundays. The look—after all—was so hot.

Fred grinned. "I can run." Fred made a 7:00 A.M. appointment with him for the next morning; there was a good track nearby, at a middle school. Before Fred went out to take a shower, he said, "You met Tony yet? Don't mind Tony. He gets confused sometimes."

Tony Devito, from Dayton, had the room opposite Sam's, but the first time he saw Tony was in the shul (the sign read CHAPEL) downstairs, with a yarmulke and prayer shawl on, kneeling down near the ark. Jews only kneel on Yom Kippur, and many not even then, so Sam was shocked. But over a Coke in Tony's room that night, Tony told him that his Jewish mother and Italian father had tried to give him and his sister a choice about religion. It worked, and it didn't work.

"Okay," Tony said. "So my sister's a nun. It's not so bad. I mean, she's got a steady job, and how many people can say their brother-in-law is Jesus, 'cause she *is* a Bride of Christ, you know."

Sam asked what her name was.

"Mary Rose. She teaches at Fordham University, in New York." Tony tried to say it again as "Noo Yawk."

They talked about cities for awhile and then Sam met Lori, the fourth co-op member. Leaning in the doorway, she was tall, tanned, blue-eyed and blond, with the dazed shy grace of Botticelli's Venus. Which is why Sam didn't expect her to say, "I'm so bored." He thought then of those "haughty daughters of Zion" in the Book of Isaiah, and imagined Lori hung about with jewels, shawls, corselets, and bells.

"Don't let Father Tony convert you or anything," she said, and then faded back into the hall. A door opened, closed.

"Wow."

Tony nodded. "Fred and me asked the rabbi to get another girl to cut down the competition, but you were the only one that applied." Tony shrugged.

Sam couldn't understand. The co-op rooms were cheaper than the dorms, the facilities better, more private, the building was on a quiet old street ten minutes from campus, the bars, bookstores, movie theaters.

They all met the next morning in the lounge to work out cleaning schedules. Lori picked at her blue nail polish. Fred was silent, wiped out after his two hundred morning push-ups and the seven miles he had run with Sam at the track, and Tony kept drifting off the subject, which seemed to leave Sam in charge.

"Marsha was our president," Tony explained.

"Why'd she move out?"

"Pregnant," Lori said.

"Fat." Fred glared at her. "She got fat."

"Because she was pregnant."

"Marsha did not like men," Tony said, and they were all silent, as if a detective had revealed the key piece of evidence to a roomful of suspects.

"Wouldn't be the first time," Lori said.

"Fat," Fred insisted.

Sam never did find out for sure why Marsha, a sophomore,

had moved; each of them had a wildly different opinion, just as
they were ill-sorted in their religious leanings. Lori called Fred "Joe
Shabbat" because he thrived on the intricacies of kashrut, which
he only observed at Hillel because it had a kosher kitchen. So when
Lori claimed to be a Reconstructionist, Fred snarled, "You can't
even spell that."

"I feel it."

They both agreed, however, that Tony would either join Jews
for Jesus or become a Jerusalem black-hatter, throwing stones at
cars driving on the Sabbath and spitting at women tourists in short
skirts.

"I don't spit! Do I spit?"

Sam supposed he fit in with them. His grim bar mitzvah, the
Hebrew school, and the Yiddish classes his parents made him attend
(while they sneered at his teachers) were all like transplants he had
rejected—nothing took. He guessed it all gave his parents more
proof that American Jewish life was an oxymoron.

"This is an interesting place," Rabbi McGee said on Sam's
second evening. "There's more jewelry than Jewishness on campus.
It's a challenge."

The rabbi had found him in the lounge reading the *Plain
Dealer* (which seemed like a college paper compared to the L.A.
Times), and had stopped, to be warm and confiding, Sam guessed.
McGee explained that Case was not the most prized post for Hillel
directors, despite Cleveland's rich cultural life and strong Jewish
community. The students had very low Jewish identification, apparently, and the only other applicant who'd competed for the post
had been a former Black Panther converted by a "mitzvah mobile"
in New York's diamond district.

Why was Sam there? It was the fall after Israel's invasion of
Lebanon, and their campus had been full of leftist and Arab students
ringing buildings with DEATH TO ISRAEL picket signs and cries of
hatred. The campus paper printed endless tirades against Israel,
punctuated by an occasional letter protesting that words like *geno-
cide, Nazi, fascist* had very clear meanings that were being distorted
by flinging them at the Israelis. Sam just got fed up with fellow
students saying "Boy, those Jews—" when they talked about Israel.
He was angry, but felt he knew only what he read in the L.A. *Times*
his folks had given him a subscription to (as an incentive to stay for

summer classes, he bet). There in Ohio he felt exposed as a cam-
ouflage Jew. In L.A., crowded with Jewish names, jokes, faces, and
concerns, he had fit in because he was never really challenged.

He couldn't tell this to his parents because it would have been
taken as criticism of them, which was unacceptable, since they had
their own parents' pre-War European ideas of how he should "address" them. His mother and father were often saying, "Don't talk
to me like a servant." It opened up a whole different world he could
hardly imagine.

Sam tried sharing how he felt about being Jewish with the co-
op members. Lori was not interested, Fred was clearly restless to
be working out, and Tony told him more about Mary Rose, the
nun.

"She says God talks to her, through music. John Denver's
Greatest Hits."

Tony then tried explaining the Sorrowful Mysteries to him,
with the adolescent enthusiasm of a kid taking driver's ed.

At his interview to get into the co-op, Sam had told Rabbi
McGee that he felt pretty ignorant—Judaicly speaking, that is. He
knew from an introductory psychology course that "I am pretty
ignorant" from a nineteen-year-old would've seemed like obtuse
bragging. He just wanted to get in, thinking it would be difficult.
And he wanted to learn something about being Jewish.

He supposed McGee thought his "search" would change the
co-op; the Jewishness there was one of tacit bland concern for Israel,
worry about anti-Semitism, a Jewishness of atmosphere, jokes, self-
parody. Any bargain, for instance, any advantage, offer, or change
for the better was greeted with "Such a *deal.*" Tony said it firmly,
Lori dropped it like a dull postcard, Fred made it sound like a
mantra. And all three tried for a "Jewish" accent, which would
have annoyed Sam's parents, who proudly spoke half a dozen languages between them, with no distorting accent in any.

The four of them shopped and cooked dinner in pairs, and
given their class schedules, Sam wound up with Fred, who wasn't
of much practical help in the kitchen. He could make origami birds
out of napkins, and at his cardiologist father's parties in Shaker
Heights, Fred had once seen a caterer's assistant run a fork down
and around a cucumber to leave the slices ridged, flower-shaped.
He insisted they always have a salad, so he could serve his specialty.

It was their first night cooking, two weeks before Rosh Hasha-nah (which was late that year) that Sam found the cross carved on the inside of the building's back door. He'd gone out to get the last bag of groceries from Fred's Audi and had to kick the door closed because it was sticking: that's when he saw it. The foot-long cross was not very deeply cut into the center of the door, but he had a sudden terrified flash of some movie with a plain swept by horsemen, cossacks, maybe, their brandished swords slicing the air as they charged. When he told Fred, and Fred was done running a finger along each arm of the cross as if tracing a map route, he said, "It wouldn't be Tony."

Which, of course, made Sam think that it *was* Tony. At dinner, though, when Tony heard, he had the sick look of a child who has seen his first accident; it didn't seem like guilt.

"The building's open," Lori complained. "It's a public build-ing, except at night." She was right. McGee taught some classes there; people were always coming by for information, counseling, schedules, with questions about Jewish observance or history.

Fred objected. "Public doesn't mean nuts with knives."

"Yes it does." Lori popped a red grape into her mouth as if practicing to be Alexis on *Dynasty*, gave it a crunch. "Yes it does."

"Someone should do something!" Tony spoke through a mouthful of salad.

Lori shrugged. "So what else is new, anti-Semitism, in Ohio."

"Go dye your hair."

"Well is it?" Lori asked Sam, as if he was an expert. "Is it new?"

"No. Of course not. But—"

"See?" Lori raised her eyebrows at Tony as if the weight of her disdain could bring him to his knees.

"Someone should do something," he insisted.

They talked then about cemetery and synagogue desecrations they'd read about in Cleveland's Jewish newspaper, like a circle of campers telling ghost stories at a fire they can trust.

Rabbi McGee informed the Anti-Defamation league and seemed pleased to have taken an official step; he also called in a carpenter to repair the damage. For a few days afterward, Sam imagined that anyone he passed on campus or at a bus stop could be the intruder. He wondered if that wasn't partly why his parents had never traveled to Europe, not just because their families and homes there were lost, plowed under, but the murderers, the witnesses, could be next to them at a café, or snapping photos at a famous monument, holding their chins up in the breeze of a river crossing to mask their shame. The scene of the crimes would not be empty and fixed for retrospection.

Nina, Rabbi McGee's secretary, told Sam that this wasn't the first incident at all. Cars in the lot behind the building had sometimes been vandalized; last year a brick had gone through an upstairs window over Christmas break when no one was around, and there were phone calls, cursing usually. In her late sixties, model-slim, with a face scored by smiles and attentiveness, and trim in bright linen suits, Nina did not seem fazed by much of anything.

"The best calls are the real ones, though, like from the Christians, the born-againniks?" She stroked the white phone machine on her desk. "Last Passover, someone called to find out the schedule for the Paschal Lamb sacrifice, and could non-Jews attend? I'm serious! I wanted to say, Darling, since the Temple times we only do a symbolic ritual, you know, pour a glass of wine on a sweater." She grinned. "Virgin wool, of course."

For some nights after the incident, they all stayed up late, Sam noticed, doors open on the hall, radios and stereos low, drifting in and out of each other's rooms, comparing assignments, talking about movies. They were all so different, Sam kept thinking; you could see it on their walls. He had posters of freeways and the Hollywood sign. Tony's walls were full of family pictures, but especially vacation shots of his sister in Rome, Paris, Chartres, anywhere there was a church or cathedral.

"She sends me Christmas cards, too," Tony said, sitting back on his bed. "She wants to save my soul."

"What do your folks think?"

"About my soul? Oh, Mary Rose . . . Well, my Dad's proud, sort of, and I guess he's happy she didn't marry some jerk. She dated jerks in high school. My Mom had trouble; it's not like she's real Jewish or anything, but a nun, even if you're not real Jewish, a nun's pretty different."

"But your sister's Jewish, since your mom is."

Tony shrugged. "She got over it."

In Fred's room, which smelled of sweat, mostly, and was

crowded with barbells and a weight bench, posters of Bruce Jenner, Arnold Schwarzenegger, Mark Spitz, and Greg Louganis plastered the walls.

One night, Fred asked Sam if he'd ever had a vitamin work-up.

Lori leaned in at the door, clutching the frame as if she were a kid on monkey bars, and jeered, "Pizza, Twinkies, nachos, beer . . ."

Fred gravely shook his head.

She laughed. "Have you ever noticed how nobody smiles in a health-food store? Know why? They're all afraid of dying—that's why they eat that crap."

"She's right," Tony called from his room.

Fred snarled, "Fuck you, Your Holiness."

Lori drifted to her room and Sam followed. Like the cool inside of a shell, it was all subtle gradations of rose and ivory. There was only one picture, a matted and framed print of that sad Manet bar girl.

"Why'd you move in here?" Sam asked.

Lori eased into her fat pink and white striped armchair. "Because Marsha was my friend."

It occurred to Sam then that for all four of them, being with Jews was not just the clearest way of being Jewish, but a substitute for it. And his parents? Well, they were survivors, refugees, like villagers who flee a volcano, they had escaped the flames, the rocks, the death-dealing lava and gas, but they had not left the disaster behind them. They may have made lives of dignity in the United States, his father as a chemist, his mother as a translator, but they were still citizens of the lost and magical Jewish kingdom spread across Europe, shaped by its passing. Sam had no such inheritance and had always resisted creating his own.

The co-op building unfortunately lay along a stretch of streets between some bars and a handful of fraternity houses, which was most obvious Thursday and Friday nights and weekends. It was like being at an opera before a big crowd scene—roaring offstage that swells into curses and boasts, then eventually recedes. Sometimes guys pissed or threw up on the lawn; mostly, they just left beer cans.

Other people's drunkenness can be disgusting, especially magnified by crowds and a reproving nighttime silence, but Sam's room was at the back, so he didn't hear as much as Tony and Lori did. The night the police came, though, they were all in Tony's room, making popcorn and listening to the new Stones album.

"Here we go," Lori sighed at 11:00 P.M.

They heard the usual strident shouting and then a chorus of "Oy-oy, oy-oy," which faded quickly. Dogs were barking.

"Jewish sailors," Tony quipped, turning up the stereo, but none of them smiled. Fred was flushed and Sam felt trapped, suddenly, wanting to move, disappear, but feeling something awful would happen if he left the room.

Lori hissed, "I hate it."

Tony cleared his throat. "Being Jewish?"

"No. Being here, inside. I want a gun. I want to stand there with a machine gun and go, 'Say it again, asshole. Come on!' "

They stared at her.

Tony whistled. "Lori the Barbarian."

"Well, don't tell me I'm the only man in this place!"

Fred nodded. "I hate it, too."

The record had stopped playing. Tony reached for more popcorn. "They're just dumb farm kids. Hicks."

They heard more shouting then, something about killing Jews, which turned into a loud and solitary "Go back to Auschwitz!"

Fred was out the door and tearing down the stairs before anyone could move. The front door slammed open; Sam heard shouts, and then a harsh cry. When he got downstairs, with Lori and Tony tumbling behind him, Fred's right hand was bloody, and there was no one in sight. "I got one in the jaw pretty good. I dragged him." Lights were coming on all up and down the street. Sam and Tony stood out on the lawn looking at Fred as if he were a massive war memorial; Lori went in to phone the rabbi. Someone had called the police, because before McGee got there, a car pulled up, the flashing light staining them all with bursts of crimson. Rabbi McGee arrived when the gray-haired cop was done taking Fred's statement. Fred's hand was cut and swollen, but he could move all his fingers without much pain.

Rabbi McGee sat him down in the kitchen with an ice pack. "So what happened? Why did you do it?"

"My mother was in a concentration camp." Fred glanced down

at his reddened hand, then up at all of them, a wide-open look of defiance and pain.

None of them had known. Sam and the others drifted off to bed, leaving Fred and the rabbi talking in the bright and empty kitchen.

No one filed a complaint against Fred, though he was sure he'd broken some of the guy's teeth. Sam began to feel ashamed that his first impulse hadn't been to follow Fred onto the street. After reading a featureless blurb about the incident in their campus paper, Sam sent in a letter deploring the catcalls and all the other incidents Nina had told him about. He ended saying that his parents had lost all their European relatives in ghettos and concentration camps, that Auschwitz could be a joke only to a very sick mind.

It appeared within two days, and the Jewish friends Sam had, was coming to have, congratulated him. He was proud to feel part of a group, its representative even, but all that praise for a one-page letter was excessive, undeserved. It was as if his cool prose had redeemed the violence of the evening for them, but Sam still felt unsettled.

A week later, his parents called.

"We got a letter," his mother said. "Yesterday. Block print. The postmark is Cleveland. It says: 'Too bad they didn't gas you, too.' There's a swastika, and both *toos* are spelled wrong: *t-o*. I don't—"

His father cut in. "What the hell's going on there?"

Sam explained about the drunks, about Fred, Fred's mother, his letter.

"*Shoydelech*," his mother said in Yiddish: terrible. But Sam didn't know what seemed worse to her. "How did they get our address?"

He realized that anyone could find his name and home address in the student phone directory.

"You shouldn't write letters," his father said.

It was the voice that had always cautioned him against signing petitions, any petitions, against demonstrations, no matter what the cause, against joining groups of any kind, no matter how innocuous, against being too free about what he said on the phone, because "you never know."

"I'm sorry."

His father snapped, "Don't be sorry. Just don't be stupid."

"He means don't do it again."

"No," Sam shot. "How can I promise that? I'm glad Fred punched that guy. Next time, I will."

"You're crazy." His father hung up and his mother tried to apologize for him, but it wasn't easy, since she clearly believed he was wrong and had to say so.

They were afraid, Sam thought, when she was done. They'd always been afraid, and he was finally learning what that could feel like.

As soon as he hung up, he went to tell everyone what'd happened, find out what he should do next.

Tony was the only one there, down in the shul, without a prayer shawl this time, but on his knees again near the ark.

"Get up!"

Tony turned, ready to smile at a joke.

"Don't do that here. Jews don't kneel."

"But Yom Kippur's coming—"

"This is just Wednesday, that's all it is. Get up."

Betrayed by
David Bowie

When I met Jeff, I was not on the run or even searching for anything—I was tired. Tired of living in the rowdy dorm where I had started to drink and smoke pot more than study, and hoarded my haphazard encounters with guys I met at the track or in the sauna at the gym, like a widow saving pointless bits of string. I resisted the temptation to date women as a cover; I didn't care what people in the dorm might think of my being gay. And with a single room, there was no roommate to lie to.

But I needed a change, even though it was my senior year, so when I heard about a vacancy, I applied to move into the Jewish students' co-op at the Hillel Foundation building, a large brick house five minutes from campus.

Downstairs at Hillel was the rabbi's office, the chapel, the public rooms for talks, meetings, films, upstairs the four co-op rooms. I got the high-ceilinged room opposite Jeff's, with two windows facing north, full of grandmotherly furniture: mahogany wardrobe, bed, and mirrored night table. People were always donating old furniture to Hillel, so the house was full and comfortable, but very eclectic, almost bizarre. Jeff's room had boxy modernismo white furniture that looked like a child's plastic toys all blown up, but it fit him, set him off. Jeff DiMarco, dark-skinned, with piercing eyes, had been lifting weights since eighth grade to make up for being only five six, and he was as darkly rich and gleaming as one of those stores that sells luxurious leather briefcases, wallets, bags. He seemed incredibly, inhumanly gorgeous to me—and at eighteen, only a sophomore, *so young*.

"You like Bowie?" was the first thing he said that nasty February afternoon I moved my carload of stuff from the dorm. I hadn't met him when I interviewed for the spot.

I shrugged. I was actually into Poulenc back then, so Bowie was as uninteresting to me as Loggins and Messina.

Jeff waved me into his room, made me sit opposite the professional-looking stereo system, and played Bowie all afternoon, talking about the songs and himself as if there were no distinction.

While he spoke, I was mesmerized by Jeff's heavy, weaving hands that sculpted the air between us as if turning ice into fountains, arches, swans. He looked like Franco Nero, I decided, with the same masculine, seductive face.

I wondered if his last name was Sephardic, which would account for his looks.

"Just Italian. Half—This one is terrific—listen to the break!" He turned it up.

I found myself captured by the dry whimsy of early Bowie ("Andy Warhol looks a scream, hang him on your wall"), and the dark visions ("Smack, baby, smack, show me you're real"), the talk of "Homo Superior," the complete fantasy of Ziggy Stardust, the wild changes from album to album, but always that eerie, distant, sexual voice. Bowie's latest, *Diamond Dogs*, knocked me out— cold, jagged music on the edge, Punk before people slam danced and dyed their mohawks. Jeff even had some bootlegs and we listened to "John, I'm Only Dancing"—which ends with Bowie *shrieking* to be fucked—years before it was commercially released.

So I sat opposite beautiful cross-legged Jeff in his white Stony Brook sweatshirt and tight gym shorts while he told me what he thought every song meant, where he was when he first heard it, how Bowie did them in concert, and what he wore onstage. And when Jeff played "Rock'n'Roll Suicide" from the *Ziggy Stardust* album, with its chorus of "Gimme your hand, 'cause you're wonderful," he told me he was gay, and that he'd never said it before.

Jackpot! I thought. Then I smiled. "Once is enough."

Jeff got up to close the door and then pulled off his shirt and shorts. "It's two," he said. "I have to do my push-ups."

I must have looked incredulous at the sudden shift, because he flushed a little.

"I do four sets a day, of a hundred, always at the same time, if I can."

And so I watched him in his black bikini briefs drop to the floor and shoot back up one hundred times, shoulders bulging, sweat dropping from his hair onto the red and black rug.

When he leapt to his feet, wet, grinning, he said, "How 'bout a towel?" His dark nipples were gleaming and tight, riding on a *sea* of muscle. I got a white bath towel from his closet door, brought it over, and he turned, stretching his shiny hard back to me as if it were as hot and life-giving as the sun. I wiped his back and arms dry, excited by the feel and the heavy, almost vegetable smell of him—like fresh grass cuttings.

"That feels good," he said, turning, and I dried his thick neck and chest, on which the hair foamed in little curls like paint flung on a canvas, down to his groin.

I knelt with the towel to dry his heavy thighs and he reached down to pull the towel away, tossing it on the bed. While Bowie was singing "Boys, boys, it's a sweet thing," Jeff brought my head to his bulge, shoving my mouth against the damp cloth. I slid the briefs down and he thrust into my mouth, already hard, sawing back and forth, hands painfully tight in my hair. His cock was small enough for me to suck him without gagging, or even thinking of it, and before I had gotten used to his jagged, fierce rhythm, he breathed in deeply and came.

"Gotta shower," he said, getting his red and white robe. He left.

"Do you want me to jerk you off?" Jeff asked when he was back from the bathroom.

"It's okay." I'd already done it myself, too hot and frustrated to wait.

At first, I thought all his showers were connected to the weight lifting somehow, but soon I realized it was sex itself that he found disturbing, unclean. If we got off by rubbing on each other, for instance, he grabbed a towel as soon as either one of us came, dabbing, rubbing, like a criminal frantic to erase fingerprints at a murder scene.

"It won't burn," I said once, trying to get him to laugh. "It's just cum. It even tastes good."

No response. The one time he went down on me (after I had to beg him), eyes closed, face scrunched as if expecting to be struck, he freaked out when I came and didn't give him time to pull away. He spit and gagged as if poisoned, glaring at me, outraged. As for fucking, he wouldn't try it, either way, seemed almost hysterically against the *idea* of it. "That's what they do in prisons, it's sick." I didn't argue.

After that first time with Jeff, Bowie often entered my dreams, thin and magnetic, singing a song he'd written just for me, or that only I could understand. He represented what I hoped for from Jeff, maybe, but also the time, those years after Woodstock and before *Saturday Night Fever* turned disco respectable, boring, and white, when being different, being *extreme* was still a great idea. Bowie became a symbol for me, a talisman.

The other co-op members hated Bowie.

"He's so *phony*." Tammy, the stunning redhead, was a second-generation vegetarian and made all her own clothes.

"But that's the whole point!" I countered, and Jeff agreed.

Dennis, the runner who looked like Keith Carradine in *Nashville*, just sneered, which he could do in French, Italian, and Spanish.

The four of us got along fine if Bowie wasn't mentioned; we cooked and ate together, kept to our kitchen and bathroom cleaning schedules. We were also more than perfunctory Jews, unlike most kids our age. We attended lots of the Hillel functions downstairs and even went to services Friday nights and had *Shabbos* dinner afterward. Through his father, Jeff was a *Cohen*, descended, so the belief goes, from the Temple Priests in ancient Jerusalem. I was a *Levi*, descended from the Temple functionaries, and on Yom Kippur, *Levis* still washed *Cohens'* hands (though there was surprisingly no special blessing for it)—something I joked about to Jeff. He told me to shut up. I was surprised at how seriously he took services, and even more the first Saturday morning that I saw him *shokeling*—the swaying back and forth that intensely religious Jews do, which I had always found a bit alien and repulsive. But in Jeff it was very sexy, imbued with all the power of his beautiful body. I suppose it also made him more unknowable, almost romantic: the man I'd sucked off was at that moment no longer an individual, but an *expression* of faith and tradition.

Despite Jeff insisting we never sleep overnight in the same bed, and his never letting me touch him at all when other people were around (and not much when we were alone), we were clearly a couple at the co-op, and Rabbi Lieberman didn't seem to mind. He was a veteran of the civil rights movement and had marched in the South, his wife was active in NOW, and both had fiercely protested the Vietnam War, so how could he have condemned us and meant it? We were so good, too, never mistakenly bringing anything nonkosher into the kitchen or mixing meat and dairy dishes, pots, or cutlery; we set up chairs and cleaned up after the Hillel events we attended.

Whether Bowie was bi or gay, what made him greatest for me was that he said he liked men, and did it openly, in the press. It permeated his songs. He was exotic, he was brilliant, he was strong, and Jeff and I wanted to be as cool as his sax on the *Pin-Ups* cover, as lewd as the boys who "suck you while you're sleeping," as funky and dreamy as "Fascination." We never just listened to one of his albums; we entered each song, and traded lines as if we had written them: "Turn and face the strain," "Watch that man, oh honey, watch that man." We were the Bewly Brothers, the Diamond Dogs, the Spiders from Mars, and Jeff told me that he liked those images better than the bar mitzvah picture that his parents treasured and reframed every year, and the other one, the one of him under a wedding canopy that would someday fill their photo album with continuity, the future.

When the *Young Americans* album came out that spring of 1975, I talked about getting gold bracelets just like the one Bowie wore on the smoky, romantic cover. Jeff said, "No way." For one thing, it was just too obvious. But worse—for me, anyway—was that I discovered Jeff was not a person to buy little treats for; he'd unwrap the book, the pottery, the paperweight suspiciously, as if it were a subpoena forcing his appearance in court. Jeff didn't seem to know how to be grateful, and after the first few tries, I stopped. It was just too annoying watching him peer at the present I had imagined he would fondle and delight in.

Instead of getting bracelets, we went in to New York to see Bowie at Radio City Music Hall, and spend the night at my sister's in Forest Hills. The stately, sweeping lobby that for me had always led inside to Disney delights and holiday pageants was that night

full of guys and girls costumed in all of Bowie's previous incarnations
(Jeff had refused to dress up or even put on eye glitter). I rushed to
the stage during a wild version of "Suffragette City," imagining Jeff
up there, naked, sweaty, shoulders gleaming in the stage lights,
pounding away at bongos. I was hoarse when we left the ecstatically
romantic, Latin-beat show, and strangely purified, as if I'd run some
kind of marathon; Jeff seemed happy too, but more quietly, like
someone too old to risk intense emotion.

My sister Laura, a biochemist, a folky who still dressed like
Mary Travers did in the sixties and even looked a bit like her, didn't
know what questions to ask about the concert, and Jeff was not good
at making conversation, so our night there was strained. We slept
in her guest room, but chastely, like brothers, even though Laura
was clearly—perhaps too clearly for Jeff—not disturbed by our relationship. "He's very quiet," she said when we had some time
alone. I took that to mean she didn't like him much, found his too-
perfect body and face off-putting. "He seems scared."

"Of what? You? Me?"

In the morning, Laura had coffee ready for us out in her tiny
garden, where the rows of daffodils along the fading brick wall were
already quivering in the sunshine, the green and white bishop's
weed starting to mass at their feet. Jeff just read *The New York Times*
while Laura and I talked about school and our folks, who were
vacationing in Hawaii.

When we left, she squeezed my hand and whispered, "Next
time it'll be better." I hoped so. I hadn't even gotten together with
any friends from college because Jeff had seemed reluctant, embarrassed when I brought up the idea, just as he avoided parties
where everyone was gay.

Besides Hillel functions, Jeff and I went out a lot with Tammy
and Dennis. Jeff was uncomfortable about going into the city or
even anywhere nearby for a gay bar or disco, but sometimes, if he
was drunk enough, he would dance with me at mixed parties where
no one minded. He was a very hot dancer, locked in the beat, and
I loved watching the sweat start to gleam on his broad dark forehead,
his shirt start sticking to that chest of mathematically precise twin
arcs, loved when he pressed against me, eyes closed.

Jeff was always talking about his parents' summer place near

Providence, so one weekend at the end of May, we decided to go up there. The night before we drove north, we left a terrific party at about 3 A.M., weaving out to Jeff's Triumph. "Keeping dark is *hate*ful," Bowie sings in "Time," and when Jeff leaned down to point his car key, there on the dark, residential, respectable Long Island street I grabbed him, pulled him around for a kiss. A car slowed down, someone shouted "Faggots!" Dogs started barking in a widening circle from where we stood.

"What's the matter?" I roared after the guy. "You afraid someone wants your ass? You're too ugly to shit on!"

Now lights were coming on up and down the street and I heard some windows opening. Jeff was drunker than I thought, so I pulled the keys from his fist, pushed him inside the car, and drove back to the co-op. He was silent all the way back, and I was still muttering threats when I got him to bed in my room.

"I feel so *gross*," Jeff said before he passed out. I couldn't sleep. Dennis had a girl over, and through the wall I could hear his bed steadily creaking. After a while, he gasped like a succession of camera flashes and she let out a staircase moan—rising, building, higher.

On the ride to Rhode Island, I could no longer see Jeff as just the guy I wanted to hold: he was something grander, more elemental, freedom from all the ugly shouting in the world. His beautiful body, his glossy dark skin, his gesturing seemed more compelling than ever. But I felt uncomfortable, on the spot, as if he was silently criticizing everything about me. Luckily, Jeff drove, because I was unable to notice road signs or rest stops. The car could've been stationary, with the New England spring unrolling in front of us like the film in an arcade game that tests your driving skill. I had already learned to keep my hands to myself when we were driving. If I even tapped his shoulder or thigh, he'd hiss, "Stop, people can see!" "Right," I would jeer, "they're hanging from the trees." But I did stop.

Jeff talked a little about his father and the DiMarco restaurants in Boston, Providence, and New Haven, about having waited tables the previous summer, and that he wasn't looking forward to joining his father in business, but it sounded like he was trying to keep himself from thinking too much.

"You're upset," I said. "Last night?"

"What if those guys in that car know me, were in one of my classes or something?"

"What if? Now they know you better."

"Don't joke about it, they could *tell* people."

"So then *they*'d know you, too. You might make the news: Queer Kisser Sighted in Town!"

Jeff shook his head. I wished that we'd made love the night before, that I hadn't just let him slip off into whatever nightmare and tension had claimed him, only to see him in the morning wake up unhappily surprised that he was in my room.

"Come *on*, Jeff, you're not even sure who that guy was!"

The house was very large and bland, a lone white and green waif fronting the Atlantic, which always seems bluer, more intoxicating off New England than anywhere else. Inside, the house seemed ready-made, ordered: One Summer Home, Medium Deluxe, dense with wicker, cheerful chintz, afghans, needlepoint pillows, and moldy paperbacks, their pages yellowed by sunshine, their covers worn by carelessness and sand. We hadn't stopped to eat, so we hurriedly cooked some steaks we'd brought, wolfed them down in the cold kitchen, and rushed to bed in Jeff's uninteresting room, where we could watch the cloudy sunset and wait for the heat to warm up the house. In bed, we had lots of Lambrusco, and I got Jeff really drunk by the time it was dark. When I greased our cocks with K-Y, I also shoved some into my ass. His eyes were closed. Just as we were about to come, I pushed him onto his back, crouched over him with one hand around his cock, and skewered myself on it. He went crazy, humping into me, screaming "Fuck—fuck— fuck!" With his hands grabbing at my ass, I thought, *There's nothing else.* I shot all over his face just as he came, and in a minute he tore out of me, rushing for the shower. He left the bathroom light on when he came out at last, unsteadily, drying his face and crotch as lugubriously as a riot victim, hoping there won't be more blood, more pain. He said nothing, just crawled into bed and fell asleep.

Later I woke him up. "I love you."

He rolled over and fell back asleep.

In the morning he seemed very upset, making blueberry pancakes as if he were a museum figure behind a wall of glass, demonstrating something I could understand only by reading the plaque.

I said, "You're letting one word get to you."

"You mean *faggot*? Or *love*?"

When we weren't out on the rocky beach, roasting, we had sex recklessly, as if to prove or destroy something. And now Jeff was fucking me with gusto, bending me over a table, a chair, ramming his cock into me, drumming at my shoulders and back when he came. I loved it.

I told him about my very first time, with my friend Bryan at a Zionist youth camp. Slim, blond, dark-eyed, a counselor-in-training, Bryan was always slapping my back, squeezing my shoulders and arms when we worked out together at the little gym, and when he spotted me on a machine, he stood close enough to kiss me, urging me to do "Just one more," in a husky, commanding voice. In the showers, he soaped his long thin cock until it was almost ready to spring up against his belly. I was uncertain how to begin, and finally he broke up one of our frequent private wrestling matches to say, "I know what you want."

"And he did," I recounted. We snuck out to a field that night, it was all clear in the sky, you could see the Milky Way. He had a picnic blanket, and some vaseline, and it was terrific, looking up into his eyes, into the constellations.

Jeff had actually had sex with more men than I, but always furtively, and that weekend he told me he wished he was a Catholic so he could confess and be forgiven, saved.

"I forgive you."

Jeff frowned. "Not funny."

"But I wasn't joking."

Jeff was amazed that my sister, even my parents, knew so much about me, and weren't shocked or disgusted.

"Hey—don't be hateful, like Bowie says."

He shrugged.

Even though it was never really warm enough that weekend, inside, Jeff didn't bother with clothes, and I studied him: the rich, curling Botticelli hair, the small high-arched feet, the enormous haunches and dark handful of cock and balls, the heavy shoulders tapering down to an impossible waist, like one of those vase paintings of Minoan athletes. But like those paintings, he was stylized, one-dimensional, a type: beautiful young man. He had kept his body impersonal, and the distance between us, I suddenly felt, was as chilling to me as the ocean which we had been unable to swim in.

Jeff had brought a tape player and we listened to *Hunky-Dory* (my favorite early Bowie album) until it could've been a script we were learning for a play. I reveled in "Oh! You Pretty Things" with its prediction of gay triumph, but Jeff kept wanting to hear "Quicksand," with its grim chorus of "Don't believe in yourself, don't deceive with belief. . . ."

It wasn't until the ride back to Long Island that we talked about the summer. Like the other advertising majors, he had been interviewing a lot for an internship, but he hadn't wanted to discuss his plans, even though we had shared interview strategies. I loved how he looked in a suit, all hidden and contained, as if his tie were the cord on a magnificent sheeted sculpture, and with one yank, everything would be revealed.

I told him I wanted to go to Europe. "My Dad never got to college, and he said if I kept an A average for at least two years, and stayed away from heavy drugs, I could spend a summer there when I graduated. The money's already in my account, but I've never wanted to go alone. I guess I've been waiting for you."

Jeff was not excited, but as silent as someone who's just been told, "We have to talk."

I began setting names out like a caterer creating an elegant and tempting buffet: Athens, Florence, Avignon, Madrid, on and on until he said, "Sounds great."

"But better with two, huh? There's enough money for both of us."

Was he too proud to accept this offer? No, that wasn't it at all. He just couldn't imagine himself traveling through Europe with me; everyone would know; it would be too obvious; it would be hell for him. Where I saw adventure, he saw shame.

I had been trying to release the playfulness I assumed was inside of him, by showing him how to let himself enjoy men, enjoy *wanting* them, by joking in the car about guys we saw jogging or walking by, sometimes threatening to stop and offer them rides or just plain howl things like "Prime Rib!" or "Lieutenant Sulu, turn on the tractor beam!" Because I had never made myself sleep with a woman—as Jeff had, hoping to purge himself of being gay—my desire for men was more unclouded, and I thought that Jeff could be just as free. I wanted to *save* him. But it didn't work.

My sister may have been willing to accept him, and my parents, too, but I realized at last that Jeff could never invite me home for a Passover Seder (he found the idea disgusting), get an apartment together, buy groceries, be a couple that was open, public, relaxed. And I wanted *all* of that.

We managed to get through the end of the semester with only one blowup, when Jeff said he still wanted to be my friend. "What kind of bullshit is that?!" He couldn't explain. I could tell that Tammy and Dennis, even Rabbi Lieberman, wanted to find out why Jeff and I weren't talking much, why I was so moody, but I resisted their sympathetic glances inviting me to open up.

I helped Jeff pack up his car to go back to the parents who believed he was just a nice Jewish boy. I asked him not to write me or call. What else could I do? My sister at first said "Try," but I didn't want to end up desperate, hungry, strained—and when I explained Jeff's attitudes toward sex, and about being gay, she agreed: "Nobody deserves that—thank God you got out."

I was not feeling very thankful.

I kept my Bowie albums, and as each new one came out, I pictured Jeff somewhere absorbing it into his private universe of admiration and fear. When the amazing *Heroes* appeared in 1978, I imagined myself and Jeff there in West Berlin, shouting at all walls, all oppression, affirming, "Yes we're lovers, and that is that" (I was ecstatic the Gay Pride Day in New York when Blondie sang "Heroes").

I eventually went to Chapel Hill for my Ph.D., feeling like Bowie's Thin White Duke: angular, tense, remote. I always made sure that Stony Brook's alumni office had my current address, and scanned their class reports for Jeff's name.

I finally read about Jeff around the time of Bowie's "comeback," the weak *Let's Dance* album and tour, the *Time* and *Newsweek* covers, and that vile *Rolling Stone* article, "David Bowie Straight." Suddenly everybody, including Bowie, was saying that the androgyny, the bisexuality had only been poses. A new biography claimed that he'd only been to bed with a man once or twice, as a "lark," and that anyway, the sex stuff was just cooked up to get press attention—and not even by Bowie himself.

I couldn't buy the new album. I waited for Bowie to clarify, to say that he wasn't denying his past, that this was all just some kind of intriguing retranslation of himself, like Ziggy or Major Tom. I wrote angry letters in my head. Bowie was more popular than ever before and his music was the least original of his career. He was claiming to be just like everybody else; forget about "Queen Bitch" or wearing a dress or going down on Mick Ronson's guitar at more than one concert, or singing about trade, a "butch little number," cruising, "the church of man love" being "such a holy place to be," all of it, the obvious and the metaphorical. "The Man Who Sold the World" was selling himself and everyone who'd believed in him.

I read about Jeff in Santa Fe—that strange ocher and gold town of looming mountains and low, secret-looking buildings, the streets awash in rich tourists—where I had my first academic position. Jeff's name popped up in Stony Brook's alumni rag, but not in the 1978 graduates column, in the deaths: "After a brief illness," it said. "Pneumonia. In San Francisco."

AIDS. It was now more than a threat to defend myself against; no matter how high I built my walls, the enemy had tunneled underneath.

I canceled my office hours and went home to play my Bowie albums the rest of the day, crying at the lighthearted "Fear is in your mind, so forget your mind, and you'll be free," wishing that I could've known, could've helped him. For a long time after Jeff and I broke up, I had kept away from men because I was so angry; he had seemed as ungrateful as Lord Douglas after Oscar Wilde was freed from prison.

Jeff was the very first of my friends and acquaintances to die of AIDS, and when I read the news, all I could wonder was this: did he die alone, still hiding, or had he discovered how hateful "keeping dark" really was?

Fresh Air

Sometimes, watching Mom at dinner, I pictured the wheelchair at the hospital, in which she'd sat shrunken by fear, and I felt afraid myself.

Dad yelled at her, of course, as soon as we knew there was no concussion, no internal bleeding, no visible medical change or problem.

"How could you drive through a red light? Twenty years driving and a red light you forget?"

Mom shook her head, all the energy of Dad's words dissipated by her awful doubting voice. "Maybe I'm going crazy," she murmured, like a defeated little girl. The accident had not aged her but torn away the years of work and stability. Mom taught Hebrew and Jewish history in our Queens congregation's Sunday school, and she always looked so firm and settled, buttoning the last button of her suit jacket on the way to classes—as if the neat little woman she was, curly dark hair cut close at the sides, freckled face patient, serious, had never known another life, had never walked down any street uglier or more dangerous than Queens Boulevard. She was at those and other times like a wonderful bright porcelain doll, shiny, untouched. But the accident, which happened near home, had come like an invisible hand to mangle that doll.

"What's the matter with you?" Dad blustered. "You're not crazy!"

If I'd expected the accident to change him, I was wrong. Dad was one of those short stocky men, broad shoulders and neck tensed forward, who seem to push themselves through life as if it were an unruly crowd. His words and looks could fall like hammer blows, pounding at your smiles or opposition. He was not a kind man— or better, he didn't know how to be kind, it was not one of his languages. And though he hung over Mom at the hospital as oppressively as stifling dusty drapes, and tried to care for her at home, the anger lurked in his ominous heavy hands and mouth, his jerky hard eyes.

"You're not crazy!"

"I am. I must be."

"What's wrong with you?"

Her helpless pained shrug disgusted him and he shook his head at me as if to say, "See? See what I put up with?"

I didn't see, I never had. Dad's criticism of Mom was persistent, historical, like the character of a people or the climate of a land. Whatever she did or said in her quiet efficient way irked him and they always seemed to be wrangling somewhere in our dark, cool apartment that faced the back of another, almost identical six-story building of postwar red brick. Mom would sometimes explode and practically bark at him, her thin voice high and stretched, but mostly she ignored his pounding questions or seemed to filter the words from the contempt and anger.

They had met in Paris, after the liberation of the concentration camps. From the pictures in their black photo album with its crumbling sheets of sepia-colored protective paper, they seemed as ill-matched then as later: standing on broad avenues, under lampposts, near monuments, they could have been two strangers brought together by a photographer's whim.

But then *I* had not survived bombings, beatings, typhus, near-starvation, and the death of all my family and friends, so what did I know?

"I didn't want marriage," Mom once said quietly after I'd come home with the news that my seventh-grade math teacher was engaged. "It didn't mean anything," she went on, smiling as if surprised by her recollection. We sat in the cozy eat-in kitchen that was like a warm quilt drawn around you at night.

"But your father wanted a new start, and children."

Whenever she called him "your father" to me, Dad sounded like an idea, not a person.

"Then why—?"

She shrugged. "We had to. To make up for what was lost, all the dead."

"One kid isn't enough!"

She nodded, and I felt then more intensely what I think I always did with my mother, that I was not her son, not even a child, but an adult whom she spoke to across a distance no one could ever cross or comprehend—especially not me.

I wasn't angry being told that I'd been wanted not for myself but for reasons that transcended individuals. I could feel myself shrug inside, saddened by the truth, but not really shocked.

It was later that same year—I was twelve—that I raged at something she said. We'd been debating abortion in social-studies class because of the Supreme Court decision legalizing abortion, and I asked Mom what she thought.

"Of course it isn't wrong. I had one." And she said it so calmly, the way you'd mention something that had merely brushed the edges of your life.

"When?"

"Before you. When we were still in Paris. We couldn't afford a child."

"You didn't want one."

She accepted the correction. For days I wouldn't talk to her. I was so mad, I failed two exams that week, the numbers and words I had to work with boiling on the page.

It could've been me.

But I brought myself out of it, remembering how Mom had said they chose to have a child, for reasons of history.

So I was a child of necessity, of duty to the past, named not just for one lost relative but a whole family of cousins in Lublin: the Franks. Frank. My incongruously American first name was their memorial. Perhaps that explained my mother's distance, my father's rage—how could you be intimate or loving with a block of stone?

People like to look back and say "I saw it coming" after times have twisted in upon themselves, but I saw only what I saw and didn't look ahead.

One Wednesday afternoon of my freshman year in college, I walked down our tree-graced clean street to find my mother upstairs, in the bathroom, on her knees, scrubbing the tile floor with a heavy old brush. Beside her, a pail of soapy water sweetened and steamed the air.

"Mold," she said, pushing her hair back with her free arm.

From the kitchen, I heard her scrub for almost half an hour, and the broken hissing was like a curse on that floor.

When I went in later, the grouting did not look much different, but I wasn't sure, and felt foolish for not having really noticed.

"It was the smell," Mom said over dinner. "It wasn't strong, but—"

Dad glared at her. "What?"

"Mold. There was some—"

"What are you babbling?"

Mom changed the subject and Dad was soon reading aloud from the *Daily News*. Accidents and crimes, he savored them, blaming strangers for not being more careful. "They should know better." Maybe he lived in that violent little black and white world because America had not freed him from his past, had been only a change of scene. Sometimes I wondered how it wasn't him in the paper, thundering his delivery truck into a wall, a house, lying splintered and triumphant in the wreckage he had made. I could see it happening.

But people said he was a "sweetheart." Mom told me that without irony. Who could've said it? Other drivers? A union boss? Cops?

The mold was not the end.

Mom seemed to be doing loads of wash whenever she wasn't cooking or preparing for her Sunday classes. At first I thought she had changed her routine, but she still did laundry on Tuesday and Wednesday afternoons, wheeling the loaded shopping cart in which blaring boxes of detergent and bleach bobbed and settled like buoys in their sea of wash.

I offered to help, but she only smiled and said I did enough around the house. Her extra washing wasn't really excessive, just curious, I thought.

Then she threw out all our towels and bought new ones.

"You did *what*?" Dad was storming at her.

In the kitchen before dinner, he had said, "Feh, it stinks in here." Dinner was overpowered by ammonia and other vicious cleaning odors.

Mom shrugged. "After a day in the truck, of course."

"Expert," he shot.

I said nothing. I didn't want to be his target more than I already was that year. I kept changing my major depending on how well I was doing in a course, and had already gone through history, sociology, French, and linguistics. My silence in response to his needling only provoked him more.

"So? What are you today? Haven't made up your mind?"

My Regents scholarship and work study paid almost all my school expenses, and I reminded him of that.

"*Svolitch!*"

That was bastard, in Russian, I think. I flushed and went on eating, red with shame, unable to look up from my plate or even see anything.

"And who said we needed all new towels?" he went on.

"They wouldn't get clean."

"*I* never saw."

The silence seemed to echo and mock the assertion. He never saw. Not when Mom bought a new lamp, cut her hair a little differently, lost weight, framed a museum print, bought flowers. He never saw.

I didn't understand why he was so upset. Who cared about towels; they just had to be dry and reachable. So what if Mom had bought new ones? Dad accused her of wasting the money he earned with his blood, his *blootigeh gelt* in Yiddish. She didn't say that she earned money, too.

That night, if they argued any more, I didn't hear. I retreated to my stereo headphones, playing the Stones's *Exile on Main Street*, loud.

Our bathroom, windowless, was at the center of the apartment, off a small hallway. I was so used to it that the opaque windows in friends' bathrooms had startled or amused me. So I was surprised when Mom started complaining.

"We need fresh air," she said, and so, three weeks after her accident, in the morning, the windows in every room except mine were ripped open even though it was November and curtains flapped and flared at themselves.

"It's too cold!"

"We need fresh air."

"In Queens? There isn't any fresh air in Queens."

My alarm clock became the sudden temperature shift in my room as Mom's fresh air surged under the door to banish the night's heat. The windows were down when Dad got home and I never said anything. I was still at the age where—for most kids, I guess —parents are hardly individuals, but a grab bag of traits and quirks and expressions, most of them annoying. Mom's sudden concern about the air didn't disturb me, just added itself to the private condemning list adolescence writes with such exactitude. She was strange? Well, parents *were* strange. Besides, she'd had an accident that shook her up.

Our words for other people's pain are sometimes criminally vague; this was such a time.

The windows were followed by an ugly whirring blue plastic air filter, hunched atop the toilet tank, that turned on noisily with the light. It nagged at me each time I even passed the bathroom. Mom just said that the overhead fan wasn't enough.

"What are you throwing away money for?" Dad challenged, the night of the purchase.

Mom slapped her hands together, hard, like an angry magician forcing something to disappear.

"It stinks in there!"

"What?"

"You don't care, you don't notice anything!"

Mom fled the dining room table, wrenched a coat from the hall closet, and rushed out of the apartment, the slam of the heavy metal-cased black door her last word.

Her exit proved Dad right; that's what I read in the self-consciously satisfied way he finished his dinner and washed the dishes. Each one he stacked seemed to me a smug "I don't need you" to Mom. But she would probably come back from her walk or flight to a neighbor's—wherever she'd gone—and not pay attention.

Because I never confided about my parents to anyone, partly, I think, to protect their past and their pain, that night's incident registered inside of me but wasn't connected to anything else. I didn't imagine myself discussing, analyzing, recreating, mocking: I simply went to my room and tried to study.

What would my room have told you about me? All the paperbacks were alphabetized by author and subject (and the subjects were alphabetized, too), so were the albums. The rug was always spotless and the pictures paralleled one another on the sky-blue walls: chrome-framed prints of Impressionist landscapes, shimmering fields and trees. Blue predominated in that room that I thought was cool and ordered, but now I wonder. It was an attempt at control, a bastion, a room that ultimately failed because it summoned its opposite—chaos—unintentionally.

What upset me most after Mom's accident was the new perfume she bought. Small and almost dainty-looking, Mom had always used unobtrusive scents, but suddenly she had all the brashness of a gleaming cosmetics counter in a department store. The laundry, the gaping windows, the air filter seemed somehow a part of the heavy perfume that almost made me dizzy.

I was worried.

Mom seemed unable to concentrate on her teaching, was taking lots of baths, where before she'd preferred showers; she stayed up after Dad was asleep, sitting in the darkness, with her perfume as strong as the sansevieria blossoms that bloomed once a year, drenching the living room at night with their sweetness. The picture of her alone in the dark pushed me from my comfort and reserve. One December night, before Chanukah, I rose from my bed, slipped on my robe, and went out to her.

"Mom?"

"What?" Her voice was hoarse and unfamiliar.

"Are you okay?" My eyes began to find her in the dark.

"Why shouldn't I be?"

"That sounds like Dad."

I think she chuckled.

"Mom? Can I sit with you?" I felt like a shy little kid at the playground, desperate to make a new friend.

She patted the couch and I moved carefully across the shadowy strange room where everything was blurred in the night.

"You never talked about the accident," I began, surprising myself.

"No."

"Why not?"

In the silence, she breathed in, and I could see her white white hands clasped in a fist. She sat head down, legs tightly together in her gray wool robe.

"I'm not crazy, and it wasn't an accident. I saw the light. I went through on purpose. I wanted to kill the man crossing the street."

I asked who.

"A camp guard. The one who killed my brother Yossel. He's here, somewhere in Queens. A Nazi. He stepped on his neck, choked him down in the mud. . . ."

I had never heard how her brother died.

"You saw him?"

"He was here, in Queens, crossing a street, in a nice suit. I went through the light to kill him. I shouted 'Murderer!' He knew. He ran away, and I hit the light pole."

"Nobody saw?"

"You know . . . only a kid was a witness. She was too young."

I shuddered. "Are you *sure?*"

"Such a face you don't forget."

There in the room that seemed darker than any I'd ever known, the terrible sick past threatened to swallow me up. I felt I could go crazy; I wanted to, wanted to surrender finally to the madness, to purify myself, to drown out all the voices and the noise, but Mom kept talking, and that saved me.

"You don't know what it was like, Frank. The filth, the piles and piles, worse than death. The smell. Books can't tell you, film is nothing." She started to cry, hesitantly. "It came back. The smell. And now it's on me," she stumbled.

"No."

"It's on me. I can't get it off—" And those hopeless words broke through the night. I reached out to hold her, and for the first time in my life, Mom cried in my arms, heavily, with the desperation of an abandoned child.

I was terrified.

When she stopped, at last, I brought her tissues from the kitchen.

She asked, "You think I should see a doctor? A psychologist?"

"Yes."

"Will you help me find one?"

I squeezed her hand. "Sure."

"Don't say anything to Dad. Not yet. He won't talk about the War, won't listen to me, and he thinks doctors are crazy. Maybe they have to be. There's so much," she said softly. "So much to tell."

"I'll help you," I said, not knowing how or when—only wanting to so much.

"You know," she said, as if surprised. "You're a good son."

It was my turn to cry.

Another Life

Send me out into another life
Lord because this one is growing faint

W. S. Merwin
"Words from a Totem Animal"

Nat had not started coming to Michigan State's small Orthodox congregation two years ago to look for a man. He expected to feel safe there, hidden, because it was not like his parents' huge suburban synagogue outside Detroit—all gleaming polished oak, a theater, a social hall, a stage. In the Jewish Students' Center at the edge of campus, they prayed in a bare, high-ceilinged, narrow room that was like an exercise in perspective, drawing your eyes inexorably to the plainly curtained ark in front. His first time, he'd sat in the last row, on the men's side, alone, after putting on his prayer shawl and slipping a prayer book from the crowded chest-high bookcase behind him. At the small slanting-topped lectern, a man was praying aloud wrapped in an enormous black-barred wool prayer shawl as large as a flag. Nat's little polyester one, gold-embroidered like a sampler, seemed incongruous, almost ugly—though it was what he'd always used since his bar mitzvah. The man came back to shake Nat's hand at the point where waiting for enough men to continue with prayers began, and got Nat's Hebrew name for when he would call him to the lectern. Nat always regretted just being a *Yisroel*, one of the vast majority of Jewish men. *Levis* claimed descent from the Temple functionaries who sang the psalms and were entitled now to the second Torah blessing at services. *Cohens* were descended from the priests and had the first Torah blessing in synagogues. Nat liked this remnant of the Temple hierarchy even though he was at the bottom (his sister, Brenda, said, "Well then, that leaves *me* underground!").

Only six of the thin-seated black plastic and chrome chairs

were filled that first morning, by guys who would have been unexceptional on campus or in town but here looked costumed and
exotic in prayer shawls and skullcaps. They all chatted for a while.
Most were graduate students, but for Nat they had the authority of
much older men, because of their deep Jewish knowledge and the
way they prayed.

The few women—wives, a girlfriend—were pale, plain,
undemanding. Nat was glad they were on the other side of the five-
foot-high wooden barrier—the *mehitzah*—separate, even after services, even talking to the men, still as private and inaccessible as
ducks brooding by the river on campus. They came to consider him
shy, he knew, because he seldom initiated a conversation.

Nat had always watched other men pose, lean, grin, and entertain women, as if from a distance, thinking they looked like
clownishly intense animals in mating desperation, all puffed up on
display. Nat couldn't mimic the flattery and ogling, because women
had never stirred a desire even to pretend in him. They were merely
figures in a landscape.

The Orthodox service on Saturday mornings was very long,
almost four hours, and some of the prayers and melodies were
unfamiliar at first, but the direction and sequence were similar to
the services he'd grown up with, and coming every week, he began
to fit inside this new structure for belief. Nat's Hebrew, always better
than Brenda and his parents knew, blossomed, until he felt confident
enough to offer to do part of the service. It was such a small congregation, usually less than fifteen except on holidays, that praying
here was intensely private for him, thankfully not a time to see
relatives, friends from high school, or be shown off by his parents
as a faithful son. Sometimes he was so moved, he covered his head
with the large new prayer shawl he'd bought in Southfield, shutting
the world and everyone out as the truly Orthodox did.

The singing, the absence of English, the spiritual
concentration—*kavannah*—seemed beautiful to him, as if they
were all, at the most powerful moments, the fabulous gold cherubim
on the Ark of the Covenant, over which hovered God's presence.
Sometimes he felt *that* holy, *that* moved beyond himself—but who
could he tell? The few Jewish acquaintances he had at State weren't
interested in hearing about his discoveries. Most people would just
class him as a fanatic, as his parents seemed to (Brenda listened,

but not with enthusiasm), and even the congregation's regulars stayed away from talking about feelings or anything verging on mysticism. For them, the service was simply the right and only way to pray.

Yet he welcomed their self-absorption. He had really come here, at first, before he was seduced by the service itself, hoping that the Orthodox congregation, the *minyan*, might be a bath of acid in which he could burn away like verdigris from a bronze his obsessions about men. He'd heard about druggy friends saved by joining Orthodox communities in Brooklyn, lazy and almost criminal "trouble" students at his high school straightening out in Hasidic enclaves of Jerusalem, and had hoped for a similar miracle. Nothing else had worked.

Acting had not helped him lose himself, but brought him into a terrifying world of men who blared their availability and were always making reconnaissance raids on guys who didn't. Learning French and starting on Russian had only given him new words, not a new identity. Running did make him fit, supplied a hobby and completely new range of conversation—shoes, tracks, breathing, diet, shin splints, marathons, stars, books, and magazines—but he was still only Nat for all those miles. And he only admired other runners more, became a connoisseur of those wonderful high round asses, those long and heavy thighs. When he watched track and field events on TV, he waited for close-ups or slow-motion shots to see the heavy weight inside a favorite runner's thin and clinging shorts whip and swing from thigh to thigh.

Even at services, alone with the other men, trying to stay deep in prayer, his thoughts sometimes wandered: to a barefoot guy in cutoffs hosing down his car across the street, who'd glanced at him one morning as Nat entered the building; or two wide-backed, tanned bikers damp with sweat and exhaustion shouting to each other as they cut down the street; or even Italian-looking Clark, who helped run the *minyan*, Clark whose weight lifting had left him as bulging and tight as a tufted leather sofa. Nat's private gallery. He felt then lonelier than ever, tracing the path of his unquenched thirst for men, to be a man (was that different? the same?) back to childhood. When he had not felt this way? And what would it be like never to look at men but only *see* them: pure registration without excitement, interest, pain? He was always feeling helpless, like turn-

ing a corner in town and almost bumping into a guy in sweatpants
with those seductive gray folds, whose belly seemed harder, flatter
over the shifting, jock-rounded crotch, or watching someone's tight,
jutting ass in the locker room at the gym as he bent over to pull up
his shorts.

Still, he could lose himself in prayer often enough, long
enough. And then his sister, Brenda, finishing her Ph.D. at State,
began to join him at services after he'd learned the cantillation for
reading the Torah. With her, he felt more anchored, sure this might
be an answer if only he waited. Brenda wasn't pleased with sitting
on the women's side at first, but she respected what he'd learned,
or at least all the weeks of practicing at her apartment with a tape
recording, chanting to himself there because it drove neighbors at
the dorm crazy. And *he* was pleased that his pretty sister drew
attention from the men, as if her presence made him less of a shadow
or a blank, less suspiciously alone. With Brenda at services, he felt
he could be normal—or seem that way—and sometimes it was
easier to concentrate. Thoughts of men were not so intense; she
was like a powerful signal jamming pirate broadcasts.

"I didn't think I would, but I like the service," she admitted
after a few months. "I don't even mind the *mehitzah* anymore. I
don't get distracted looking around, like back home."

At men, he thought, wondering what she had guessed about
him.

Perhaps she knew everything and didn't want to mention it,
like the Jews in polls done by national Jewish magazines, who
overwhelmingly supported civil rights for homosexuals but didn't
want to have to *see* what that meant in their own lives. This unspoken
demand for invisibility was more enlightened than Judaism's traditional distaste for homosexuality, but Nat could not find the difference very comforting.

Nat watched Mark's strong shoulders inside the black-striped prayer
shawl on Mark's first *Shabbos* at the Orthodox congregation. Mark
read Torah with a slow, persuasive rise and fall, beautiful large
hands flat on the lectern, rocking softly, and Nat found himself
staring at Mark's smooth thick lips when Mark brought the Torah
around and he touched his prayer book to the velvet-sheathed scroll.
Mark nodded.

Mark was a *Levi*, and Nat imagined him in the Temple, strong feet bare, curly hair and beard fragrantly oiled. With those deep-set blue eyes, beard growing high on his cheeks, and the muscular frame, he looked distant, romantic, like someone's burly wild grandfather in an old photograph: a man who had disappeared on an adventure in Australia or Brazil. Nat drank Mark's every movement on that criminally hot and dusty June *Shabbos* Mark first came to services. When Mark kissed his prayer book on closing it, or bowed during certain prayers, the gestures were smooth and authentic expressions of a certainty Nat found seductive, and that made Mark unlike anyone else he knew.

In the little crowd after services, they discussed Mark doing part of the service next week. Mark talked briefly about having just taken an administrative job at State, after a similar position at Penn, and Nat told him about being raised Reform. He described their invisible choir and organ, the three gowned rabbis who had seemed like Hollywood extras, watching them high on their stage from a sharply raked auditorium. It was theater to him back then, distant and boring.

Mark smiled. "So how'd you wind up here?"

Nat hesitated.

And Mark invited him back for *Shabbos* lunch after they chatted with Brenda, who assured Mark she had other plans.

They walked the mile or so from the Jewish Center in an almost incandescent heat—even Nat's skullcap seemed too warm and heavy to be wearing.

Nat did most of the talking, and felt very young again, excited, as if he was on the verge of a birthday present, or a longed-for trip.

The air conditioning had left Mark's place blissfully cold. "This is just temporary," Mark said, explaining the boxes all over his featureless apartment. "I'm looking for somewhere nice."

They set the table and Nat tried not to falter when he handed Mark the silver laver at the sink after washing his hands and drying them while saying the blessing. Sitting opposite Mark, Nat watched him say *Hamotzi*—the prayer over bread—long hands on the swelling, shiny challah. Mark sliced a piece, salted it, and gave Nat half.

"This is beautiful." Nat fingered the linen cloth, the silver.

"Wedding presents." And then he shrugged. "That was a long time ago . . . it's not important."

After lunch of a traditional *Shabbos cholent*—the meat and beans stew that baked overnight—and singing the prayers, they played Scrabble and read the Detroit newspapers in a silence so comfortable, Nat felt as purified and free as after an hour in the campus steam room.

"Why don't you stay?" Mark said near six o'clock.

"For dinner?"

Mark smiled and slipped off his skullcap, then shook his head. "Stay with *me*. Aren't you gay?"

Eyes down, Nat said, "I've never done this."

"But don't you want to?" Mark came to hold him tightly, stroking his hair, his arms and face, taming the wild beast, fear, and then led him into the bedroom. Mark stripped. His body was statue-hard, blazingly dark and public—as if all the men Nat had ever gawked at padding from the showers to their lockers; or lifting weights, shoulders and face bulging as if to hurl themselves up through the roof; or lounging near the pool in bathing suits no larger than index cards—as if their essence had been focused like a saving beam of light into this room, for him.

He pulled off his clothes and moved to hug Mark, entering that light which seemed now to blaze up inside of him as he rubbed himself against Mark.

"Wait."

Mark led him close to the mirror on the closet door, slipped behind him. "Look. *Look.*" With one hand, he held Nat's head up so that Nat was forced to see his own wide eyes, and Mark's guiding him. He leaned back into Mark as if cushioned by water in a heated pool, floating, hot, abandoned, as Mark lightly ran fingers along his sides, down to his thighs, and back up, circling, teasing, calling up sensations from his skin like a wizard marshaling a magical army from dust and bones. Nat watched his body leap and respond as if it, too, were urging him to keep his eyes open and unashamed. Mark slipped one dark and hairy hand down from his waist to grasp him; the other stroked his chest. Mark kissed his neck, his ears, his hair.

"Don't look away."

The words came to Nat as if in a dream in which he was a solitary tourist lost in some vast but familiar monument whose history and meaning he strained to understand in a shower of pamphlets. He struggled, he gave in, staring into Mark's eyes watching *him* watch an incomprehensible act that ended—for now—with a savage rush as he came, and Mark grinned, laughed, right hand wet and white.

Later that night, they took a walk to campus, and it was a bit cooler where they sat by the river.

"Sometimes I feel transported, completely," Mark told him, explaining why he was often intoxicated by *davening*—prayer. "On Rosh Hashanah once, I saw my shadow on the wall in shul, yarmulke, beard, and it didn't look like me. It could've been anyone, any Jew, who knows where, how far back."

Ducks, white and startling in the dark, idled against the river's current. Nat breathed in the faint sweetness of Mark's skin and hair, wanting to brush a hand in his beard.

"You know," Mark began, "There's a legend that the Torah is written in letters of black fire on white fire. Sometimes I can almost see it."

Nat admired how for Mark, being Jewish was home, not a foreign land to be approached with guidebooks and a map.

He thought about black and white fire the next *Shabbos*, and found himself crying when they sang *"Av Harachamin,"* Compassionate Father, before the Torah was taken out of the ark, their voices blended and thoughtful, not loud as usual. As Mark's soulful voice rose above the others, Nat felt open and faint, wanting to rise, enter, disappear.

When Mark blessed the wine after services, he was beautiful in his brown slacks and beige shirt, brown and beige Italian silk tie, not at all like the other guys in the *minyan* whose shabbiness was almost boastful.

"Are you okay?" Brenda asked Nat. "Are you getting a cold or something?" She was their family's smart one *and* the beauty— slim-hipped, gray-eyed, magnetic in a bikini, with curly, almost red hair, face wide and kind and striking, with Dad's strength and Mom's charm, but Nat no longer felt like her plain and umimpressive tagalong little brother.

"I'm great," he said.

Nat helped Mark move to a larger apartment farther from town. It was splendidly cool, neutral-toned, all gleaming glass and brass, a construction, perfect and complete. And with its balcony view of a man-made lake, it was like a brand-new eraser wiping Nat's ugly dorm room from a board like a hopelessly misspelled sentence. He hated leaving Mark's place, which felt like his first real home.

At the dorm, he had to laugh at the jokes about getting laid, about faggots, had to be careful not to stare at anyone getting out of the shower or even stare into the mirror at the reflection of someone half-dressed, or nude under an open robe, shaving, spitting, scratching, praying for consciousness. Here he felt safe, could shower with Mark, stroke his back, go nude, bite Mark's ass in the kitchen, be completely free, or at least *grow* toward that freedom. Because even when they just went out for dinner, or to a movie, he was not relaxed. He felt stared at, wondering if they looked like more than friends.

Mark insisted that here in a college town it was different than in New York; most people wouldn't assume two men together were *together*: "Look at all those jocks, and the fraternities." But Nat disagreed, worried about the ten years between them, wishing that he, too, were big, broad, and dark, bearded, blue-eyed, hairy, so that they could look like brothers or cousins.

Nat's fear led to their first explosion. Mark had bought them expensive seats for an upcoming Chicago Symphony performance on campus—an all-Russian program of *Russlan and Ludmila*, *Le Sacre du printemps* and Prokofiev's Fifth Piano Concerto. But Nat just set aside the card with the tickets and didn't smile at his surprise that came with dessert.

"That's a *date*," he said. "Everyone will see us."

Mark was silent after that, rinsing off the dinner dishes in their sink of soapy water, starting the dryer, wiping the counter. He hung up the dish towel, his movements heavy, admonishing.

Nat sat at the table, waiting out the silence, feeling like he'd entered a room of celebration with news of someone's death—important but guilty.

Leaning back against the sink, thick arms crossed, not even looking at him, Mark almost spat out, "What is *wrong* with you? Why is everything so fucking secret? You won't even tell your *sister* about us!"

"We're not in New York, this is Michigan, and we're Jewish, and it's wrong."

"Sure! And tell me you voted for Reagan! Is it wrong for *you*, does it make you a monster? Will you stop lighting candles, stop being a Jew?"

"Sometimes at services, I feel like I shouldn't *be* there, shouldn't kiss the Torah or do anything."

"That's what your *parents* would say, your *rabbi*, not you! You don't believe that, you *can't*. When are you going to stop *hating* yourself?"

Mark went on, and Nat hardly listened, but he felt the passion in Mark's voice and felt near tears, wishing Mark's message of acceptance was not like the anguished cry of someone aboard a ship that was pulling out to sea who called back to the dock, "Jump in, hurry, *swim!*"

And then he *was* crying, and Mark handed him a napkin, and said, "Oh *fuck* the concert."

"No," Nat said. When Mark had wanted to fuck him on their first night together a month before, Nat had pulled away as if slapped. It seemed impossible—too brutal and strange, and painful proof of how far he would have traveled from his incoherent fantasies of being with a man. He said no then, and had kept saying it, but now his fear of what it meant, what it would feel like, fell from him in a rush, like the fan-shaped leaves of his parents' ginkgo tree, which could drop in one cool fall day. He smiled. "No, fuck *me*."

With Mark's weight around and inside him, Nat felt like all those characters he'd never understood in *The Rainbow* and *Women in Love*—annihilated by sex, transformed beyond words.

When Mark was finally asleep, Nat imagined his parents bursting in on them, Brenda horrified, old friends nodding, "Sure, I always knew." What could he tell them?

It was oddly like the first time he had prostrated himself on Yom Kippur at the Orthodox services during the Service of the High Priest, the only time Jews ever did that in prayer. The service described in lavish detail the High Priest's preparation for entering the Holy of Holies and everyone, many *thousands* of people at the Temple mount throwing themselves to the ground when the Priest pronounced the Name of God in a way lost to history and the multitude crying "Praised be His glorious sovereignty throughout all time!—*Baruch shem kavod malkuto layolom vaed*." With his forehead touching the floor, tired, hungry from fasting, intent, awed by the moment kept intact through two thousand years, Nat had known that his final, unexpected willingness to surrender to something beyond his understanding was a border, a crossing that would always mark him as different from what he had been.

Lion's Den

"Young man—I may be old, but I'm not *dead*."

Those were Ray Howard's first words to me outside of class. I had come to his office on a hot Friday afternoon in May, late in the semester, wearing sandals, T-shirt, and running shorts, armed against his criticism and his fame with my only weapons. You see, I was, at nineteen, indisputably good-looking and well built, just as I was indisputably not very insightful about modern American literature, or much of anything.

"Wear some clothes next time—this is not a gym. Close the door."

Howard leaned back in his leather swivel chair, the wall of gleaming books right behind him like a peacock's magnificent spreading tail.

It was my sophomore year at Cornell, and I had been watching him from the first evening of class. Even at fifty-five, Howard was striking in his elegant Italian suits and shoes, his silk shirts: a large square-faced man with pale blue eyes and thick graying hair, a tight tennis player's body, with an almost European stateliness of gesture and tone, though he was originally from Buffalo. He *looked* famous, exactly what I expected of an editor who had built the careers of many writers and playwrights, and who had known most major American writers since the end of World War II. He came up once a week from New York to teach at his alma mater, and even had a house in town, where he spent many of his weekends.

I had not felt Howard pick me out from the others in class. We all seemed to amuse him, quietly; it was our youth, I guess, our nervous egotism, our haphazard admiration of him, our fear of being foolish. In class, he never cut anyone down, no matter how stupid your remark, and in his long pauses you could sense Howard marshaling years of politeness and professionalism. There were many professors in the department who announced in hallways, on the stairs, in elevators that the world was tough and it was their duty to make us suffer—which was often achieved by humiliating diatribes in front of as many classmates of ours as possible. Howard was different; his harshest comments were always private, written down. But in his comments on *my* papers, there was something else: "Don't be so goddamned clever!" "You're too cerebral, stop making yourself smile." They were like the admonitions of a fanatic coach who believes that only abuse will bring out the best in his team—and that affection between men should be loud, hard, aggressive.

I certainly liked being reached out to, but hadn't known how to respond. I wanted to look good when I finally went to his office, so I waited for the warm weather to tan myself diligently on the banks of the river that cut through campus near my dorm.

That Friday afternoon in May, Howard asked me if I wanted to be a writer, or critic or "something."

I shrugged.

"Well, even if you work eight hours a day, you might just end up somebody who writes."

Flushed, I asked what the difference was.

"Passion—stubbornness—balls—bad luck. You've had it too easy, you're too caught up in yourself."

I told Howard that an acting teacher in my freshman year had said something similar, that I didn't like or understand other people enough to lose myself in a part.

Howard smiled. "Is that bait?"

"It's true."

"Oh, it had to be. Sensitive-young-man-reveals-secret-fear-that-he-can-never-love. Bullshit."

I shook my head.

"Listen, Tony, why don't you cross your legs and we can get to work." Plucking open my folder, he talked about my papers for two hours, taking them apart more thoroughly than before: line by line, exposing weak arguments, straw horses, flaws in my logic, cheap witticisms. I felt like the French cavalry at Agincourt, their invincible armor pierced by English archers. In high school, I'd always been praised for the "sophistication" of my prose, but Howard showed me what I most feared to see (because I knew it was true): I was a facile writer, shallow, consistently taking the easiest route. There was no real cruelty; Howard would just read some line of mine aloud, look at me and say, "This will never do." He was taking me seriously.

"Are you angry?" he asked at last. "Maybe that'll get you off your butt." And then he smiled. "You know, I don't socialize with my students, but when finals are over, give me a call."

He nodded and I left him, walking back across the teeming, verdant campus as if I'd flubbed an audition.

I spent the last weeks of the term reading about him in the library: the wild marriage in his twenties to a poet who'd died in a plane crash; his heroism in the Pacific; the years as a journalist; his growing reputation as a "Pulitzer-maker," since so many authors he'd discovered won the prize; the one or two discreet references to male "secretaries." Howard had never said anything in an interview about his sex life more personal than "Don't be banal." I suppose that was an answer, of a sort.

I was trying to bring Howard down to the level of an individual, but all the articles, the photographs at banquets, parties, and museum openings made him larger, historical, thrusting him further away from me than at the semester's beginning.

Spring at Cornell was dazzling, with everyone "laying out" in the sun, ducks, rabbits, and squirrels everywhere, and thousands of bushes and trees wild with bloom—forsythia, azalea, rhododendron, lilac, quince, redbud, cherry, magnolia. You could get drunk on the successive waves of color and the smell, and I was, almost, when I met Howard in town for the drink we had arranged. I wore pants this time, loafers, and a pink Lacoste; I felt too warm but liked Howard's quiet nod of approval. He ordered Seagram's and I had a Manhattan.

He grimaced. "You should drink something *real.*"

I nodded, eyes down.

Howard went on to ask me so many questions about my classes, my family and home in Syracuse that he could have been a writer wondering if I had possibilities as a character in his book. But with each answer that I gave, I felt diminished, reduced; clearly, I did not impress Howard, and there was nothing I could drag out of my past or my family's past to shock him with: no cousins who had set themselves on fire, no lurid divorces, nothing. I felt utterly bland and inconsequential.

After three drinks, Howard said, "I think I'll take you home now."

On the drive to Howard's house at the edge of town, he only said, "I'm trying to figure out if you're worth the trouble."

It looked like an ordinary Colonial on the outside—but inside, the living room blazing with books was two stories high, heavily curtained and furnished in green velvet. "*Gone With the Wind.*" Howard laughed, mounting the dining platform and passing through to the kitchen, and I remembered Vivian Leigh and her desperate interview with Rhett.

Standing there in the softly lit gleaming room, I felt stupid and helpless. Howard whipped up fettucine carbonara and we ate that with a bottle of Fleurie by the empty fire. I studied the label, and the blue-green marble of the grate. In class, Howard was sparing of anecdotes and never made us drool by referring to well-known writers by their first names. Now he talked idly about some home repairs he was thinking of, almost as if I wasn't there.

When Howard led me up the freestanding black spiral staircase to the loft bedroom, everything seemed reversed somehow. I wished *I* were the one in control, cool and demanding. But when Howard stripped, I couldn't help falling to my knees, embarrassingly hungry, worshipful.

"Not that. No," he said, pushing me onto the large high bed. I surrendered, with Howard's hard and hairy chest on my back, one hand busy with oil. That night I felt like a galleon becalmed in one of those Errol Flynn movies, boarded by swarms of pirates, plundered, wrecked, dispatched.

In the morning—it was a Saturday—Howard brought me a bed tray of pancakes, bacon, coffee, and pineapple juice. It was like one of those shiny nightmares where you're forced onto a stage you know you should find familiar and you can't remember your lines. I had sometimes imagined breakfast in bed as part of an affair, a real affair, not just sex, but now I felt like an invalid, trapped.

Howard sat opposite me, nude, in a large wicker chair, and lit up a Gitane. I watched him. In the strong light, all the muscles in his taut, well-exercised body, especially his tight, deep chest, seemed tensed for some overwhelming attack, almost brittle, as if he were a beautiful but gnarled apple tree exposed to the coming shock of winter.

He smiled. "You're not *un*likable, you know." He stubbed out his cigarette and came to take the tray, though I wasn't done. "Wonderful thighs," he said, pushing my legs up and back.

Later, stroking my flushed shoulders and chest, he said, "Why aren't you circumcised?"

"My parents hated it—they're Czech."

"It's charming, a nice surprise, so Euro*pe*an."

I didn't know what to say. The sense of Howard's long and probably rich past with other men rose around me like the enchanted forest burying Sleeping Beauty's castle in thorns. But before I could say anything, Howard rolled on top of me, covering my mouth with greedy lips. "I like having more," he murmured, grabbing my head and holding it tightly, as if I might try to pull away.

So what had I expected? Once I'd decided that I wanted to sleep with him, I guess I imagined that Howard would go crazy for me, buy me clothes, a Patek Philippe watch, introduce me to famous writers or take me to Europe.

I had never imagined that Howard would make me feel like I was a servant on one week's trial, invaded and controlled. He never suggested I come to a department party, or meet any of his colleagues or friends at Cornell, or spend time down in New York with him. We never even went out to dinner or a movie; Howard always cooked something French or Italian and we watched television, and went up to bed.

What I hated most was when he got calls from his staff, from writers, agents; his face would close to me, he'd wave me away from the phone as if I were a little kid, sometimes even suggesting I go back to the dorm. I wanted him to talk about what it was like to enter someone else's work, to build a relationship with a writer, about mistakes he'd made, anything that would help me understand what was most important to him. I never saw any of the manuscripts he read through; they were always piled out of sight.

Until then, my sex with men (mostly handjobs) had been

sporadic, accidental, happening when I was drunk after a party, or pretending to be asleep in a tent on a camping trip, or getting offered a massage after a wild game of touch football, or letting jokey wrestling turn unexpectedly serious and breathless. It was easy for me and the other guy to pretend we hadn't really hoped it would happen, or even enjoyed it *too* much. But Howard was so imperious (and I'd never been fucked before) that I couldn't pretend I had stumbled into these moments; this was *desire*, premeditated, lingered over, too substantial to be a surprise. I found myself dreaming about him, and when I was at his house, I had to keep touching him, feeling the dense hair on his arms, following the curves of his ears, rubbing his chest and back as if I were a sculptor patiently coaxing clarity and form from anonymous clay. He was a man, like me, yet completely different—maybe because he was older and his body was poised on the edge of surrendering to gravity and time. He was as exciting, in a way, as a boy about fifteen or sixteen—you know, when the flesh seems tight, almost bursting, and still somehow incomplete, on the verge of a *different* transformation.

Though Howard cooked for me, held me close in the shower—at least while he thrust into me and jerked me off—he was always, always detached. His appetite for sex seemed enormous, impersonal, a need for release transcending who I was or what I had to give.

At least he never said I was dispensable, and I found that reassuring. I needed reassurance. There was no one to talk to about him, because no one who mattered knew that I was gay. I needed a good gay friend, or an older sister with whom I could lay out each possibility, study his every gesture and word the way "Kremlinologists" used to analyze official pictures of Soviet leaders—before *perestroika* and *glasnost*—to see who was standing where at state occasions and then spend hours, days guessing what it meant. I needed to talk about what was going on so I could understand myself. Did I love him? Was I just stuck with Howard because I was really afraid to be involved with someone my own age, someone I could have a future with? Was I just like the women who consistently sleep with married men, afraid of commitment even when they gripe about not being able to find it?

It was impossible to figure out, and I was completely alone, with no one to help me. It may have been 1987, but I was not liberated. I was Catholic and terrified of being condemned and destroyed. And there was so much homophobia on campus, sparked by AIDS; you were always hearing rumors of people being hassled or beaten up. Howard and I had talked about AIDS, but not much, since he had tested negative, and I had never done anything that would have endangered me. Almost all of our conversations about being gay sputtered into silence. He hated the word *gay*.

"It's not what I am," he kept saying. "It's just what I do."

I think I wanted him to be open and brave, to make me feel less like hiding—but he wouldn't help. He wouldn't even work with gay authors.

"I was almost arrested once, back in the Fifties, when I was twenty-nine, working on a newspaper in Albany," he told me. "It was a setup. This attractive man at a gas station asked me to meet him that night at his house. He looked like Jimmy Dean, so I did. And when we started necking, a cop burst out of, well, out of the closet. Call that droll, I suppose. I spent the night in jail. My father wrote me out of his will. My mother fell ill with a pinched nerve, stayed in bed for two years, my sister left town and never talked to me again."

"Doesn't it make you angry?"

"Tired," he said. "Just tired."

He wouldn't say anything more, and I felt sure it was because I had made no real impression on Howard. I was like an amusing TV show you enjoy for a season but know you'll never miss when it's canceled, or a light summer read, a paperback you don't mind having forgotten on the beach.

It was too bad we never had anything to fight about—rage might have made a difference.

Once I managed to ask, "Do your relationships usually go like this?"

Howard grinned. "I see you've taken Intro Psych."

And I *had*. Everything I said or did seemed to place me in a group for Howard, a negligible class of individuals. When I got him a birthday present, a month after that first night, Howard wouldn't open it until I left. When I was next over, the hand-turned walnut hourglass from England had already joined other gifts and mementos, anonymous on its shelf.

Howard didn't gossip about students, professors, writers, or

other editors. Was that a deliberate holding back, or some plan to
destroy my mind? Wasn't I interesting enough to share Howard's
life, his work, even circumstantially? A few times, I had vaguely
mentioned that I might want to be a playwright, and Howard only
laughed. "All you kids are the same. You don't want to really *do*
something, do *anything*. You just want to *be* it, you want to have
the career without the work!" Occasionally, he made general remarks about writing that I held on to as long as I could. Like: "Lots
of people do their best work when nobody cares, nobody's interested.
It hurts, and it's good, and when the praise and recognition come
their way, they end up with too many smiles over their shoulders
when they type, too many pats on the head, not enough doubt and
too much goddamned fear."

"Why fear?"

"Fear they'll blow it, be a disappointment. The writing be-
comes a game, like Bowling for Dollars—camera, crowds, tight
lips, tension, oohs and aahs."

After six weeks, Howard told me that he was going to England
in a few days to visit old friends.

"But I extended my dorm contract through the summer!"

He murmured something that might have been "Too bad."

We were in bed, the lights low, the stereo playing "Think of
Me" from *Phantom*, which Howard had seen in England.

I asked, "How long?"

"As long as I can."

I felt too proud to ask him for an address or phone.

When he left, I tried hating Howard, imagined his publishing
firm being bought up by a conglomerate, and him being fired and
replaced by someone young and dynamic—me, of course—a fantasy as crude and implausible as Eliza Doolittle's "Just You Wait,
Henry Higgins."

All I got was a postcard from Cornwall: "D. H. Lawrence was
right."

For weeks I felt depressed, abandoned, unable to decide what
to do with my summer, with my money running out. I bought the
Phantom album and played it until I had memorized every line,
crying sometimes at the Phantom's chilling plaintive "And now,
how you've repaid me, denied me and betrayed me." What was

worst was thinking Howard would find me sentimental and ridiculous, because I certainly did.

And then another postcard came, from London this time:
"Change of plans. Returning." I didn't know if that meant to New
York or Ithaca.

Two days later, Howard phoned me. "I'm here, why not come
over?"

I drove so erratically from the half-empty dorm that I was sure
I'd be stopped and arrested. I screeched into his driveway, and then
sat in the Honda Civic, trying to force myself not to feel excited.

When at last I got out and knocked, Howard called from inside:
"The door's open."

Howard sat on the green velvet couch, one arm along the back,
the other arm ending in a large drink. I had never dared mention
that his drinking worried me, because Howard always drank with
bravado, as if daring you to tell him to stop, to slow down, to
consider the consequences. But now his drink seemed like an af-
terthought, or a prop. He looked so large, so present in that slightly
musty house that my anger and confusion drifted away like the
pieces of a letter ripped up and tossed from a bridge.

"Drink?"

"Not yet." I was afraid to move closer.

"Sit down, Tony." But I couldn't. He went on, not quite
looking at me: "There's something you have to promise. No one
else will do it, they'll think it's crazy, or just wrong. There are letters
in the gray file cabinets in my bedroom closet, photographs, all
kinds of stuff. I want you to burn them out back when I ask you.
No one will really notice; they'll just think it's yard work."

Howard nodded then as if I'd agreed. "In London, an old
friend, a doctor, asked me when my last physical had been. Well,
of course, *years* ago. So we did one, the usual, and the X-rays were
very bad. I have bone cancer, inoperable. Chemotherapy might
work, but not for long."

Now he looked up.

"Tony, I've seen so many friends on chemo, it's terrible. It
wipes out a week at a time every month, maybe more: nausea,
fatigue. If I thought I could live through it, maybe it'd be worth
writing about . . . a diary. But I don't want to hang around like

leftovers, stinking up the refrigerator, the whole kitchen, every time you open the door. And then get thrown into the garbage. I want to die."

I turned away and heard Howard set down his drink. He came over and hugged me.

"It's rough, huh?" Howard's voice had all the tenderness of a cabdriver bitching about life in The City, but his arms and chest, his whole body, drew me in.

"I want you to fuck me now," he said. "At least twice. And then later we can have veal marsala, okay?"

Upstairs in bed, plunging into Howard for the first time was not a triumph over his distance, but a commitment, a promise. Howard beat at my ass like a conductor driving a crazy orchestra.

Over dinner, he asked, "The Picasso near my bed?"

I loved the Minotaur lithograph whose stocky hairy figure had Howard's fleshy presence.

"Take it home with you tonight, whenever. *Soon.* Later, people will say you stole it."

"You don't have to do that." And I cursed my inability to say something that echoed what I felt.

"Send in the violins." Howard laughed. "Fade out."

Then he reached over, stroked my hair. "I *am* sorry. This is a lot to dump on anyone. And it's so crazy. All these people have died of AIDS and when I tested negative, I thought, well you're safe now. I guess I forgot you can die of other things."

I thought of some lines from *Giovanni's Room* about not many people ever having died of love, but multitudes perishing for the lack of it. I didn't tell Howard, who would probably accuse me of being too literary.

"Why won't you do chemotherapy?"

"Because that would only make it easy for everyone else, not me. They would think I'm brave, they could help, they could worry, they could talk about it. You're not supposed to agree to die, you have to fight. Hell, I don't want to, not that kind of fight. It's a sucker's game."

"Will you tell anyone?" I knew that his parents were dead, but little else about his family.

"I have to. The department here. And at work. Close friends. My dear sister." He rolled his eyes.

I had never met Maria, who Howard called "The Ice Queen." In her pictures, she was a large, unsmiling, clear-eyed, heavily beautiful woman, a bit like that Seventies model Verushka, swathed in shawls and turquoise jewelry. And she *had* modeled before moving to Arizona to paint. Howard heard about her now and then from friends, but never directly.

Before Maria flew out from Tucson, and before Howard grew weak and couldn't leave his bed, I burned the papers he asked me to, and more that he'd brought up from New York. Howard sat out on the deck lined with large oval English terra-cotta pots of hot pink impatiens. He was smoking, drinking Jim Beam, nodding as I brought out one pile of letters, cards, journals, and photographs after another to the little bonfire I'd started with leaves and fallen branches in the middle of the summer-seared backyard. The thick walls of privet hedge made me feel I was in the center courtyard of a prison.

"What is all this stuff?"

"The past," Howard said. "Nastier parts of it. Letters, diaries, everything an archivist would kill to get a hold of."

I stared at him. There he sat, tanned, fit, beautiful, and commanding in his lawn chair, like a British diplomat calmly having an aide destroy classified documents during some colonial uprising before the embassy compound could be "compromised." In a month, two at the most, he would be dead, but it seemed impossible to me. He looked only a bit thinner, not doomed. Too soon, I thought, too soon for me to even think of what I had to say to Howard before the end.

I wiped charcoal smudges from my bare chest and belly.

"I'd like to burn the whole house down," Howard muttered. "Would you do that for me?"

I nodded.

Howard didn't smile. After a moment, he went on, "Burn some more papers, Tony; I like to see the sweat at the small of your back when you bend over."

"You're doing okay with this," he said when I was finished and the pile reduced to feathers of smoke. "No questions about saving anything for posterity?"

"It's private, it's yours."

Howard peered at me. "That doesn't sound like a curious college kid who maybe wants to write plays."

"I would have cared before, but now—"

Howard was apparently too dazed by the sun and booze, or too pleased with the destruction, to ask what I meant. I sat by him, drinking what he drank, and hating life.

"Where is everybody?" I asked. "Your friends? Your authors?"

"Out of town. Out of the country. Or just out. Some can't deal with it and probably won't see me till the funeral." He shrugged. "Well, that's not exactly true. This is your day, I asked to be left alone." Howard looked right at me, smiling as if to say there wasn't much time.

There wasn't. When his sister arrived, she enacted a quarantine, saving him from friends, who would be "overtiring." The first time she came to open Howard's door, I was surprised to see that she looked like someone very ill. She could have been one of those beautiful Renaissance statues in some polluted Italian city, features and outline, runny, blurred, and worn away.

"I'm Tony."

She nodded, eyes blank.

"Your brother's student. His friend."

"Raymond is asleep."

I said I could wait but knew it was hopeless, so I left and never saw him again. She would barely let her brother talk on the phone, and I felt strangely disgraced, exiled like a legionnaire forced into the desert without water. Howard's sister turned me away twice, though she accepted my flowers, and trying to talk to her through the screen door or even face-to-face was like scaling a cliff wall without pinions or ropes.

Howard's last words to me on the phone were a feeble "Call me tomorrow." But he was dead by then.

I read all the obituaries, the articles reviewing his career, but felt cheated. There was talk of a biography.

I was surprised he had asked to be buried upstate and not in New York. At the university chapel, I sat in a sweaty daze through a dozen reminiscences by his coworkers, colleagues at Cornell, and writers from New York, wanting to burst through all the literary references and nostalgic joking with a cry of "I knew him, too! I *fucked* him." But then I suppose I was not the only one who could shout that in the crowd of several hundred.

I filed out with everyone else into the neon-bright day, tugging at my tie.

Heading to my car, I heard someone call me. It was Maria. "Come," she said, pulling me over to her shiny blue Volvo, waving off people who wanted to talk to her.

She seemed serene the way people are when they talk about death being part of life and all that crap. You bitch, I thought, you fucking vampire. *I* should have been with him when he died, and before that too, all the time.

She opened the trunk and brought out a parcel wrapped in brown paper and thick string. "He wanted you to have this. Here, it's the Picasso."

She handed it to me with great care, watched me tuck it under my arm.

She closed the lid. Quietly, she said, "He was a failure, you know."

"What?"

"He could never let himself be homosexual all the way. Every-one *knew*, but still he had to hide it, or try. He ran away from you to England. He might have loved you," she said. "But he probably didn't know."

I turned from her, as speechless and overwhelmed as the flood survivor asked by an eager young reporter, "Now, can you tell us what happened to you, sir? How do you *feel*?"

That New York Fear

My sister, Becky, was a reluctant New Yorker. She would've been happy spending the rest of her life in Traverse City, Michigan, where our folks had moved in the early fifties from Ohio. But she married Carl, a pianist, and his hopes of a concert and recording career took them in 1975 to New York, which she had never accepted as her home. She was like one of those decrepit White Russians sighing in a Paris café, insisting that the Czar, *some* Czar would return to Russia because the people missed their Little Father. Becky knew that Carl would never leave, except for vacations and family visits (and even then, reluctantly), yet she *believed* she would return. Someday.

And her apartment, despite its stagy magnificence, seemed to prove that. With the help of an inheritance from Carl's grandfather, a cardiologist, they'd bought an enormous co-op on Riverside Drive in the low Nineties. It was like a movie set of grand and spacious rooms flowing into one another, with pillars, French doors, elaborate moldings, rich-grained parquet floors, window seats, a marble-topped fireplace, and closets as big as studio apartments on the East Side.

Built in 1920, their building was like an enormous thick wall blocking the New York it faced away from, the New York that was only traffic noise fifteen floors below. Most guests found the co-op quintessentially New York, and when people told her the view was "fabulous," Becky glanced critically out at the Hudson and murmured more often than not, "But you should see Lake *Michigan*."

This amazing home was decorated, like our parents' house in Traverse City, in Colonial, with maps and scenes of Michigan framed in almost every room. There were duck decoys, framed samplers, embroidered inspirational pillows, wreaths from Mom's garden, ferns in baskets, quilts, afghans—all of it as incongruous in that Twenties splendor as a Grateful Dead T shirt spread across a Louis Quinze bergère.

"I want people to feel at home," she insisted. *People* meant family and friends from Michigan (she hadn't quite decided how to classify New Yorkers). And we *did* feel at home, though I was her most frequent visitor from Michigan. The rest of the family tended to view Becky and Carl as scientist-explorers who had gone to live in an impenetrable forest or on the edge of a volcano to prove some fanatical theory about plant-spore migration, asteroids, or the ancient Sumerians.

Becky was always asking Mom to send her Michigan cherry preserves and maple syrup, and that delicate thimbleberry jam from the Upper Penninsula. She had never quite gotten used to the crowds in New York, was still unwilling to "cope" with the rudeness (or hauteur, if you like) of saleswomen, or with brusque cops who called her "*Lady!*" Worse for her, though, was that she was often afraid; she called it her New York Fear.

"Okay," she told me one night after we'd had lots of seven and seven's, "it's quick, sharp, a stab, sort of, like when you notice your subway car is getting emptier and there's this (small *p*) punk kid looking at you. Or worse—*not* looking. Or late at night walking up the block and you can see the doorman but you hear footsteps— and should you run? Or when someone all funny in the eyes stops and you don't know if he's going to ask for the time, or a cigarette, or yell about spaceships—and does he have a knife? It's like everything you hate about the city just bunching up in this gigantic fist that's ready to *pound* you. I feel like that when Carl hasn't called and he's late from a recital."

Still, she could joke about it sometimes: after all, she and Carl had never been mugged, never had their car stolen or vandalized, their apartment broken into, or a wallet or purse grabbed during the Christmas rush on Fifth Avenue.

"But that isn't the worst fear," she would say only to me, grinning: not like having a job that treaded water while your friends ascended into gleaming comfort and even a certain small fame with the tender self-assurance of a Poussin Madonna. Or the fear of always seeing *the* play, reading *the* book, knowing *the* club or piece of gossip a day too late to be impressive—or unimpressed. For Carl's friends, she said the greatest fear was of missing vivid obscurities, like not having heard the bootleg recording of the Bulgarian recital of a little-known opera by an unknown composer that featured the First and Most Ineffably Dazzling Performance of a Fabulous Soprano of Later Historical Magnitude.

Becky was sorry that Carl had become an accompanist. "God, I wish he were a singer instead. I'd take a singer any day. I could handle the temper, the depression, the sadistic voice coach, the vocal nodules . . . but an accompanist? You not only live with *his* ups and downs, but everybody's he *plays* for. It's geometric group therapy! Those people scare me. I can't believe the things they say, the things they do." She added, "Even the things they *say* they do." This was, of course, before AIDS. "They're all *crazy.*"

I could see her point. I'd been to one party she'd thrown for Carl where two marriages seemed about to collapse—before dessert, even. A couple disappeared into the study, closed the door, reappeared after an hour, flushed, clothing disarranged, while their spouses were still snarling in the kitchen about whose fault it was; other guests had drifted in and out to offer sympathy, advice, drinks, helpful plans for revenge, or themselves. A week later, Becky saw all four at a concert. Beaming, they apologized. They also told her in vivid psychosexual detail how revitalizing the experience had been, and hoped she'd have them back. Soon.

"I am not that sophisticated!"

For a time, she wasn't at *all* sophisticated, trotting around New York in Grandma's handwoven cardigans sprigged with deer and wreaths and a white wool stocking cap with a worn pom-pom that she thought was "precious."

I would tweak it when I came in to visit (at home, it didn't look so shabby or strange). Though she eventually gave up the hat, she resisted changing the way she looked, wore her blond hair bowl-cut, as it'd been since she was four or five, and favored plaid skirts, like Mom.

Carl did not seem to care what Becky wore. A big gorgeous Swede with lake-blue eyes, he had stopped *seeing* his wife years ago,

I thought. Their love was solid and comfortable, even mildly celebrated among their divorced or squabbling friends. But at the parties
I'd attended at Becky's, I sensed that people's smiles and comments
were a bit patronizing, as if to not be tormented, caustic, and bitchy
in New York was to settle for a diminished life. And wasn't it "sweet"
that Becky loved Michigan and their apartment was done in what
one guest had dubbed "Early Daniel Boone"?

"I couldn't live like that," Becky was often saying in response
to Carl's friends; as, for instance, when dinner guests served up
gossip about a famous conductor sleeping with young Guatemalan
men, about a diva drunk at rehearsals, about a cellist beating his
wife. "*My* life is an open book," she would add demurely, like a
Henry James maiden gathering up her shawl.

"*Rebecca of Sunnybrook Farm*, love," a drunken Australian
tenor once asked, "or *Tropic of Cancer?*"

"Well, I know they dish about us," she told me once. "But so
what? So I still have my Michigan '*a*' and I say 'grosheries' instead
of 'groceries,' and so I don't dress like a million skinny women in
New York. Honey, I've *been* skinny and it made me mean."

I remembered how thin she had been that first year after moving
to New York, model thin, smoking two packs of Kents a day, rocking
in Grandma's handpainted chair, nervous about Carl's career, about
the incredible rents, about shopping in dirty and chaotic super-
markets, about the cockroaches, about the rusty water, about jun-
kies. I had thought her very glamorous then: my grown-up sister in
a grown-up apartment, with a husband who was going to be *famous*
(we didn't think there was any other reason to leave Michigan).

It didn't happen for Carl. And from Michigan, we watched
Carl's career settle into the coarse weave of insignificant engage-
ments he tried to pass off as cloth of gold, like so many other
struggling artists who not only weren't at the top but didn't even
know anyone who was. What a cruel city to just be "good" in. We
heard he was a terrific teacher, but he didn't enjoy having students
who might outshine him. He and Becky fought a great deal those
early days before she found a job in publishing, and Carl realized
he wouldn't be reviewed in *The New Yorker* or the *Times*, would
barely be reviewed at all, would probably leave no more mark in
New York than a cigarette butt tossed from a heaving, crowded bus.
Becky often talked about my successful teaching career at the Uni-

versity of Michigan (I'm co-chair of Romance Languages) as if it were some lost chapter in a people's history, dazzling, romantic: "*We* could have had that life."

Things started to improve for Becky, if not for Carl: she got a job as a reader at an academic press and then became an editorial assistant. Before that, though, our folks were very worried about her. Dad thought she might have a nervous breakdown, and this made her seem even more glamorous to me. I.. Michigan, people shot themselves in the barn, had a snowmobiling "accident," ran off with a neighbor, or disappeared in the woods; a nervous breakdown sounded wonderful and exotic. That's what they *do* in New York, I thought; it'll be an *experience* and we can all be brave for her. I pictured Becky off in Connecticut in this enormous white-on-white rest home surrounded by a glowing park out of a *Masterpiece Theater* series, with statues and duck ponds. She would have a soothing and wise German psychiatrist who had fled the Nazis, whose great healing sympathy came, somehow, from a tragic vision of life.

But Becky remained a Michigander ("Michiganian" is too chic for me) in this way above all others: she never did therapy in New York—not psychoanalysis, Jungian, primal scream, Gestalt, Skinnerian, transactional analysis, none of it. And I guessed that her friends and Carl's thought her odd, like someone at a buffet table passing up the truffles or the pâté for bean curd.

"I think people should help themselves," she'd say, "or their friends should." Even *I* thought this a bit insensitive. But whether she believed it or not, it was the voice of Michigan, the voice of our parents: to pay someone to listen to your problems seemed crude, shameful. And dangerous. One distant cousin's wife had been institutionalized after only a month of therapy, and when the husband objected (so the story went), *he* was put away himself. His parents were so terrified *they*'d be next when they came to get him released, they hardly said a word!

"Listen," Becky told me, "everyone's always 'making progress,' and 'finding themselves slowly,' and 'getting better,' and 'learning to listen inside' . . . but doesn't anyone ever get well or just *stop?* They move to a different therapy, like changing your nail polish. Look at their faces when they talk about it; they're either bragging about how they can stand all the ugliness, how tough they are, or they look wasted, like they just got out of the Black Hole of Calcutta. Not for me."

So, she missed Michigan, had no therapist, was not married to a famous pianist, not mixing with stars, not becoming one herself. I guess in New York that makes you only moderately miserable. None of it prepared her for Joselynne's book.

Becky called me late one May night in the thirteenth year of her life in New York. I wasn't surprised or scared to hear from her at 1:00 A.M. We'd always liked talking late on the phone, with our different worlds gone quiet and remote. Hearing her voice, distilled out of the room she spoke from, what she was wearing, the Petoskey stone earrings I'd given her years ago, our bond seemed sometimes painfully strong, as if we were too close to see how separate we were.

"Something terrible happened, Dave. It's Joselynne."

I had not heard her mention Carl's first wife in that tone; she made the name sound, well, *important*.

"What's going on?" I sat up sharply because I'd just seen *Fatal Attraction*.

"Dave, she wrote a *book*, a novel. It's terrible, all about us, Carl and me, no it *isn't*, but she's taken all this real stuff and made up horrible things, I can't believe—"

"Whoa! Take me through this slowly."

She tried. But first she had to remind me about Joselynne Douglas, whom I'd never met or even seen a picture of. For Carl at twenty-three, Joselynne had seemed the ideal wife: beautiful, gracious, gentle, sensitive—she was always telling people how much she valued being sensitive to people's feelings—aware, and alert. But it was clear, Becky said, in only a few months that the marriage was impossible. Joselynne needed to plan and control everything in Carl's life, and her "sensitivity" was a mask for the stifled outrage of a criminally frustrated child.

"She was the Alarm Clock from Hell," Becky explained. "Do this, do that, *now*. But *so* sweet, nice, understanding, only Carl saw it. Everyone else thought she was an angel." Now I had certainly met people like that; they spoke so quietly, so unassertively you had to lean forward to hear them. They didn't interrupt, because they'd tell you conversation was not combat; they just waited, blaringly patient. I'd always mistrusted this display of harmlessness and seen it as the fiercest egotism.

Still, I understood that whatever Joselynne was like, *this* was, of course, how Becky would have to see it. Carl was so phlegmatic when it came to anything outside his fervid musicians' world that I could imagine a more organized and demanding woman than Becky (who claimed to be as easy to live with "as a goldfish") finding his calmness dreary, like a week of summer reruns.

They had all known each other at Michigan State University, and that was apparently where the novel was set, in the late Sixties.

"There's all this *sex* in it!" Becky wailed. "Stuff I've never even *heard* about; you'd have to give me an instruction book and I'd *still* get it wrong and end up in a hospital. And I'm horrible in it, just like Joselynne, a real cold smiley bitch, manipulative, with no sense of humor. She says I stole Carl, like he was somebody's bicycle, or a gold watch. I did not steal him, I helped him escape!" After a silence, Becky said, "My name is Betty, Carl's is Mark, and hers is Linda. I mean, you don't have to be real smart to figure it out if you knew us."

"But you told me she was a hairdresser or something, how'd she get to be a writer?"

"Ask me if I care! Maybe she met Joyce Carol Oates on a subway. Maybe she took night courses. Maybe she's a medium and the book was sent from the spirit world. Does it matter? It's out, and I'm *in* it!"

"Where did you find it?" I imagined some tiny paperback rack at a supermarket under blaring headlines about Atlantis, Miraculous Weight Loss, Siamese Triplets Born to a Three-Year-Old Midget.

"Doubleday's. On Fifth Avenue."

That threw me. But I told her that there must be *thousands* of books published every year in New York, and most wound up on jumbled sale tables, stamped $1.29. No one would ever hear of Joselynne's book. Becky was in publishing—didn't she know that?

Becky gulped, or sobbed, or maybe just took in a lot of breath to help her expel the following words. "It's published by Random House. It's been reviewed in The *Times*. They said it was a 'wickedly barbed cultural document.' "

She stopped me, of course. I have that Michigan respect verging on suspicion and dread of *The New York Times*, and have always thought of its power to make people and events important as practically invincible.

"What if Mom and Dad read it? They'll think I'm a monster."

She wasn't inventing the possibility. They might buy the book, because our parents had some peculiar idea that you not only had to be nice *to* a relative's ex- but nice *about* the man or woman. And keep everyone informed. They ran into Joselynne or her mother every now and then up at Charlevoix and always passed on the news to Becky, who would usually not sleep much that night, after calling me to shout something like, "What do they want me to do! Invite her to Thanksgiving?" Carl never had any contact with Joselynne, and the news items didn't seem to bother him.

"Now listen," I said, and went on to be stern. All our lives, I asked, hadn't everything we'd feared come out wildly different from the way we thought it would?

"Yeah," she muttered. "Usually worse."

Right then, she was inconsolable. She created for me a nightmare vision of everyone in New York reading the book, people pointing and staring at her on the number 5 bus, abusing her like a bad woman on a soap opera whose viewers think she's *real*: a viper, a witch.

Still, I tried to soothe Becky, and promised I would talk to our folks and call her the next night.

They called *me*.

"David," Mom began, "that Joselynne sent us a book she wrote. Isn't that nice? It's called *Revelations*, but it doesn't seem to have anything to do with Scripture that I can tell."

"Wordy," Dad said on the extension. "Too damned wordy. Too many *words*. Those long sentences I hate with the semicolons."

Even in retirement, Dad read only one or two books a year, usually sports biographies. Mom read little besides mysteries.

I asked how far they had gotten.

"First chapter," Dad shot. "Gave it up."

Mom clucked. "It's not what I would choose for myself, but I'm glad Joselynne got herself a big—One of those—"

"Advances," Dad filled in. "A big advance, she said. Might move to New York."

Becky was relieved to hear that Mom and Dad would probably never read enough to discover their daughter was a fiend. And even if they *did* get further into the book, I insisted, they wouldn't believe Joselynne's portrait was accurate—but they also wouldn't dislike

Joselynne. Mom and Dad could only ascribe ugly motivations to politicians and other public figures, rarely to people they knew (Dad, for instance, was convinced that *Johnson* had masterminded JFK's assassination). If they saw a distorted image of Becky in the novel, they would most likely conclude that Joselynne was "confused" or "unhappy." And leave it at that.

These comments were the first I made about the novel that slowed Becky down, that made her feel like she might not be swept off her little atoll of accomplishment by a tidal wave of shame.

"You're right," she kept saying. "You are *right*."

I did not tell her that Joselynne "might move to New York," and when Becky, in her new spirit of optimism, said, "And Carl's friends won't get to it, they only read music, and each other's reviews," I agreed.

I found Joselynne's novel at Border's here in Ann Arbor the next evening and read it straight through. In one way, it was pretty damning. Becky/Betty did drugs and sold them; slept with half the English department at MSU, generally in groups of three or four; stole people's research and published it under her own name; came to classes she taught stoned. But she was so stereotypically a Sixties flower child/operator on speed, devious and dazed, that I wasn't convinced people would recognize the character. Maybe it had a name like Becky's, and a matching physical description, but this was simply a portrait of a young American girl ninety years after Daisy Miller. I even liked the combination of Philip Roth's rage and Len Deighton's plotting, with dashes of Barbara Cartland. What a brew. For Becky, I said it was trash.

When Becky called to tell me that Carl had read the novel and found it unrealistic, boring, I was relieved. I had wondered if that sleepy exterior (moved to expression only by the impetus of grand fulfilling music) could be stung into some kind of operatic lust for revenge. But there were no family reverberations, no lawsuits, no public humiliation. It probably *would* sink like all the other well-reviewed but forgettable books of that year, I concluded.

Then Becky called with good news, and bad.

"I saw her on Oprah," she dropped, like a gambler betting a last chip, unemotional, resigned.

"Doing what?"

"Talking about the book. It was a show on writers who had

been in other professions. One was a plumber first, another a
teacher. She looked like Joan Collins—you know, tarty, with lots
of bust and hair, and some weird accent that I think *she* thinks is
what people expect Michigan to sound like."

I didn't know what to say, and waited for more bad news, for
Becky to tell me *she* had been asked to appear on Oprah, for a show
of Real People into Fiction.

"You won't believe this, Dave, but I got promoted, with a huge
raise. I'm an acquisitions editor now. Guess why," she breathed.
"My boss read Joselynne's novel, and he knows Carl, knows we
went to State, and put it all together."

"No."

"I'm telling you he *did*. He said so." She laughed a little. "He
looks at me differently now, like I'm more interesting, or something.
The guy who cuts my hair is spending more time on me, doing a
much better job. Even the salesgirls at B. Altman are more attentive,
I *swear*. I saw one had the book in her shoulder bag when she was
going out to lunch. People *know*. And Carl is getting more work,
more students. His friends *all* treat me different, like they're waiting
for me to swing from the chandelier or rip my clothes off at dinner
and go wild in the salad."

"It can't be the book."

"People think we're exciting, for the first time. *And* successful.
Really, Dave, I *feel* it. I guess *being* in a book is more status to lots
of New Yorkers than writing it, I mean, you don't have to do any
work, you're just yourself. It's wonderful!"

I tried to think of something sensible to say that would quash
this fantasy of Becky's. If she started feeling like Joselynne's book
was bringing all this into her life, she'd end up so grateful that
Joselynne would *surely* get invited to Thanksgiving. I couldn't stomach the possibility; I was not that sophisticated.

"Now don't yell at me, Dave, okay? *Okay?*"

I mumbled "Sure."

"The book is starting to sell really well, but I'm worried that
no one will buy the screen rights. What do you think?"

The Prince and
the Pauper

Paul knew that his mother would not have liked Claudio. His mother suspected all handsome men, as if they were representatives of some furtive agency of terror. And gay or straight, she dismissed them as "pretty boys."

But her contempt was a mere child's pail of sandy water splashed against a cliff, and she knew it. They existed, they endured despite her.

So Paul did not tell her why he had decided to move from his efficiency apartment near the University of Michigan to share a house at the very edge of Ann Arbor with Claudio and another graduate student in their program. He did not say that he had watched Claudio at parties. Or that once, the previous spring, in a Women's Literature seminar, he had gradually edged his chair closer to Claudio's at the table to try breathing in the rich smell of that bare, thick, tanned neck rising from a loose T-shirt like warm new-baked bread.

Paul did not say that he had studied how Claudio sat: still and impassive, legs uncrossed, never stroking his close-cropped black beard or resting a hand on his knee, his heavy-lidded brown eyes large and demanding in the broad face of a Renaissance prince, with a high forehead, dense shiny black hair, thin nose and mouth.

Paul did not mention that once, on the way back from a movie and dinner near Detroit, with five people from their program jammed into a VW, he had fallen asleep next to Claudio. It was the hot, crowded little movie theater, the drinks afterward, and the long monotonous rush of trees and highway lights. When he woke up abruptly at a sharp turn and raised his hand for balance, Claudio surprised Paul by clasping it to steady him, smiling, letting it go. Afterward, when Paul found himself staring at the hand Claudio had taken, he thought, Oh honey, you are *gone.*

His mother never knew how happy Claudio had made him, but as if she had guessed everything he hadn't told her, she said on the phone, "Paul, be careful."

"I'm just moving into a house, Mom."

"You and two men is not a house, it's a *situation.*"

"I'm an adult, I know what I'm doing."

"That's just what I said when I married your father!"

As soon as he'd arrived at the University of Michigan for a master's in English, he started hearing about Claudio, the star of the doctoral program. Claudio had already published half a dozen scholarly articles and was only twenty-six, not even finished with course work for the Ph.D. Claudio was studying D. H. Lawrence's short fiction, and Paul thought that said something wonderful about him.

"I hate our department sometimes," Claudio told him a week after Paul started renting the second bedroom in the small white Cape Cod house Claudio's parents had bought as an investment. It was at the top of one of Ann Arbor's steep and lovely hills, on a street lined with old and well-kept brick homes fronted by neat gardens.

The other housemate, Dean—a slim, silent doctoral candidate—lived in the finished basement and worked so much on his dissertation that Paul had hardly seen him.

"Listen to them, Paul, they're students of literature and what do they talk about? Caulking their windows, that's the married ones; scoring dope, that's the ex-hippies. Where's the passion?"

Paul kept scrubbing a plate.

"How can they read anything if they don't feel?" Claudio pressed.

Paul had to admit that his fellow students were somewhat dull, at least in class; outside, he thought them very friendly and relaxed.

"I hear them talk about *Women in Love* and I want to choke. They don't understand a word of it."

Paul was glad that *he* wasn't in that Modern Fiction seminar; Claudio would probably lump him with the rest. Lawrence had always perplexed and amazed him, with all those people speaking the terrible truths of the blood. He thought of Glenda Jackson in the movie of *Women in Love,* demolishing her lover with a soft, almost good-naturedly destructive "You *waste* me, and you *break* me, and it is *horrible* to me." Paul went red in the small tiled kitchen hot with steam and Claudio's probing voice.

"Maybe they're afraid to feel," he suggested quietly.

Claudio sneered. "Bullshit. They *can't* feel."

But despite disliking the department, Claudio gave frequent parties, perhaps to show that *he* wasn't dull, so Paul worked hard for the next two weeks to avoid feeling guilty having fun at Claudio's first party of the semester.

The Saturday morning of the party, as Claudio stood stirring a large pot of meatballs, his sleeves rolled up, dark arms spotted with sauce, Paul found himself watching one spot, pictured wiping it, brushing it away.

"Taste the sauce." Claudio held out the wooden ladle to him. Startled, Paul focused on the long, steaming red oval, blew on it, and tasted. It was very good, he said.

Claudio agreed. He was making lasagna too, would have garlic bread and salad, and afterward pass around fruit and cheese.

"I love *occasions,*" Claudio explained.

Claudio's best friend, Lana, got there early to help set up, she said, but she just drank rum and cokes while they worked. A fifth-year doctoral student, Lana was a large brunette whose nervous good looks seemed a perpetual irritation to her. She wore stylishly extravagant clothes as if to lose herself in their brutal elegance, and had recently taken to layers of shawls, and slit skirts, like Faye Dunaway in *The Eyes of Laura Mars.* Paul shared an office with her and some other graduate students, but she wasn't like any of them. Morbidly self-important, Lana stalked the department as if trumpeting her own fame, each long stride a proclamation, and a promise of bedroom wealth, though she frequently warned she would never sleep with any of *them.* She enveloped professors with flattery and smiles like a flock of anxious birds, hands and shoulders wiggling, wheeling, darting. She used their first names, throaty and intimate, and always sprayed her wrists and throat with YSL when she went to talk to her adviser.

The other graduate students hated Lana for her flirting, and for her perfect grade point, her Phi Kappa Phi award, her fellowship, her articles in scholarly journals, and the claims people *said* she'd made (Paul had never actually heard any from *her*) about sleeping with a number of well-known novelists, like Barrett LeGrand, the minor Southern novelist who'd just won his second Pulitzer. Next to Claudio, Lana was the department's star, and whenever Paul saw them together, they were usually running down everyone in the department.

The evening of the party they were talking about the East Coast, oohing and aahing about their favorite places in Boston. Paul knew that Lana had done a B.A. at Barnard, an M.A. at Brown and had often heard her deplore the University of Michigan and the state.

"It's all so gray here—no color, no life, nothing to do," she moaned several times. "Ann Arbor is not a place but a *reputation*."

"False, too," Claudio added, scraping out a pot. He was from Vermont.

They were right, up to a point, Paul thought. Lots of people at the University of Michigan seemed to believe they really belonged at Harvard, but he hadn't been able to figure out why.

He didn't bother giving Lana and Claudio his Michigan spiel. He was apparently one of the few graduate students from New York who was happy there. New Yorkers tended to stick together like suspicious tourists whose bus had broken down in a Mexican backwater, only they made no loud pretense of finding the locals "charming." Paul thought Michigan people were friendly compared to New Yorkers, and the state was incredibly beautiful. But Lana and Claudio were not interested in hearing about beaches or camping or winter sports or Lake Superior or the glories of Big Ten football.

It bothered Paul that Claudio liked Lana so much. And that the only thing she had said to *him* in the kitchen was, "You have very revealing eyes."

The music Claudio played on his gaudy, gleaming stereo that night was thankfully *not* the *Saturday Night Fever* sound track you heard at every party that year, but Aretha, James Brown, Eddie Kendricks, Marvin Gaye. And so they all seemed to dance more freely in the small gray and green living room with its ranks of plants guarding the windows. Paul watched Claudio move, admiring the play of muscles underneath his black crew-neck sweater, the heavy biceps (Claudio had thrown the discus in high school), the tilt of his head, and the steady churn of his slim hips. When everyone, blissfully drunk, was gone at 4:00 A.M. and Paul had helped Dean downstairs, he forced himself to start washing up.

But Claudio came out to the kitchen, stood behind him, breathing deeply. "Why don't you stop that?" Claudio's hands dropped onto his shoulders like snow thudding off a roof. Then Claudio was pushing him down the hall, into Paul's room and on the bed, wrenching at his clothes, turning him over.

Claudio had Paul's legs spread, was stabbing at his ass with an angry tongue, forcing him open. Then he was off the bed, ripping through drawers. "Cream," he demanded.

"Top drawer," Paul said. Then, "That hurts!"

"It's supposed to," Claudio laughed. "That's how you know it's good." And Claudio proceeded to cover Paul's mouth with one sweaty hand while he fucked deeper.

When Claudio slipped inside him a second time, heavy, insistent, silent, Paul begged, "Say something."

"Shut up." Claudio reached underneath to jerk him off.

Paul came into Claudio's hand, and Claudio wiped it on the pillow, pulling out with a wrench. Paul asked where he was going. Wasn't he staying the night?

"Forget it. I won't sleep."

Claudio was soon taking a shower.

Paul had not known enough men to be so casual about sex. Jerry, his first lover, in high school, had been so magnetic that other guys were uninteresting to Paul until sophomore year of college. Jerry had come back one summer from two months at a baseball camp, burnished by the sun, taut and muscled, and grinning. "I saw these two guys," was the first thing he said. "In the shower. One was *doing* it, I mean, he had his dick right up the other guy's *butt!*" And Paul had stared, unable to believe his luck. The year before he had written Jerry a poem about life and rivers and friendship, which Jerry had said was "neat," and tucked into his ring-leaf binder. Ashamed, Paul never talked about it or tried to maneuver Jerry into staying over, or wrestling, or reading *Playboy* together, anything that might have broken down the walls that were as much inside Paul as between the two of them. But now Jerry was describing two guys actually fucking!

"And it slipped out and was shooting all over." Jerry laughed, obviously waiting for Paul to laugh, but he was too breathless. They were in Jerry's bedroom hung with Yankees posters, sitting on the floor with their backs to the bed. *Say* something, Paul cursed at himself, but couldn't speak—his mouth had gone dry. Jerry leaned closer, eyebrows waggling. "It looked like fun," he said. And in that spirit, they went into the bathroom to shower together (well, they *had* been shooting hoops in the park, and they *were* kind of grungy). In the shower, Paul closed his eyes, let Jerry do everything, soap them up, bend him over, probe and then try to push in, and then step out to find some vaseline—"or something"—to make it easier. With the water and Jerry's soothing hands on his shoulders and back, Paul felt like Columbus discovering America—amazed, transfixed, a *success*. Though Jerry was always laughing about their sex (and they started sleeping over at each other's houses), it was not because he discounted what they were doing, but because he was so happy and released. Sometimes he'd sing to the Monkees' theme song, "Hey, hey, we're the fuckers—people say we're fucking around. . . ." with all the zest of a college fight song. Paul *wished* he could be that free.

Jerry's father got transferred to Hawaii in their senior year; the letters didn't last long, and no trip out to Hawaii ever came through. Still, Paul thought of him a lot, and how much he looked a bit like Michael York, and all the times he'd say, "Let's go to the *moon*" —and how he took Paul there. So he wasn't much interested in finding someone else. Until his sophomore year at Hunter, in the theater department's costume room, when Peter Texeira, slim and pretty, half-Portuguese, half-black, a sweet, sexy-eyed guy in charge of costumes, had locked the door and simply fallen on Paul in a whirl of hands and exclamations. It turned out that Peter was given to endless discussions about what their relationship meant to each of them at any given time, as if they were scientists charting microscopic changes in a cell. But despite all the attention, it lasted two years, and Bill, his only other lover in college, an aspiring painter, had championed monogamous commitment as "maturity with poetry." Paul had done Christopher Street and the bars only as a tourist, not a resident alien, always returning with Peter, and later Bill.

And then there was Paul's mother, who had announced from

the beginning that she would never draw back or reject him, but whose acceptance had shaped his relationships with men because she took it all so *seriously.*

"I'm not crazy about this," she said after he came out to her in high school when he knew he could no longer pretend he wasn't dating girls because he was . . . shy. "But, it could be worse," she'd added. Which meant his alcoholic father, who'd lost his real estate business, his marriage, and then his life in a car crash—all before Paul was five years old. He had few good memories of his father, mostly pictured a large, handsome man breaking or hurling things—dishes, vases, books, shoes, whatever, and shouting like a train wreck.

Paul's mother liked Jerry a lot. She found books on homosexuality as readily as someone going back to school after thirty years, and discussed theories of sexual development, homophobia, and gay liberation with Paul. She seemed to welcome this new opportunity of sharing his life, one even more intimate than the milk and cookies talks in grade school when he sat in the sunny kitchen kicking at the table leg and she cooked dinner. He knew that all this research was her way of dealing with the unexpected; in any crisis, his mother was always thorough and kind, and hungry for information. But they had spent so much time talking about his being gay that he hadn't had much chance to live it out. Once he'd said, "We're not cramming for a test, Mom!"

"No?"

Jerry, Peter, and Bill had all been surprised that she let them in the house after she knew about their relationships, and that she even made little jokes about it. Paul was grateful when he thought about *their* parents, who would never want proof of what they must have already suspected about their sons. That struck him as fatuous, like a little kid with his hands over his ears making loud "I can't hear you" noises.

The morning after Claudio fucked him, Claudio was nonchalant, no different from any other morning. Paul did not try to touch him, barely smiled. On campus, in the student cafeteria in their department's basement, he drank six cups of miserable coffee and decided that *he* would be nonchalant, too.

But that night, he couldn't sleep, and found himself in the

bathroom, preparing himself with vaseline for Claudio's wide cock. He stood outside Claudio's unlocked door waiting for his hands to feel steady enough to open it quietly and slip to the bed. He would kneel on the floor, he thought, reach in under Claudio's covers, stroke him while he dreamt, gently, entering and changing his dream, and then when Claudio was ready, Paul would crawl in and pull him on top before he was awake. Maybe Claudio would never know it was real.

He stood outside the door for most of the night, possibly, terrified of going in, unwilling to return to his empty bed. Was this like the times his mother had tried to get his father to leave a party or a bar by the sheer force of her love and concern for him? Paul was trapped there until he heard Dean coming up from the basement, for a drink of water, he guessed. He hurried into his room. There were a lot of nights like that.

Paul tried walking around the house just in silky gym shorts, bending over a lot, changed his after-shave and tried to radiate desirability, but nothing worked. Claudio treated him like a regular roommate. Then, one night Claudio offered to give him a back rub, and Paul thought it must be code, that Claudio had changed his mind. He made himself walk into Claudio's room slowly, as if he had merely come to look at the Salzburg Festival posters (Claudio was a Mozart freak). Paul took off his shirt and lay across the bed as solidly and seductively as he could. But he also wanted to blend in, to look natural there, and to register. Claudio was utterly silent crouching over him, using a heliotrope-scented oil. Claudio's heavy dark hands were like the sirens' song luring Odysseus into the sea. While Paul's body surrendered, his thoughts raced on past each circle of Claudio's finger: *Now*, he'll roll me over *now*. He'll slip my jeans down *now*. But Claudio stopped after a few minutes and told Paul he had work to do. More code, Paul thought, waiting up in bed for Claudio. Eventually, he fell asleep.

Why couldn't he talk to Claudio? He wanted to call his mother and see if she could tell him, but each time he imagined her resigned silence, he gave up even thinking she could help.

Stifled by his own desire and shame, for the next two months Paul forced serenity on himself at every meal, in every conversation, when what he most wanted was to beat at Claudio's beautiful untouched face. Dean's writing wasn't going well, so he spent much more time upstairs after meals, watching television, reading. Dean looked at Paul sometimes, puzzled, perhaps, but never asking a thing.

Three days before Christmas, when classes were almost over, Paul went to a professor's party in a barn of a house filled with books, antiques, and drunken graduate students. He wore his Jim Morrison black leather pants and a white T-shirt stretching across his chest, and got compliments all night more intoxicating than anything he could have drunk or did drink. I am *hot*, he kept thinking, passing from one beautiful noisy room to another, slipping in and out of conversations he never understood. It was all like far-off music, lovely and undemanding. Stopping at a long gold-framed mirror, Paul saw his mother's dark eyes, thick reddish-brown hair, and felt pleased at the resemblance, pleased that what was most womanly in her made *him* look more like a man.

He found a room full of dancers and moved to join them, laughing now with release. It didn't matter, it didn't any of it matter. He danced by himself, with couples, anyone, the faces and moves all blurring together into one admiring glow. He felt terrific, desirable, could feel the certain heat of praise. "Under my thumb," he sang, even when the song was over.

"You're drunk," Claudio was saying. "You need coffee."

Paul stuck his tongue out, kept dancing, shaking his ass at the world.

"You should go home."

Paul danced away. "Dean'll drive me back."

"He's gone." Claudio tried to grab him by the shoulders. "You need coffee." Claudio succeeded in taking his hands and pulling him from the music. When Claudio found their coats, Paul didn't care anymore if he stayed or left.

They drove for a few minutes in a stifling silence until Claudio pulled the Mustang over, glared at him, hands on the wheel.

Paul forced himself to say "What do you want from me?"

"Nothing. We're friends. Friends can sleep together, it's no big deal."

Paul leaned against the car door, right in line with a jet of smelly hot air from the heater, blind, wanting to rush out into the night and bury himself in a snowbank.

Claudio started up the car and when they pulled into the narrow driveway, said, "Let's fuck." Paul followed him inside like a chastened puppy with no will to be bad anymore. Inside his room, Claudio ripped off Paul's shirt, yanked down his pants, and then pushed him down on his knees and shoved his face down on the bed. He held Paul's hands out as if to tie them to posts and crouched behind him, trying to force his hard cock inside, without any cream, without anything. "Relax, goddamnit!" Claudio kept pushing until finally Paul felt his body painfully give way and Claudio was inside of him, riding, thrusting as if to burn this moment into his flesh. Near tears, Paul thought of Oliver Reed pounding blindly at Glenda Jackson's body, wasting and breaking her, falling on her like an avalanche. He was biting the quilt, Paul realized, suddenly tasting it, when Claudio collapsed on his back, sweaty, with a triumphant groan.

Claudio didn't touch him after pulling away, but Paul didn't say a word.

The next day, Claudio left for the winter break, packing quickly, methodically, strong back bent over a dark leather suitcase. Paul stood in the doorway of Claudio's room, trying to chat, feeding off so little, so very little: Claudio's voice, the hands folding and stacking, the rich line of his neck.

"Are you okay?" Dean asked when Claudio was gone, bringing his mug out to the empty living room, where Paul sat staring at the plants, wondering why he didn't know what any of them were.

He looked up. "How's your writing?"

Dean settled onto the rug and launched into a monologue about his dissertation. It was psychological criticism and Dean spoke of the Jacobean plays he was examining in terms of fixations, complexes, obsessions, networks of wishes and fears.

"It's so dark," Paul brought out. And yet the plays had the truth of nightmare—like the woman in *The Changeling* getting a man she hated to murder her fiancé and then being forced to sleep with the murderer to make him keep the secret.

Dean shrugged, and said, "I could always lighten things up with a snappy title. How about 'The Penis as Protagonist in Renaissance Drama'?"

Paul suddenly pictured Dean—with his enormous grin—as a happy runner bounding to the finish line, supremely confident that he would break the tape. Claudio had so quickly become all Paul could see in the house, that Dean had felt like a shadow to him, a wraith, despite the laundry they'd done together, the shopping, the chores. But his smile was so wide and warm. . . .

"You hungry?" Dean asked. "How about Small's . . . unless you don't like veggies?"

They bundled up against the wind and snow and had a quiet dinner as soothing as a loving hand on your forehead, stroking away a headache, and decided to see a Chevy Chase movie afterward.

But Paul couldn't fall asleep later, wondering what would happen, what he would tell his mother when he went back to New York in two days for the winter break.

It was a strange time: lost on Fifth Avenue amid thousands of Christmas gift-seekers, nervous with his friends because he didn't want to mention Claudio, yet had little to say about school. Everyone else had jobs; Paul was the only one of his group to have gone on to do graduate work, and he felt his conversation at a New Year's party was a disappointment: he had nothing new, stirring, insightful to say, no adventures to share. His friend Jim was trying to set him up with his cute puppy-eyed cousin from Baton Rouge, but Paul was not at his best, and even the languid way Jim's cousin spoke (*Paul* had two syllables with his drawl) was annoying. Paul felt shrill, hurried, unable to relax, like the city itself. Seeing relatives was even worse, like going through a fun house, distorted faces popping out at you from every angle.

"It's not good, is it?" his mother asked when he was packing to drive back to Ann Arbor. She sat on the edge of his bed.

"You look like a mother on a TV show—" he started, but then gave up and sat by her, tried to explain what had happened, what he felt.

"No, cookie, that's not love," she insisted, hugging him. "That's never love, it's a problem. There's something in you you're working out, Claudio just represents it."

"But what?"

"If I knew, I'd be one of those TV mothers, right?"

No one was at the house when Paul got there and Dean had left a note saying he was going to stay in Miami a week longer than he'd planned.

Paul unpacked with the radio on, recalling his mother's last worried smile and little slow wave, which made her seem like the wife of a Confederate soldier leaving home near the end of the Civil War. Paul spent the next few days reading for the coming semester, drinking lots of cocoa laced with rum, rearranging his room, clearing out some of the kitchen cabinets, dusting, doing wash, watching television, avoiding even a glance at Claudio's room.

What would he have done in there? Looked for a diary, read Claudio's letters, desperate for some proof that he had meant something, desperate to know who this man was? Or would he simply have rubbed his face in one of Claudio's flannel shirts?

The day Dean was due, Paul drove into town for a haircut, decided to make a quiche for dinner, but it was Claudio who arrived, standing there with a girl dressed in early Grace Slick.

"This is Molly; Molly, Paul." They stomped their boots and Molly nodded hello. They helped each other off with their coats, draping them on the nearest chair.

"My car's in the shop; Molly gave me a lift."

From Vermont, Paul thought, a lift.

Some kind of conversation developed, despite Molly's indifference. Once, only once, she looked right at Paul, seemed to smile, and mouthed, "Sorry."

It was that obvious.

He did not go out with them for dinner, but read for hours with a furious lack of concentration, eventually fell asleep, woke feeling cold and sweaty, pulled the quilt up, fell asleep again, and woke, sure it was very late. Breathing quickly, he gathered the quilt around him, managed to pull on boots, and stumbled from the oppressive house outside, down the icy gravel path, the cold like a nightmare, down to his car. He yanked the door open and plunged inside, his breath shooting white clouds into the startled air. Eyes closed, huddled, he rocked jerkily to lose the pain, quicker, hysterically now, eyes sore and heavy. He wept thinly, the tears like a trickle of blood from a wincing cut.

The front door opened, closed, there were footsteps, and he stared with blurry eyes to make out the figure.

Dean came around the hood of the car and got in on the driver's side, shivering. "Out for a spin?" he asked.

"When'd you get back?"

"Just before. Didn't you see my car?" He pointed. "How about a drink inside? The service is lousy here."

Paul let Dean walk back first so he wouldn't see how ridiculous Paul looked dragging the quilt. Shivering, he left it on the couch and followed downstairs in his shorts and fleece-lined boots. Dean kept his heat up pretty high in the basement, so Paul was comfortable.

"You look like a raunchy Eddie Bauer ad." Dean handed him some tissues and a shot of Jack Daniels.

Paul wiped his eyes and nose, grinning, unembarrassed now, enjoying the attention. He was pleased with his body because of Peter, who had said in sophomore year at Hunter, when Paul thought he wanted to be an actor, "*Girl*, you don't look half as good as you could and you won't get any hot parts in shows here unless you *do* something with yourself." Thin, sleek, elegant, Peter wrote him up an exercise program, went jogging with him, advised on caps and contacts and bought him a subscription to GQ.

"I'm trying to figure out how your books are organized," Paul said from the fat green armchair, holding out his glass for a refill. Freud was next to Hemingway, which was next to Milton and James Clavell.

"It's a diary." Dean waved at the well-stuffed brick and board shelving. "It's all in the order I read them, so I can go back, remember where I was, who gave me the book, why— But *I'm* trying to figure out how long you're going to let Claudio screw up your head like tonight."

Paul looked away, drank without tasting.

"I take it you mean Molly," he said.

"I do."

"And?"

"Well, face it, he just wants to irk you. Come on, I met Molly—okay, briefly—but I can tell the girl does *not* have a rich internal life."

Paul howled "Yes!" and spilled some of his drink. Dean leapt up from his disordered bed.

"Would Monsieur like me to wipe his briefs?"

Paul hesitated, realized Dean wasn't exactly joking, smiled. "At least." Paul set his drink on the floor, nodded, closed his eyes as Dean crouched between his legs, gently slid the white shorts away from his body, down his thighs. When Paul grabbed at his head, Dean said, "Slow, slow."

"You're so dark," Paul said, with the covers thrown back, stroking the tan line just above Dean's pubic hair and at the top of his thighs. He shook his head. "Florida."

"I didn't think you were gay," Dean said. "I mean I wasn't sure at first, until I watched you and Claudio, the way you look at him. Hungry, down."

"Is Claudio gay or what?"

"Well, he's fucked almost everyone in the department, except me. Guys like that are whatever people think they are. Which means nothing, really."

"My mother said something like that."

"Smart lady."

Paul stroked Dean's hairless taut thighs, feeling warm, familiar, as if released from an exile where he hadn't been able to speak his own language.

"Molly won't be the last overnighter, you know, woman *or* man." Dean ran a finger across his lips, as if asking the words to wait.

"But what can I do? Move?"

"Why not? It's between semesters, you could get a single at the grad dorm easy, and nobody'll notice. You can say it was too far from campus here, rent's too high. You never signed a lease, right?"

Dean kissed at his neck and chest.

"You'd help me move?"

Dean said, "Sure." He grinned. "He can always get Lana to take your room. . . ."

"What?"

"Bad joke, sorry. He dumped her the night of the party, and she's been telling people in the department coffee room that he stole all his articles from her. She's psychotic. Haven't you heard all this?"

They slept until Paul woke from a dream of calling Claudio, the phone's harsh, insistent jangle bruising the air, but Claudio wouldn't answer.

"What do I tell Claudio?"

Dean shrugged. "He'll be pissed we have to find another room-mate, and that he can't toy with you; he'll probably want to fuck you again, to see if he can, but it's just a stage."

"For him?"

"For you. It happens to everybody. They get trashed—"

"By Attila the Hunk?"

"Right! Mostly, you recover."

"And then what happens?"

"If you're lucky, you meet someone who's not so amazing, but nice."

"Do you read palms, too?"

"Boy," Dean said, sliding on top of him. "I read everything you've got."

Paul supposed he was like most people when it came to thinking about breaking up with someone: you fantasize that they'll simply be shot into outer space and you won't have any awkward read-justments, any pain. But it didn't end so neatly with Claudio. The day after Paul moved out with Dean's help (while Claudio was at the library), Claudio called and asked him to come over to talk.

When he said he was going, Dean stared at him from above a half-unpacked box like the wife of a criminal, convinced there was no such thing as "one last job."

Paul told him that he needed to feel he wasn't a coward, but that was bullshit. He wanted to see Claudio alone, and perhaps what he hoped was that no one had ever walked away from Claudio before and the shock would have made Claudio see him as lovable, or at least important.

When Claudio met him at the door of the house, he had just gotten out of the shower. ("What a coincidence," Dean would later say.) He had on only a small towel, bulging at the crotch. Water still spotted the dense curls on his deep-muscled chest, and his thick hair hung wet across that princely forehead. Despite the near-nudity, he looked armored, with muscles like impregnable chain mail, a body to keep the world away, adoring, not to welcome it or give anyone joy.

Their talk in Claudio's room was scattered. Claudio dropped the towel and stood for a while brushing his hair dry in the mirror, "profiling," as Dean put it when Paul got back to the dorm. Claudio was so big and dark and meaty—but everything about his body seemed to distance Paul now, not reel him in on Claudio's line.

"I just don't think it's a good idea for me to stay," Paul kept saying, like a little kid sure that the same words of a lie, infinitely repeated, can keep punishment away.

"Why not? We can be friends now."

Paul shook his head. He wondered if Claudio was really waiting for a confession of love, or just desire, a weepy capitulation.

"It was okay," he told Dean when he got back after only half an hour. "Nothing happened."

"You think D. H. Lawrence is so great—well, there's a line in *Kangaroo*," Dean said. "About a dog going back to its vomit."

"And you thought that was me?"

He and Dean understood the first guest lecture of the semester, on "The Literature of Uncertainty," in waves, like nausea, but Lana loved it and slept with the lecturer—she said. Bill Judson from Yale had seemed perversely cryptic to Paul, a sphinx without a riddle, but not to Lana.

"Oh Pauly, he was wonderful," she crooned a few days later, leaning back in her swivel chair as if into Judson's short arms, her big-toothed smile gulping the windowless office. She sighed. "We had a fa-bu-lous dinner. . . ."

"*Paul*," he corrected. "No one calls me Pauly."

Lana smiled brightly, as if pretending interest in someone's tropical fish tank.

Dean had told him that he couldn't stand Lana, not because of her snobbery but because of her constant talk about sex, which seemed almost a parody of the very real sexual tension between graduate professors and their students. The department was long past the days of Sixties wife-swapping, serial divorce, and lesbian love-ins, but things did happen. Dean had told Paul on their first night together, in between climbing all over him, that he had been forced to shuffle his doctoral committee membership because two members—a woman and a man—came on to him.

"At first, I didn't pick up on it; I was too nervous about grades and papers," Dean said. But the woman had taken a number of opportunities to give him rides, and her blouse was always unbuttoned enough to reveal a great deal of her amazingly large and firm breasts. "I thought she didn't know, I mean, buttons can pop open when you're built like that—" When they had coffee to discuss his work, though, Dr. Slate freely talked about her "dreadful" marriage and several "tempestuous" affairs she'd had.

And the man, Dean's committee chair, fiftyish, handsome, slim, married, had started pressing Dean to come play squash with him at his health club, or use his sauna at home. Dean had gone over just once, thinking Dr. Viorst's wife would be there, too. But she wasn't. "And he took off his bathing suit!" Dean blushed with the memory. "So I left. I mean, his thighs are his own business, and so is everything else."

Both professors had resisted the committee change, firing off angry letters to the department chair (who looked like Dr. Smith on "Lost in Space" and was just as cowardly and deceitful), accusing Dean of sloppy scholarship, threatening to strip him of his teaching assistantship.

"So I went into the chair's office—that geek!—and told him that I'd go to the ACLU and file a suit if they didn't back off, and I told him why they were hassling me. He sputtered, and he shut them up."

Lana sighed again now, while Paul got ready to meet Dean for lunch. Lana reminded him that Barrett LeGrand, the novelist, who she said had "a dick of death," would be reading at Michigan in a month. Dean called LeGrand's work Faulkner-by-numbers (a little miscegenation, some old folks yapping about the past, tormented souls and sentences), but Lana adored LeGrand's work, had all his novels on her office desk. It was quite a desk, too: more loaded than all the others the teaching assistants used, the broad top a blur of Xeroxed articles, crushed index cards, coffee grounds, clippings, memos, pink or green tissues, open books, combs, pen tops, moist towelettes.

Lana said very little about LeGrand in the department, merely smiling whenever his name came up, as if lost in unspeakable gorgeous memories *they* could never share. The rumor was that she had been the cause of LeGrand's first divorce when he was a guest lecturer at Brown.

The February snow came before LeGrand did, waves of it like shock troops, brutal, deadly, crazed. They all bore it as usual, trying to find some humor in their discomfort. But Lana whined and complained about the traffic, the slush, the roads, the wind, as if no one else were battered or harassed.

One blazing white afternoon, a few days before the reading, Lana, resplendent in red and black down to her rings, slapped a book down on her raving desk.

"Claudio is such a schmuck!"

Paul didn't turn from his desk. He had seen Claudio all around campus, and still could not even look at him or smile—let alone chat!—without feeling nervous, even guilty.

"He thinks he's such a hotshot critic, well, *I* gave him the ideas for half of his articles, the phony, and in bed, too. He's like a spy! The only big thing about him is his prick, and *that* won't last forever. I'd love to see him try to raise the dead at sixty!"

Paul flushed, remembering the last time he'd seen Claudio's dark fat cock, and Lana plucked her coat from the rack and left the office.

That was the first time she had mentioned Claudio to him in any way; he wondered if she was mocking him.

LeGrand gave a pleasant reading; his round sarcastic voice made the opening of a novel-in-progress sound far less baroque than it would probably seem on paper. But Paul couldn't follow what LeGrand read, because LeGrand was so much more magnetic than his dust-jacket photographs hinted: dark-eyed, elegant, a slim Dana Andrews. Paul kept hoping LeGrand would move away from the lectern so he could see if he was really as hung as Lana had said. Dean watched Paul watch LeGrand, and Dean patted his knee. "Down, boy."

The garishly lit lecture room in their department building held over two hundred people, but no one seemed as happy as Lana, arrayed in black suede boots, thickly woven black sweater dress and shawl, and purple earrings, lipstick, eye shadow, and nail polish.

"She looks like a bruise," Dean whispered.

After the rich applause, LeGrand was surrounded by professors and students waving books at him to be signed, chatting, laughing, fawning. Lana hung at the edge of the crowd, poised, radiant, as if she and LeGrand were Maria and Tony in *West Side Story* and the crowd would freeze as soon as their eyes met.

Paul headed for the nearest john. While he was combing his hair, LeGrand came in and Claudio followed. In the wide mirror, Paul watched Claudio take the adjoining urinal and eye LeGrand while standing well back, exposed, getting hard. LeGrand was watching Claudio—and Paul. He caught LeGrand's hot inquisitive glance back at him in the mirror. He was too embarrassed and surprised to leave. While LeGrand and Claudio were washing their hands, the novelist nodded to Paul, and then he simply steered Claudio out, an arm around his shoulder.

In the hallway, Paul almost bumped into them talking to the chairman, who glared at Paul as if wondering just who the hell he was.

With an arm around Claudio, LeGrand was saying, "This *charmin'* young man has read *all* of mah books and has some *very* astute insights I'd like to hear him *dilate* on, so I hope you won't *mind* if he drives me to your lovely *home* tonight?"

When Paul found Dean, Dean said Lana was furious; she'd told everyone she and LeGrand were going out after the reading, before the party, that he couldn't wait to see her again, had sent her flowers!

"Is it true?" He recounted what he'd seen in the bathroom.

"They're incredible," Dean said, "Claudio and Lana. He's doing this to make her crazy, or just to show he can."

At the party, Paul watched LeGrand locked in conversation with Claudio and a succession of professors, while Lana pretended that she wasn't staring at them, glittering, drinking, laughing like a figure in an opera throwing herself into life to hide some deep abiding sorrow.

At one point, eyes heavy with drink and expectation, Lana said to Paul, "I'm meeting him at his hotel later."

Looking for a bathroom a bit later, Paul met LeGrand weaving in a darkened little hall. LeGrand pushed up against him, grabbed a hand, and brought it to his bulging flannel crotch.

"Jesus," Paul breathed.

"Now *you're* the one I really want." LeGrand smirked. "Such a sweetie." And he pushed Paul down the hallway into the bathroom, closing the door and leaning back against it. LeGrand said, "I just did you quite a favor, son. I told your chairman you had the makings of a critic of professional stature. Sounds nice, don't it? He thinks you are a jewel in the rough, thanks to me. You're *mine* now," LeGrand said, unzipping his pants, and Paul knew LeGrand wasn't drunk, and he wasn't charming.

"*Get* on it," LeGrand said, holding out his swelling cock with two hands, pulling back the foreskin as slowly and reverently as if it were some sacred glowing object in an ancient religious rite.

"No." Paul felt himself turning red, but he knew he had to be as calm as possible. He said it again, more softly, "No."

And he was surprised when LeGrand moved away from the door, cock drooping, face suddenly closed, exhausted. Paul slipped past him out of the bathroom, hoping no one would see him.

He grabbed Dean as soon as he found him and said, "Let's go." When Dean asked what was wrong, Paul just said, "I gotta get out of here. I'll tell you later."

Back at the dorm, Paul just sat on his bed, unable to say anything, let alone get undressed.

Dean didn't fuss, didn't sulk, just waited.

Finally, Paul told Dean what had happened in the bathroom, feeling that he had seen something as ugly and clear as a horrible deformity flashing out from a black and white photograph. "So Claudio went after LeGrand because he wanted to piss Lana off, besides just being Claudio. And LeGrand probably figured it out and wanted to mess them both up by getting it on with me? It's like a soap opera, it's sick."

Dean nodded. "Some people live their whole lives like that."

"Not me!"

Dean grinned and pulled off his shirt. "Not you." And the clean, simple lines of his body were as beautiful to Paul then as a well-farmed landscape seen from a plane: rich and regular, ordered, promising.

"My mother would like you," Paul said.

Dean sat on his lap, began to stroke his face. "Why not? I'm a pretty likable guy."

Inheritance

I was lucky when my mother died. I was alone, in another state, and I didn't know that my mother had left me "the German money." That money—reparations from the West German government—and her years in concentration camps had never been something to talk about. For a while in high school, Simon, the youngest, read everything he could find about the camps, and in the bedroom we shared, books stamped with swastikas, barbed wire, blood-red titles, and broken Stars of David leered at me, brutal, deranged. I avoided the subject, which was easy, because Simon's silence was heavier than usual. But Dina, the middle one, exploded: "Don't read that stuff . . . it's over! It's crazy!"

Simon said he had to.

I don't know what my brother learned and I never asked Dina if he talked about it. The darkness of my mother's past was too frightening for me. I do know that my father resented Mom's savings account and she never spent a deutsche mark of it—even after he died and things were very tight.

I was alone, camping in a state park, on the Lake Michigan shore just south of Charlevoix when her car skidded and hit a punishing light pole on the FDR Drive in New York. It was early June, early in the season, and my beach site was cold, especially at night. For two weeks, I sent no postcards, made no calls from the phone near the ranger's cabin, hardly even talked to the cashiers when I drove to the huge mall market ten minutes away—a glare of food, appliances, drugs, and sale clothing—to stock up on steak meat, thick soups, and bread. The drive north, on 27, up to the hills and farms and then west to the lake had stripped from me people, time, words. I read very little, never listened to the radio I had almost forgotten to bring. Mostly I just walked the shore, satisfied, quiet. Despite its size, Lake Michigan is finished, bounded: you can comprehend it in your mind as well as on a map. Even though I'm from New York, the Atlantic has always seemed more like an idea of water, a theory or example.

If I'd stayed home an extra day, I would have gotten Simon's call and flown to New York. And because Dina was off in Maine, angry at her current boyfriend (I picture her glaring at gulls at the end of some dock), Simon had to handle everything. He functions so well in emergencies he hasn't created, I think, but afterward grinds himself down with self-hatred and criticism, a slave to what he *should* have done. Looking at his slim frame and youthful face, you'd never guess he harbored such savagery and loathing inside. All the disasters that had soiled his life seemed a fulfillment of some kind—as if he were working out an idea of himself so awful it could only be expressed in divorce, debt, failure, contempt.

So I was camping while Simon did everything (we had no close relatives alive) and Dina sulked in retreat from yet another man who couldn't give her what she hoped for. Our sister had made a confused career of rage—trailing broken windows, torn clothes, lipstick scrawls on bathroom mirrors from man to man, or so she said. They generally forgave her, or at least tried, because she was more confused than vicious. And because she was, as Mom always said, a knockout: curly reddish blond hair, green eyes, slim theatrical body and voice, a presence more than a woman. Dina had tried acting in college, but the lights, sets, costumes, and makeup had diminished her somehow, forced her into unaccustomed calculation. Dina's the beautiful one, Simon is kind, and I'm the brain. At least that's what our parents thought, which tells you a lot about all of us, doesn't it?

When I left Charlevoix and returned to Detroit and found Simon's telegrams and letter, I felt protected by the silence I'd brought with me from the lake, from my walks down the beach, the clear nights gaping at the Milky Way and a wilderness of stars, afternoons dozing in my tent, two weeks of peace. I read about her death, read Simon's requests for support and advice, read about the funeral and Dina's hysterics when she found out. I felt a tranquillity as deep as the grief I would have expected to feel.

I wasn't frightened. That was probably the difference two weeks at the lake had made for me. I did not feel, as Simon might, thrust into a grim adulthood, abandoned; or like Dina, deprived of a reality that had shaped her revolt. If anything, I was calm, relieved. I felt ready, and preparing to fly to New York to be with my brother and sister, I kept thinking how lucky I was that the worst was over.

I was wrong, of course—but then there's always a story if you think you can see around corners.

"Cremation makes more sense," Dina said when we came back to Simon's from the grass and stone death park in New Jersey. The flowered grave site next to Dad's had made me dizzy, and silenced us all on the ride back to Forest Hills. Dina was the first to speak, as usual.

"But she was against that," Simon objected, looking lost on his florid gold couch. I had not seen his new apartment before. It was strange, surprisingly vulgar, glittering with fake crystal, slashed with red and gold: the bad taste of someone who had known poverty, I thought, and found relief in the textures and colors of a child's fantasy castle. The thick drapes were swagged and festooned. Sitting there drinking coffee from a china cup smeared with shepherdesses, I saw Simon as incomprehensible.

"And the car burned," he went on. Dina frowned. I wondered what it had been like, if my mother had suffered, or died instantly, as we'd been told. But these questions didn't open me up—they were dry and theoretical. I couldn't connect them with the ugly new grave, with our strange isolation in Simon's living room. We hung there like the tassels at his windows: separate, senseless, linked only by events.

"It's sick," Dina charged, unable to sit. She stalked the room, angry, unseeing, her black dress beautifully wrinkled. Even her unpolished nails and pulled-at hair were attractive, demonstrative: she had the look of grief, the confused interruptions. I thought she wanted to cry, and I wanted to hold her, but we weren't like that. Dina stalked into the bedroom to lie down.

Simon started lunch and I thought of next year when I would

light the *Yortseit* candle to commemorate Mom's death. It didn't seem like enough, but then we weren't really Jewish. Dad had been a socialist, American-born son of radicals from Lithuania, and Mom's war years had made her just as resolutely areligious. As a family, we had contributed to charities, bought Israeli bonds, but the holidays had been ignored or hardly observed.

We all three had flirted with "being Jewish." In high school, Dina was involved in collecting for so many charities that we called her Saint Dina; Simon read his books; I studied Yiddish authors in translation for a year or so, contemplating doing Jewish studies somewhere—but none of it lasted. Our parents didn't seem to care; Dad, an accountant, just wanted to support us.

I don't know what Mom wanted.

Simon's lunch was delicious: cream of broccoli soup, Spanish omelettes, apple pie. Dina liked eating Simon's cooking and they hugged before sitting at the dinette table. I resented their closeness in a flash of remembered annoyance. I used to come home and find them talking and laughing in Dina's room, finishing each other's sentences, happy as lovers. When they'd invited me to sit down and enjoy an album, I felt patronized, excluded, more like a little brother than the eldest.

"So eat," Simon urged, trying to be funny.

We ate in silence.

"I cried for days," Dina broke out. "But it didn't change anything. I didn't feel better, just tired."

Simon nodded.

I said I hadn't felt anything much.

"Figures," Dina snapped, spearing some egg with her fork.

"What's *that* mean?"

She flushed. "You're so goddamned mature."

"You're upset," Simon murmured, clearing his place.

I went for a walk. Forest Hills is pleasant, with street after street of redbrick buildings of all sizes, everywhere scraps of lawn, bushes, well-pruned trees—all of it so careful, clean, well tended that Queens Boulevard's eight lanes slash through like a gross and dangerous joke.

Sitting on a bench in a tiny concrete triangle studded with trees, I took the sun with ranks of old and elderly Jews. My mother would never have this, I thought, as a Q60 bus with great staring

windows heaved past. And I felt hot with shame, exposed. I had
been so happy, at peace in Charlevoix as the metal fist of that car
crushed her life. My absence seemed disgraceful to me, and without
remedy, a fact too black and treacherous to be forgotten, or forgiven.
If they knew, I thought, almost afraid to look at the men and women
around me. I hadn't been home in two years and my mother was
dead. The noise, the heat, the scrape of shopping-cart wheels, the
tangle of Yiddish, Russian, heavy English, the sense of "The Bull-
var" (as Mom had pronounced it) as an endless scar, unyielding,
even the pretty clouds hemmed me in. New York made no sense
to me now that I'd been living in Michigan for five years. I could
no longer experience the excitement, the power I was supposed to
feel and enjoy in this city; I knew only the noise, the oppression,
the stifling weight of it all.

We'd grown up in Inwood at the tip of Manhattan in a German-
Jewish neighborhood shadowed by Inwood Hill Park, where you
could still find Indian arrowheads and where we loved peeling layers
off pieces of mica schist. It had been clean and quiet and close
enough by train to where things really happened: Downtown. But
even before Inwood decayed as the city around it seemed to smear
itself with filth, before New York had begun to seem impossible
and crazy, I had been ready to leave, ready for a new home.

Forest Hills was very clean, and walking back to Simon's along
the pavement that seemed to conjure against the city's dirt, I saw
that the three of us were no different than the children we had
been. I remembered Dina shouting and stomping little feet, Simon
offering one of his toys, infant appeaser, and me unable to do
anything but leave. Dina's anger was like the shrill of birds in a pet
store—pure noise, hard to find meaningful. In the small cheaply
paneled elevator, it was obvious to me that I'd never much liked
Dina and I didn't know Simon well enough to be sure.

Upstairs, Simon apologized.

"What for?"

"Dina. She's upset." Simon watched me unpack. I grinned at
that tactful word, wondering how I was supposed to talk to him;
Dina was usually our go-between.

When I sat on the couch, Simon asked if he could say something. I shrugged and he joined me, dark eyes bruised, confiding.
Simon had been through so many fires: drugs, drifting, car acci-

dents, divorce. He scared me. There was something almost historical about failure so sustained.

"John? Are you scared?"

I nodded.

"I can't sleep. Driving the cab makes me crazy. Dina can't help."

"She needs too much attention."

"We all do. 'Attention, attention must be paid.' Remember?"

Years ago, he and I had seen a revival of *Death of a Salesman* and gotten drunk afterward talking about Dad. Simon told me how Dad always made him feel he wasn't good enough, which was funny because I thought Dad let him off the hook too easily. That night, in the bedroom we shared, Simon had crept from his bed to hold me. All night, he hugged me fiercely in his sleep, like he did when we were little boys, muttering once, "Don't let them get me." In the morning, he looked ashamed of himself and wouldn't talk to me.

"I'm so tired," he said now, leaning on my shoulder and then putting his head back in my lap. When he was asleep, I stroked his hair, wishing I could cry for the father we had lost and maybe never had.

Later, we sent out for pizza. Dina called an old college friend and invited herself over for dinner.

That night, with Simon asleep on the couch, Dina still out, and me in a sleeping bag on the sculptured gold carpeting, I woke recalling Charlevoix. One bland sunset, I had walked along the cold water's edge, sliding, stumbling over a wealth of pebbles, the collar of my Wayne State University windbreaker snapping at my neck and chin. I sat for an hour on a thick shelf of slate that broke in steps into the lake. When I finally rose to go back to my tent for a shot of Chivas, I saw something bulky and strange caught in the rocks off to my right. A bloated dead collie, slick-furred, had somehow washed up there. I couldn't see its face and felt as much sadness as disgust. That evening, I made a boisterous fire that ripped apart the darkness of my beach site, trying to protect myself from the vision of that dog. I grilled a steak, as if that could arrange the facts for me, impart some meaning—but there was none. The heavy morning rain swept the collie back into the lake and the rocks it had been caught in were obscured by the tide.

I hadn't expected that dog to follow me to New York. I slipped off to the kitchen in my shorts to have some juice. As I opened the fridge, Dina let herself in.

"You're up. Want some coffee?" She smiled at my near-nudity.

I went to grab my robe.

Dina fumbled with the kettle, almost dropped the Nescafé jar. But there was no chance of waking Simon, who slept through anything. We sat at the butcher-block table and Dina looked tired, pulled down at the eyes, mouth, shoulders.

"I'm worried about Simon," she said at last, eyes unfocused.

We talked a bit about his bad luck with school, with women, and with life. He had never been happy, I concluded.

"So who is?"

I shrugged.

"You're cute. For a librarian." Dina reached for the kettle, poured hot water into her cup, groped for the spoon at its side. Her slightly acid sweat was mixed with the sharp perfume of alcohol and the aroma of coffee crystals.

"I don't want to go to the lawyer tomorrow," she began. "I don't want to see the apartment."

"Then don't."

"You're so comforting."

I couldn't help her; she couldn't ask for help. We had always been a family that talked a great deal but hardly listened, hardly broke through one another's words. We spoke to fill the silences, I think.

"You know, John, you can't help being cold. I don't blame you for it."

And then Dina, lovely drunken tired Dina, threw up on her hands.

"I didn't like him," Dina said in the car as we drove from Midtown, from the lawyer's office. "I never liked him."

"You never met him," I had to point out.

"Mom didn't like him," she countered.

"Dad did."

Simon just drove.

Mom hadn't liked the lawyer; that was true. The explosions over the German money had frightened us all. Dina and I had agreed the idea was repulsive, Simon was silent, Dad was furious, and Mom quivered like a tuning fork. But she did it, went through all the legal work, the medical examinations, going to the German Embassy or Consulate, I can't remember which—did it all and never spent a penny of it. I was proud of her for that, though I never said anything.

"It's a lot of money," Dina pointed out. "For us."

It was all more than we could have expected or guessed.

We drove up to Inwood different, changed by the will, the finality of paperwork. Dina and Simon were to split the savings and insurance and the contents of the apartment. Mom had left me the German money and I didn't understand. Was it a test? Was I supposed to do something with it?

"Watch out!" Dina yelled as Simon almost went through a red light behind a police car. Off behind us, brakes cursed.

Mom and I had never been even casually fond of one another. She had treated me like a poor relation she'd taken in out of pity. She was polite but fundamentally uninterested. Why leave me the money?

I didn't want to go back to Inwood; remembering the castlelike P.S. 98, the Fanny Farmer candy store on Broadway, the steep hill of our street, Park Terrace West, filled me with a sick sense of unreality. It was hard to believe this particular past. I think we all felt that and it began to make us silly. Dina started imitating a third-grade teacher we'd all had, Mrs. Zir (called BraZir), sticking out her breasts and talking fruity counter-Brooklynese—the desperate accent of people unable to escape. Simon giggled, and in the back-seat, I sang snatches of a dirty song we'd been spanked for singing at home. We chatted about what store had been where, driving up north on Broadway, north of Dyckman Street, the traditional border of Inwood, but it was halfhearted. Inwood was seedy and forgotten-looking, a place with no real purpose or identity for us.

When we finally pulled up in front of the huge mock-towered apartment building with its view of the Hudson and the Cloisters in Fort Tryon Park to the south, talk ceased. Simon had keys and he led us into the dark neglect-scarred lobby echoing past pretensions with its coffered ceiling crusted over by thick gold paint. On the seventh floor, there was an ugly silence, as if we were trespassing.

Dina grabbed my hand, then dropped it. The mud-colored

hallway, made uglier by cracked and inefficient light fixtures, was no place for warmth. Simon led us in and the scent of Mom's perfume, Chanel No. 5, assaulted me. Simon and Dina breathed in deeply, too, but said nothing as we lingered by the door.

Dina took off down the dim hall to the bathroom; Simon sat at the foyer desk, where the phone perched atop dusty address books.

The foyer was depressing: bare unpolished parquet, pale yellow-gray walls, small dented brass chandelier that looked like a carriage lamp and was over fifty years old.

I entered our old dining room, the heart of our apartment, which was always brightly lit and overfurnished, full of food and guests.

Our parents had loved company. They were constantly on the phone, clouding the air with plans, arrangements for shopping, lunch, dinner here, a party there, cards Saturday, the park Sunday, drives, walks, little visits. Their hospitality had seemed rich and European to me. Friends could stay for hours, taking coffee "with something" and tea and snacks and eventually a meal to fuel the incessant conversation.

We hadn't liked their friends; most were European Jews with embarrassing accents and prying eyes.

"It's like they can tell my weight to the *ounce*," Dina had complained. Dina was beautiful, which was appropriate for a girl, and so they evidently respected her, or at least her potential for marriage. And I was intelligent, though they thought I spent a little too much time with books.

George, a custom-tailor friend of my Dad's, well-off, always glowing with his own success, constantly asked me about my graduate work, with the smarminess of someone asking a little child, "Are you a boy or a girl?"

Dina did malicious imitations of them all in her room. They were loud, crude, we thought, too satisfied with themselves, with being alive. I think we really resented how Mom brightened with them—especially after Dad's death—how she smiled, told stories of being a girl, mentioned relatives, holidays, vacations on a farm, the Jewish section of her city, with an edge to her voice that showed me all that was real for her, everything before the War.

Simon puzzled our parents' friends, was too interesting. They avoided staring at him so obviously it must have hurt, tried to act

as if they weren't fascinated by his dark, troubled life. "So young,"
I imagined them thinking. "So young and already no good."

We never said it, but the real problem was that my parents'
friends were too Jewish and we were snobs—Dina and I, that is.
We were afraid of them.

Not Simon, though. He couldn't be drawn into mockery or
disdain. His silence shielded him from all of us, made him a mystery, unreachable.

Simon was Mom's favorite in a strange way; she looked at him
the way you'd look at a cripple, masking her pity. And Dina was
closer simply for being a daughter. So why had Mom left me the
German money?

I sat at the dusty table. I don't think Mom ever knew exactly
how to feel about me. She had two miscarriages before me and
maybe when I was born she found herself not as grateful to have a
child as she should have been, or wanted to be. If Simon had felt
not good enough for Dad, that's how I felt about Mom. Maybe I
had sensed very early that none of us were quite real to her, that
she couldn't bring herself to care about us, because she had lost
everything: home, country, people, family. Thirty-six of her closest
relatives had died in camps: her parents, grandparents, sisters, cousins, uncles, aunts. She had no pictures of them, no evidence of
her past, so who could blame her for holding on to it in the only
way she knew?

Dina joined me, eyes red. "I'm okay."

"Anyone hungry?" Simon asked from the large dim kitchen.
It was dusty and full of food, even though some things in the
refrigerator had spoiled. We ate scrambled eggs and stale toast,
waiting for the coffee to brew. Simon talked about the funeral some,
about the people who had offered to help him, help us, how he
hardly heard any of it. I couldn't feel him in his words. Dina changed
the subject.

"John, are you dating anyone?" She sounded like Mom, whose
curiosity had always been mechanical; answers in general had
seemed to interest her, but specific ones hadn't appeared to mean
very much. "No? How come?"

"Too busy."

Dina sneered, as she did at anyone who struggled with shyness,
and chewed her toast with a superior tilt of her head.

"Coffee's ready," Simon noted, clattering cups.

"I've never been *that* busy," Dina said.

"Maybe you should try it."

"Coffee," Simon insisted.

The room I'd shared with Simon was large, painted sky blue, with big windows facing south. The beds, bureau, desk, and bookcases were all the same blond wood and seemed welcoming, almost tender. The books were our oldest, *Robin Hood*, Dumas, Jules Verne, Sherlock Holmes, Oz books, Lewis Carroll, in shiny scratched bindings. The closet was jammed with old shirts, worn chinos, warped and boring records, boxes of school reports and writings from our first year of school. I didn't touch anything or attempt to sort; there was no hurry, because we'd decided to keep paying the rent until the end of the lease so we could put off moving things out. Simon stretched on his bed, hands twisting at the chenille coverlet. I knew that direct questions sometimes angered him, but I asked what was up.

"I might move in here."

I sat on my bed. Simon rarely shared his plans with me: I heard about them from Dina.

"Why?"

Simon shook his head.

Dina's small room, all yellows and red, was bright and full of her past: photos, framed certificates, dolls, unhappy clothes, a jumble of shoes, bold posters, and broken pens. She hunted through drawers, pulling out letters and knickknacks with a cry, shaking her head and tossing them back in. Watching her fun, I thought of having to clean up toys when we were kids. I'd be in charge; Dina would not want to stop and Simon would be lost in a private world with some unlikely looking scrap of a toy. Mom, finding us unruly, disorganized, would say, "You're not doing what I asked," in dull accusation. She was a frozen-faced woman, unsmiling, with small eyes, stiff gestures. No clothes could soften her thin and rigid body, or make her seem less severe. Her approval was like something you chase in dreams, something you need and fear.

"God, Mom *hated* this!" Dina laughed, dragging dress after dress from her closet. "And this one!"

I asked her, "What does it feel like?"

"To be back?" She shrugged. "It doesn't. It's not real. I keep thinking I'll hear her in the kitchen or something."

Because the bedrooms were all so close together at our end of the apartment, and the dining room was for guests, they talked in the kitchen at nights, where we could just hear a murmur of voices like the hum of traffic down below on Broadway.

"I used to wish she was dead, when I was little," she said with a smile.

Simon ambled in.

Dina shrugged. "I never thought it would be like this. All this stuff still here."

When we left, Dina brought along an old purse stuffed with things she "might need" before she came back: some scarves, a torn appointment book, loose photographs from college. There was nothing I wanted; I wasn't ready.

Down in the dreary lobby, Dina asked what I'd do with the German money. "It's a lot," she said. She looked grim, like someone planning revenge. "It's a lot of money."

Simon headed back upstairs to water the plants and we waited in the car.

"He might move in," Dina said.

"He told you?"

"I saw it, the way he looked at everything." Dina scowled at a troop of limping dirty pigeons near the car. There was not one that didn't have a battered or deformed leg. I asked why Simon was moving.

"I don't know."

"But it's not safe here, is it?"

Simon returned smiling, as if the moments alone upstairs had pleased him more deeply than we could understand. His smile upset me, but it was only when we drove away that the tightness burst in me and I sobbed.

"Stop the car," Dina ordered. She got into the backseat and held me against her neck as if she'd always been free and giving, and we stayed parked near Broadway while I felt something real at last.

Dina decided the next morning that even though she was going to quit her editing job, she wanted to go back to Boston.

"Do you miss Michel?" Simon asked.

I hadn't met Dina's new boyfriend, who was half Canadian and a graduate student at Harvard.

Simon looked hurt when she said only, "I have to go." Switching her flight was surprisingly easy and Simon drove her to La Guardia as soon as she was packed. She kissed me goodbye as if embarrassed to do it, and I decided to stay at Simon's. I was sure she was running from the threat of closeness between us, the possibility of change.

Opening a can of soup for lunch, I imagined them at the airport, fond, affectionate, holding hands. Dina's boyfriends had never liked Simon, never liked her long phone calls to him, the devotion that could send her through the epic blizzard of '78 from Boston to New York simply because he'd called that weekend saying he needed her. Dina didn't love him, it was adoration so deep I wondered if she really saw him, could separate the man from what she felt about him. She was his steady partisan, his cheerleader; nothing he did had ever seemed to shock or displease her. She was always quoting that French saying at me: To know all is to forgive all.

I couldn't feel that about Simon. I knew too much and his disasters unnerved me. I couldn't feel comfortable with his college drug dealing, his bad trips, his hippie slut girlfriends, his poor grades, his car wrecks, his brief marriage to a girl he didn't know and apparently didn't like, all the irregularities that left him untouched somehow, as if his life were a Renaissance fresco with him innocent, saintlike at the center, plagued by writhing demons. Was there something cruel in an innocence that survived so much chaos?

Mom had been afraid of him, I think, as if he was a vicious reminder of the madness in her world. "*Shaydim*," I heard her whisper more that once: Yiddish for malicious spirits. I'd woken once near dawn, years ago, to take a leak and heard something strange when I opened the bedroom door, a shushing down the hallway. I edged out and peered down it in the darkness, trying to see and hear better. It came from the foyer. I began to make out a figure seated at the foyer desk—Mom. Gradually, I saw that she was alone, talking to herself, whispering in the dark in Yiddish. "*Shaydim*" was one of the words she said. I couldn't make out the rest; I was too scared to call to her or move. The whispering stopped;

I moved back into my room and heard Mom go to bed. I don't know if she noticed me. I don't know why she sat there. *Shaydim.*

I decided to stay with Simon a little longer and he didn't seem to mind. He was always exhausted after a day's driving and went right to bed after dinner, leaving me alone with the strange garish apartment that seemed like a disguise whose purpose I couldn't guess. I did very little to take advantage of New York even though Simon kept making suggestions about museums, shows. I didn't want to go out; the city seemed unbearable to me, much dirtier and more crowded than I remembered. Maybe it had been exciting for me once, but I didn't need that anymore. The fabled cultural richness of New York can be crippling, a source of resentment, like a nightmarish list that would grow longer and more demanding no matter what you crossed off it.

I saw lots of movies, ran at night on a track at a nearby junior high, tried to write letters, and tried to plow through *War and Peace*, as if to drown in all the characters and events. There was no one in the city worth getting in touch with; I wasn't like Dina, who still talked to friends from third grade, kept track of moves, babies, promotions. I had almost always let connections fade by themselves.

"Are you ever glad they're both dead, now?" Simon asked one night in front of the TV.

"How?"

"Just glad. It doesn't hurt so much."

"What doesn't?"

"Hating them."

When the phone rang, it was Dina. She and Simon talked for half an hour before I got on. I didn't say anything sharp because I knew she was better at it.

"How's Simon?" was her first question.

"Alive."

"Mom used to say that to her friends, remember, when they asked how she was?" Dina repeated Mom's answer in Yiddish: "*Ich lebt.*"

I said nothing, feeling a little dizzy, and the line hissed.

"When I got back"—Dina hurried—"Michel was so sweet. He made this fabulous dinner. You won't believe it. There was—"

"I believe it. How're you two doing?"

"*Sensas!*" she said in the French slang Michel was teaching her: sensational.

Michel spent half his time with soccer and half kicking around ideas, Dina had said. He scored poorly either way but made up for it "personally." I assumed that meant in bed.

The rest of the conversation was just as superficial; we could have been distant relatives making a yearly holiday call.

Death had not brought us closer.

I didn't sleep well that night, even though the grotesque couch was soft, enfolding, a perfect retreat. Simon's question had disturbed me. I didn't think I hated my parents. But then my grades were always high; I had never caused trouble or talked back, never really wanted to. I'd learned to tie my shoes very early they said; I was a good boy. And if I had ended up as only a research librarian (Mom wanted me to be a Professor), it could have been worse.

Perhaps what really woke me, though, was the cigarette smoke. I pulled on shorts and followed its bite to the dark, silent bedroom.

"I smoke when I can't sleep," came Simon's invitation. I moved to his bed and sat near him. He was nude under the covers; he had a slim body, lightly molded by exercise, was probably handsome, I thought, unless it was just that the darkness was kinder to him.

I took a cigarette, though I hardly smoke. The ashtray was enormous, green alabaster.

"Janet gave me that."

Simon never mentioned his ex-wife. They'd met in Tucson at the university when he was twenty-three and finishing college for the third time.

"Sometimes I miss her. She made me laugh. No one else did. But that wasn't enough." He sounded stronger, as if my silence, the night freed him. "I needed more with a woman than that. Remember *Women in Love*? 'Star equilibrium.' "

"Is that possible?" I'd never managed it.

Simon smiled. "You're the smart one."

We talked about Dina then, wondering if Michel would make her less angry at life.

"What's going to happen to us?" Simon asked, the way you'd ask if a train was late.

I thought of Charlevoix.

Simon put out his cigarette, shifted Janet's ashtray to the floor. "John? Stay till I fall asleep?"

I took his hand and he smiled, closing those strange troubled eyes. I loved him, I thought, my gentle soft brother, betrayed by his own complexities. He withdrew into a safer world, his body twitching, then shifting into sleep, possessed by darkness now and ease.

My boss urged me to take a month's leave, so I decided to rent a house near Charlevoix. And even though it was late into the season, I found one, because for once I didn't have to worry about money. It was red-stained oak, high above the beach, swathed in pines, set far back from the narrow trailing road, and from about every room I could see the lake. Like Simon and Dina, I had fled—not to the past, or to a tempestuous affair, but away, as if I were a mystic seeking the pure emptiness of a desert in which to entertain visions. I read, I ran on the beach, I wandered the little house in which wallpaper, curtains, and rugs matched in various shades of gold and green in every room, graceful, perhaps, definitely expensive, but too methodical. I thought of crying in Dina's arms in Simon's car, and I felt humiliated. Like a child who has established an elaborate ritual of getting to bed—sheets so, teddy there, favorite rocks strung along a shelf in secret harmony—to fend off nightmares, I had grabbed on to Charlevoix: the word itself, soft, open, would protect me.

But I was wrong. My third night there I dreamt I was on a winter battlefield at night, barefoot, legs and arms frozen, struggling to dig a trench in icy ground but my shovel only struck sparks. Shaken, I turned on all the lights in the house and made myself coffee, mocha java. While grinding the beans, I slipped back to our kitchen in Inwood, was making coffee there for my mother, thinking with pleasure how the aroma would wake her from her nap, hoping that nothing else would.

For years, unexpectedly, Mom would cry out in her sleep, wordless heavy animal anguish. In the violated darkness of our apartment, we would all wait for more, but of course Dad would wake and hold her and the next day he'd look at us in warning not to mention the nightmare whose terrible shape we never learned.

Sometimes, the terror hit Mom when she was napping, and

one of us had to shake her where she slept in the living room. I had done it once, when I was only ten or so, reading *Bomba the Jungle Boy* in my room when her cry seemed to slap the book from my hand and shove me to my feet. I crept down the hall to find her on her back on the gold-threaded overstuffed red couch. Her face was foreign, squeezed, and she moaned in what sounded like Russian. Beginning to cry, I poked at her leg and she rolled onto her side away from me. I ran to the bathroom to wash and wash my hands, as if they were stained by her fear.

Now, in Charlevoix, I stripped, pulled on running shorts, and flung myself out of the house, stumbling down the dunes, to the vast blue lake, bursting into the water, my feet grabbed by rocks, splashing, desperate. I swam with fury in each stabbing arm until I felt drained.

She was dead. There on my back on the star-silvered beach, eyes closed to block out the incredible bright sky, my mother's death howled inside of me. I had not been close enough to my father to begin missing him until years after his death, but her, oh I had loved and hated her wildly, in the silent extravagance of despair.

As my chest rode waves of pain, I knew she had left me the German money for this. She wanted me to remember. And I had nowhere to hide, not even Charlevoix.

Shouts of Joy

*"Weeping may lodge with us at evening,
but in the morning there are shouts of joy."*

Psalm 30

Afterward, they would agree that Ken saw the woman first as she stepped from somewhere to fill the empty seat at his left in the noisy Hillel dining room that Friday night. She was beautiful and still, a slim redhead with bright bluish-green eyes, twenty-five, perhaps, dressed in rich dark colors—plum, maroon. There was a fine gold pattern in her hair like the gleaming embroidery on a prayer-shawl bag, he later decided.

At the long table, where everyone waited for dinner, loud joking discussions followed the blessing over the wine. The large room's baseboard heating could only tease the Massachusetts November cold but could not displace it. The woman sat, hands in her lap, smiling at the noise, the evening. When Ken told her his name and his major, and asked if she was a graduate student, her "no" made him look at her more closely. She seemed rested and very content, and her heavy cowl-neck sweater, high leather boots, and wool skirt looked a shade fuller and more luxurious than what people in their small college town generally wore.

"I'm Riva," she said. "I'm just here for dinner."

Hal and Amy, sitting directly opposite, introduced themselves.

Riva seemed so kind that Ken had an unexpected, frightening desire to tell her he was gay, which he hadn't told anyone here, had hardly even told himself. It had to be obvious, though. He never dated women and he could not stop looking at men. Everyone at Hillel, the students who lived in the co-op upstairs, those who like him came to all the Friday-night lectures and services, even Rabbi Keller, seemed to make a point of treating him casually. "We don't mind," their silence, their distance seemed to say, "but keep it to yourself." He sometimes felt like a drunken wedding guest at a reception with everyone screening him off by their politeness, muffling the explosion they feared he might make. And he was too uncertain and afraid to search out other gays, though he knew he could go to the Gay Council office at the Union Building, or to Rashid's, the local disco, for Wednesday's Gay Night, or even to the men's room in the basement of the Music Building.

Before, upstairs, at the service welcoming the Sabbath, he'd felt more lonely than usual. He wanted to share the service, to welcome the Sabbath bride not just with friends and acquaintances, but with a *man*—someone like Eric, Hillel's excellent cook. He loved watching Eric. A hotel-management major, Eric was short, tight-knit, with a mane of curly brown hair, and a broad, heart-shaped face, thick short mustache, and startingly blue eyes that gave nothing away. He handled and served food with a formality that was sensuous, almost embarrassing—for Ken, anyway. And his stocky taut body seemed terribly confined by whatever clothes he wore. Tonight he had on a sexy thick deep blue turtleneck, which stretched across his hard and perfect chest.

What would his parents say if they knew that just fifteen minutes after prayer, Ken was sitting there hoping Eric would turn around and show the crack of his tight faded jeans, which were a kind of nudity under the long white chef's apron?

He looked away, to find Riva smiling at him, as if she had seen and understood everything. Eyes soft and sympathetic, she shrugged lightly, as if assuring him the future would be okay.

"Where are you from?" Ken asked as Eric wheeled the soup cart closer to their end of the table.

"The East."

"You must hate it here," Hal said from the opposite side of the table. "There's nothing to do, and it's so goyish." Tall, freckled, glaring, Hal was Ken's least favorite person at Hillel. He was from "Lawn Guyland," from one of the Five Towns, and was constantly complaining about how Amherst was nothing compared to New York—too quiet, too dull, too WASP. He always wore an enormous gold-plated Star of David, like some beacon sending off a distress signal.

"But the trees," Riva said. "The valley. The river. All so beautiful." Ken tried to place her accent—it sure wasn't Boston. She was right about Amherst; even though the UMass campus wasn't very attractive, crossing it, you kept catching rich glimpses of the green and gold Connecticut River Valley between buildings.

Riva handed her bowl to Eric, who raised his eyebrows as if mocking Hal. The table was soon canopied by steam and the savor of lentil soup. "Besides," Riva continued, "where there are Jews is a Jewish place, no?"

Hal sneered and went at his soup.

His girlfriend, Amy, said, "I have friends in Boston."

"Yes." Riva nodded, which seemed strange to Ken, but Amy smiled as if the two women had just exchanged a confidence. Small, dark, shy, Amy had been dating Hal for a month, and next to him, her little light always seemed dimmer, almost extinguished. Ken hated how when he'd seen them walking together, Hal held his hand at the back of Amy's neck, as if steering her, or holding up a dead and plucked chicken.

The huge aluminum salad bowl lurched closer, passed by eager, unsteady hands. Ken could hear Rabbi Keller at the other end of the table discussing Carter's recent triumph at Camp David.

"What do you do?" Amy asked, sipping her wine.

"I'm a violinist—"

"Then you must be with the chamber ensemble at the Arts Center tomorrow night. I *love* the violin."

Hal speared a radish. "Why are you *here*?"

"In a strange place," Riva said, "I wanted to be among Jews Friday night."

It was said with embarrassing simplicity, and Ken felt as if Riva was speaking the truth of his heart, or at least part of it. Amy studied Riva, smiling a bit oddly, and Hal just rolled his eyes. Meanwhile, the twenty others at the table did their imitations, argued politics, panned movies, talked about "Saturday Night Live"—the easiness and warmth that made Ken feel at home. He noticed a few people eyeing Riva.

"*This* nothing little place is what you want?" Hal began complaining about Rabbi Keller, who was new. His Orthodox background, Hal said, ruined their Conservative services. "I mean, if I wanted *Fiddler on the Roof* I'd see the damned movie, all right?"

Ken didn't listen. He *liked* how Rabbi Keller led services with quiet passion and authority. He liked being able to lose himself in the service it had taken him two years to fully understand and love. As the son of Reform Jews, the prayerbook's Hebrew rows had looked like impossible walls to him, unscalable, but now he was inside them and knew so many strange things: that he liked praying, that he believed in God, that he wanted to live a Jewish life, whatever that meant.

"We need more English," Hal was objecting.

"Hebrew's beautiful," Amy pressed.

"You can't read more than a *line!*"

"I'm learning." Flushed, Amy added, "It *sounds* beautiful."

"Why do you come here?" Riva asked Hal sharply, leaning forward. "Why come if you don't like anything?"

Hal just stared.

"*Why?* To feel superior? To laugh at people?"

Hal shook his head as the table quieted down.

"You think you know all about God, don't you? People like you keep God away."

Hal flung the wine in his glass at her, spattering Ken, too. People jumped up, knocking their chairs over. Amy shouted "Stop it!" and in the sudden confusion, with knives and forks paralyzed or dropped and people standing, chattering, confused, asking what had happened, Riva was gone.

Amy stood up. "You are *disgusting*," she said, moving away from Hal.

Someone tapped Ken on the shoulder. It was Eric, handing him a washcloth to wipe his face. Eric said, "Why not help me clean up, later?"

In the kitchen after everyone else had gone home, when the cleaning was almost done, and all the co-op members were out or upstairs, they talked about Hal's mortified apology to Rabbi Keller, the small storm of gossip, with everyone wondering who Riva was, and people giving different descriptions of her voice, her hands, her hair.

"She sure got to Hal, like she knew just what would hit," Eric kept saying. "It's about time."

"I'd like to see her tomorrow, at the recital." Ken closed the dishwasher.

"You won't," Eric said, tying up a garbage bag. "She's not in the poster up in the hallway."

Ken felt relaxed, as if the wine had washed away his shyness, his longing, and he perched on the top of a step stool while Eric fixed them hot chocolate.

Eric handed him a steaming sweet mug.

Ken stirred his hot chocolate. "She didn't say she was *in* it. Maybe she's an understudy or something. No, .:at's dumb. Maybe she was sick when they took the picture. Or we just assumed—"

"—Maybe not."

"What do you know about her?"

Eric dried his hands. "I'm just guessing." The large kitchen, with its banks of cupboards, two massive aluminum-hooded stoves, suddenly seemed private and small.

"What do you know about her?"

"Wait." Eric went out to the hall closet and returned with his backpack. He fished inside for a paperback, searched for a page, and then handed the book over, open. "This is a book my sister sent me last month. I've been thinking about it ever since dinner. Look at the top on the right."

Ken read half-aloud: "Elijah wanders over the face of the earth in many and varied disguises . . . bound by neither time nor space . . . he acts as a celestial messenger. . . . He brings consolation to the afflicted and chides the arrogant and proud."

Ken put the book down. "Oh come *on*," he said. "Passover's *months* away, and Elijah's a *man*."

"So are you," Eric said, moving closer to slip a hand over Ken's where it lay on the book of folktales. Then he grinned.

Ken suddenly felt as if he was soaring up in a World Trade Center elevator, alone, rocketing so fast that nothing would be left behind, not a trace of who he had been. The hard insistent beat of his pulse seemed to rock him back and forth like Orthodox men in prayer. He couldn't speak.

"We're done," Eric said, a little flushed. "We can go back to my apartment."

Eric lived in a large studio a few icy blocks from the Hillel building and close to the tiny downtown, at the top of a house with a view of the Emily Dickinson home, though you couldn't see it from Eric's place. The furniture, drapes, and wallpaper were splashed with a floral print of orange, gold, and green. "My sister's a decorator," Eric explained. "She wanted me to feel warm all winter." Two tall bookcases were stuffed with paperbacks on Jewish history, worship, and thought, Jewish fiction—a small library almost as rich and varied as the one at Hillel.

"Have you *read* all this stuff? Really?" As Ken stood scanning the shelves, afraid to turn around, Eric came up and started massaging his shoulders, slowly, with the easy authority of someone doing Japanese ideograms—it was exciting, tense, involved. Ken leaned back into the warmth, the pressure.

"Don't stop," he said, "or I'll think of some reason to leave."

"No you won't." Eric broke away and opened the couch bed as if he were a pirate revealing his treasure. And then he stripped. Ken had seen men like this at the campus gym, had sat next to them on locker-room benches, but they were always figures, not people, not anyone looking at him with open, inviting eyes. Eric stood like a wrestler, poised, tight, his tautly muscled body hairless, except at the base of his fat jutting cock. He was as beautiful as all those men Ken had gawked at in the weight room, or biking through town, arms and shoulders bulging with force, or jogging across campus with sweatpants drawn tight across their firm asses and calves.

"Why would you want to leave?" Eric smiled. "Society? Your parents? The Torah?"

"All of that, especially the Torah."

Eric sat on the bed, legs wide. "Do you keep kosher? I didn't think so. Then why choose just one restriction to guide your life, to make you feel like dirt?"

"You've had this discussion before."

"So have you. Come here."

"I don't know what to do."

"You'll learn, you'll learn."

Eric slipped Ken out of his clothes so gently, he could have been a nurse. He pushed Ken back on the bed and moved on top of him, massaging him slowly with his whole body, kissing his mouth and eyes, his ears, stroking his hair, his sides, languidly rubbing his heavy penis up and down the length of Ken's, and across until Ken exploded from the pressure, the excitement, and the hungry, commanding look in Eric's eyes.

"You didn't turn off the lights," Ken murmured.

"There's time," Eric said, pushing a pillow under Ken's head and moving up to crouch across his chest, his cock throbbing like a slow metronome.

"I'm real close," Eric said, moving to Ken's mouth. And as Eric pushed Ken's mouth open, Ken felt his lips were as sensitive, as tingling as if he were high. He closed his eyes, licking and sucking with everything in his life somehow concentrated at that one spot. When Eric groaned and clutched the back of Ken's head, Ken didn't pull away, didn't cough or spit—he felt too peaceful and relaxed.

Eric got off and lay beside him, and Ken only knew that they had slept when he woke up near dawn, with Eric down between his legs, tongue tracing the curves of his balls.

Eric looked up, eyebrows twitching like Groucho Marx.

At services that morning, before the Torah was taken from the ark, Ken whispered, "Do you really think Riva was—?"

Eric shrugged. "It's some story, huh?"

And when the Torah was brought around, Ken was struck for the first time by the gold embroidered lions flanking the tablets of the law on the scroll's white velvet sheath. Their glass eyes were so very blue, like Eric's, like Riva's.

Ken reached his prayer book to touch the white velvet, and brought it back to his lips.

"It's a *great* story," Ken said to Eric as the Torah was borne away.

Witness

In 1945, soon after the Soviets liberated his slave-labor camp in Germany, my father disappeared. He and my mother—Polish Jews—had survived everything: it was only freedom that separated them.

"Maya, I turned around," my mother said, always describing the chaos a week after liberation with the same words, "and he was gone."

When I first heard the myth of Orpheus descending to Hades to rescue Eurydice, and losing her when he turned, I pictured the figures not in Greek robes but in those gray, horrible striped camp uniforms; my mother had kept hers, because she wore it the last day she saw him.

No matter what I learned about my father's life in Poland before the war or his sufferings in the ghetto and in camps, he was always someone who had disappeared.

"Gone," my mother would echo, as if the little word would have to explode with its own meaning.

No wonder that when she and I visited our friend Eric for holiday or Friday-night dinners a few blocks down Riverside Drive, mother would sit with her knees and heels together, back straight, gloved hands folded in her lap, her thin face resisting Eric's charm. Going anywhere seemed to remind her of her loss.

Eric would regale us with tales of his piano students and their "impossible" parents. At the table, he chatted about the old days in Vilno when he and my father and mother were students together, days that had no surviving record in photographs. Gradually, Mother would smile and laugh, clapping her hands almost girlishly.

It was only Eric who could work this magic on her; nothing *I* did could soften the woman for whom loss was not a memory but a shadow hanging over everything she did. It was sometimes in her smallest, most casual gesture that I saw this most; closing a cupboard or setting a pan in the drainer, she would suddenly blur for me as a woman, as my mother, and seem a figure burdened by history. I found it hard, then, imagining her at work in the lingerie shop uptown, with its frills, straps, and pastels. Mrs. Reisen, the bouffanted, puffy-cheeked, awkward owner, was also a survivor from Vilno and seemed to find balance in Mother's quiet elegance.

Almost every Sunday, my mother, Eric, and I went to the Metropolitan Museum. Eric and my mother headed decisively up the crowded stairs straight to the exhibit they would investigate and explore for the afternoon, planting themselves in front of canvases or glass cases, reading all labels, staring, staring, as if there were something concrete and measurable to be borne away. The way my mother dressed those days, applying her makeup with the care of a jeweler putting the last touches on a Fabergé egg for the Czar, she could have been readying herself for some hazardous encounter; Eric always wore a dark and somber-looking suit and tie. I never quite had the stamina to besiege and invest any one exhibit, but drifted, unable to be held by a single work of art for long. I loved roaming from hall to hall, consorting with Junos and knights on armored horses, consoles and urns, surrendering to color and form—the lift of a marble chin or the light on a marquetry top jostling for attention in my mind when later we finally headed out and down onto Fifth Avenue. We'd made an agreement that I had to keep checking back to see where they were, and often I'd find them both with their heads high, in challenge almost, defying a canvas, a Greek krater to resist their inspection, in a silent but somehow tense harmony.

"This was beautiful," Eric usually said afterward. "Very instructive."

Mother generally nodded, deferring to his opinions on anything cultural.

More than going to the museum, however, I loved the familiar walk down to the brownstone Eric lived in, climbing the steep, pitted stairs to the fourth floor, listening to Eric play Rachmaninoff and Liszt—big showy pieces like a carnival ride that grabbed and shook and excited you. At the Steinway given him by an American cousin—guilty, perhaps, for having spent the war in utter safety— he was commanding. With his large weathered hands and gray-streaked black hair *en brosse*, Eric looked like one of those musicians you see in movies: fiery, dramatic, obsessed.

He was actually very relaxed, and moved and spoke slowly, as if translating not only his words but himself into English. So his foreignness was ingratiating—not like Mother's, whose voice and manner were often as stiff as her lacquered dark hair. Eric made me think of Maurice Chevalier sometimes—polished and charming.

I made the mistake of telling him that once and he shocked me by saying Chevalier had been a Nazi collaborator. Such land mines were often exploding at my feet: when I bought something (like a change purse) and discovered it was made in West Germany and Mother forced me to return it; when I repeated garbled bits of history I'd picked up in school and was set right like a puppy being smacked with a magazine. Mostly it was my ignorance they criticized, and, through me, the America they both agreed was too optimistic and eager, too *blind*. In high school, I found a Frenchman in a James Baldwin novel saying, "You Americans—you do not know any of the terrible things." That voice, the voice of dark wisdom, was my mother's, was Eric's. That was what united them most deeply, I suspected, and what kept them most apart.

But Mother's knowledge was not just tragic. With her firm decisive walk and the way she never seemed subordinated or nonplussed by her stylish clothes, my mother was a monument to a different vision of being a woman. She was not pretty—her nose was too broad at the tip, her eyes dull—and yet she made herself up and held her head with complete belief in her own attractiveness and chic. It was a conviction and a dignity that I couldn't copy. I felt too dumpy, too bland. I bemoaned the pretty dark eyes that were wasted on me. And it seemed only a fairy tale that someone as prosaic as me had been born in *Paris*, though fitting that we immigrated to America when I was less than a year old. I had given up trying to learn French when my first French teacher said I had absolutely no ear, no grace, no chance: I was a *chameau* (camel, dolt).

"Maya, you don't have to be beautiful," Mother was always saying. "Be careful." But I never had the sense of detail that in her was like a language learned in childhood—the right knotting of a scarf, the balance of jewelry, bag, shoes. "Emphasize your best feature," she advised. But I had grown up in a different country, bombarded by grosser and more exacting standards for women. I couldn't even play the piano very well, though Eric was patient with me.

"You're quite competent," he said.

"You mean dull. I want to do something *well*; I want to be special."

He nodded, and I was relieved that he didn't insist, too kindly, that I *was* special. This delicacy I thought very European.

Watching them at Eric's—his hands flashing at the piano, Mother cool and composed—it was hard to picture them in a war, starved, beaten, betrayed. Yet I could see it looking around Eric's stark white-walled living room, which seemed so much a contradiction of his personal warmth. The bare lines seemed a reminder to himself, a warning not to be too comfortable. With Mother, too, there was a warning—in her posture, her dry kisses.

When I asked them direct questions, Eric spoke about the War in fragments I had to piece together over the years. Mother would barely get started before she would have to go lie down in her darkened bedroom. I tried to imagine myself with them sometimes—a younger sister, perhaps. But it was to understand *them*, not myself. I know many people wonder what it would have been like to go through the War, because those horrible years seem to dwarf any pain or suffering since. The camps were *not* a test, not a trial by ordeal, not a Hollywood movie with the heroine looking beautiful even while she's been heavily made up to look shattered, ill. By twelve, I was already writing in my diary everything Eric told me, as if to make it real.

I never asked Eric about my father or mother, because he was only comfortable talking about himself. Perhaps his own fate was still so incredible to him that he could believe it only through repetition.

Eric's mother had made a brief stir in Vilno as a pianist. But considered brilliant at seventeen, she was less so at twenty, not at all at twenty-five. When the Nazis invaded, Eric's father, a teacher, was rounded up with many other intellectuals and shot. Eric heard after the war that his mother wound up in a Latvian concentration camp, where, when it was learned she was a pianist, her hands were cut off and she died.

After the liberation, Eric was on a train bound for Paris. with other displaced persons. At some small town in Germany, a screaming crowd stopped the train.

"I could not believe my ears," Eric told me. "They lost the war and still they shouted 'Death to the Jews! Death to the Jews!' We men jumped out to beat them. It felt very good, I have to tell you. Just imagine. The war over, and still they were shouting. When they ran and the train moved on, a man in our car started chanting and then we all did: '*Alles geht vorüber, Alles geht vorbei/Deutschland ist verloren, Die Juden sind Frei!*'

"At the next stop we chalked it on the side of the train, and we traveled through Germany like this. There was no more shouting."

"What does it mean?" I asked.

"Oh, it isn't so powerful in English. 'Everything passes, Germany has lost, the Jews are free.' "

Not powerful? I thought. I was fourteen when I first heard that story and felt so moved, I hugged Eric.

He flushed. "What?"

There was too much for me to say.

It was in Paris soon after the Liberation, that Eric discovered my mother, stunned by her failure to find out anything about her husband. Had the Russians repatriated him to Poland by force, as they had other survivors and refugees? Nobody knew. No one ever heard from him again, or even said they'd heard he was alive, somewhere. Many times, when I saw a handsome, pained-looking stranger as old and refined as Eric, on a bus or in a museum, I thought that it could be my father. What if he'd lost his memory and was married to someone else? I spun endless stories in my head on this theme.

Once I asked Eric if he would ever go back to Vilno.

"Never. Europe is dead for me. They bulldozed Jewish cemeteries! My family came to Vilno in the 1600s, and now there is nothing left . . . not even dust!"

Mother nodded at that, adding they had left France because Germany was so close.

She and Eric seemed so much larger than life to me at such moments that I ached with a desire to do something, to say or create something to give their lives the most beautiful expression I could.

When I started seeing more books about the Holocaust being published in the years after the Eichmann trial, I pressed Mother to write her own memoirs. Mother scoffed at my insistence that she owed it to the world to record what had happened to her.

And Eric said, "I give what I have to my students. No more."

How could I argue with either of them? But I was afraid that something much too precious would disappear, just like my father and everyone else sucked into the black hole of wartime death. It wasn't right—silence was not right. I watched the flood of Holocaust books—history, reminiscences, psychological and sociological analyses—watched all the films with a growing fear that my mother and Eric would never be part of this, that their own pasts—and my father's—would be submerged in statistics, in summary sentences.

Then, in 1975, when I was finishing my dissertation in Jewish Studies at Columbia, Eric apparently changed his mind and finally agreed with me. He enrolled in a course at a small Manhattan college—Adult Autobiography, a class that used tapes, photographs, and interviews to help people in their Fifties and Sixties recreate the past. He was one of several camp survivors in the class, and they, too, had kept silent, out of pain, and more recently a desire not to seem as if they were being fashionable, self-important.

"Don't tell your mother," Eric warned me, and I couldn't figure out why. But almost as a bribe, I think, he showed me his first assignment—a piece of "creative writing," flawlessly typed, with no title.

She can try to forget. The crunch of boots outside. Her father being dragged away. Her friends calling from the back of the disappearing train for them to "Run, run!" But they can't. Faces all around, disappearing each day. Her world smaller and smaller and smaller. Try to forget: her mother on one line and she on another and her mother's line disappearing. "Doctor, I have nightmares." "Well it's no wonder, considering that you—" "Doctor, I have nightmares." But worse than the cold sweat that sticks to her all night afterward, worse than all the beatings, is the fear. It comes quickly, while she is doing the dishes or straightening a picture. It holds her, and she stands, paralyzed, hearing the crunch of boots. She cannot turn and she knows it is the end. It leaves her exhausted, knowing that for her there is no end.

"My writing teacher said the piece was too emotional," Eric said, frowning, "and that no one writes about feelings these days in *fiction*—they are passé." He shrugged.

"Did Mom tell you all those things?"

Eric was at the piano leafing through a book of Clementi sonatinas.

He didn't look up.

"You're in love with her, aren't you?" I felt unbelievably stupid not to have seen this before, to have always assumed they were tied only by history, by their youth in Vilno, and by *me*.

At home that night, I knocked on my mother's door after she'd gone to bed. Her light was on. She looked very pale against the dark headboard and bedclothes; a book lay open in her hand. I asked her why she didn't marry Eric.

"We never discuss it."

"Don't you love him?"

"I have no right to be happy."

"Why? Because everyone else is dead? Because of Daddy?"

Eyes down, she said, "Eric is your father."

"What!" I was suddenly like a tiny child lost in a department store that seemed larger than the world itself, too desolate to cry.

"It was wrong, but I was alone. So much death . . ."

I made myself breathe in deeply. "Why didn't you tell me? Why did you wait?"

"I was ashamed," she blurted, clasping her hands.

She looked away as I moved to sit by her. I wanted to shake her as much as hold her. I felt I was my mother's equal for the first time, not in wisdom, suffering, or even courage—but in life. It was *our* life, hers and mine and Eric's. I thought of all the times we three had walked through Riverside Park, hand in hand, me in the middle; of the years of birthdays, Passover seders, New Year's services, trips to the museum, the coffee and cake, the hours of listening to Eric play, the way he stroked my cheek with the back of his hand when he said goodbye.

"You could have had an abor—"

"Never," she said. "Never."

And that made me feel very good. Mother told me her husband was really gone not a week after they were liberated into chaos, but the very day, the very hour. Her pain had always been real, I thought, unable to condemn her for hiding the facts.

When she was asleep, I called Eric to say I was coming over.

"You know," he said at his door, regal in his silk robe. "She told you? You look different."

I nodded. "Mom told me."

We sat on the couch like two strangers waiting for a bus who have exhausted commonplaces but want to keep talking because the night feels lonely through the silence. Eric's hi-fi was playing *Sleeping Beauty* very low, and the plaintive broad sweep of the strings in steady ballet rhythm reminded me of the many evenings at City Center, high up, peering through the opera glasses Eric had given me as a birthday present. Eric and I were usually relaxed there, Mother not at all, sitting with rigid back and fixed stare, so intent on not missing anything, I thought, that I wondered what she *did* see.

"I thought you would discover us sometime, would feel it."

"Why wouldn't she marry you . . . did you ask?"

Eric nodded. "Many times. She said marriage would be pretending we did nothing wrong. Maybe she thinks he is still living somewhere."

I told Eric the fantasy of finding my father in a stranger.

"But why," I asked, "why now? Why are you taking that course?"

He smiled. "We will be old soon, all of us. No one else can tell what happened . . . not you, not anyone. It is mine to do. I am the witness." The unspoken words were: And not *you*.

I felt relieved, suddenly, of my frustrated and helpless sense of mission, which I had never shared with him, but he had obviously understood.

We were very formal that night. Eric dressed to walk me home, and I kissed him good night on the forehead, holding him by the shoulder, as if I was the piano teacher and he was the student who had just made me very proud at a recital.

Mrs. Reisen died that spring, unexpectedly leaving my mother not only the lingerie shop but a surprising amount of money. When I got my Ph.D., and a job at Indiana, Eric and my mother announced they were getting married, as my "graduation present." They moved into a huge and sunny apartment on West End Avenue with a view of the Hudson from half of its rooms.

I wondered why Eric had chosen just that particular time to risk changing all our lives. I never asked, though I kept imagining what might have happened. He must have *seen* something to embark on a course that could have left me hating him and my mother, defiant, hurtling into exile. He could have been on a bus or in a cab and spotted someone in a crowd or crossing a street who he was sure was Mother's husband, even after thirty years. I picture Eric staring, staring at the shocking, familiar face, terrified that he will lose my mother, lose me. Or does he wonder for the first time if my mother's husband had amnesia, or more likely, had *deliberately* disappeared, had fled from my mother at the end of the war because she would always be a witness to everything he had suffered and lost. And Eric, panicky, perhaps, despairing, had decided he had no choice.

I wanted to know what he had seen, but I never would. I was only an American, and did not understand the terrible things.

The Life You Have

It was a mistake at dinner for me to tell Bill that John Gardner had tried for fifteen years before getting his fiction published. He yelled, "John Gardner's *dead!*" and stormed from the kitchen. I had been desperate to say something helpful, because three of his stories had come back that morning with anonymous rejection slips, leaving him stunned.

I heard the closet door and then the front door close.

Bill disappeared down our dark silent road at the very edge of town, past the condominiums stacked like children's blocks, past the horse farm, trudging with angry hands jammed in his coat pockets. I followed for a bit, to apologize, but his small striding figure looked so sad, I trailed back to our Cape Cod to wait.

We were twenty-four when we met, back in Amherst, Massachusetts. Bill was electric, the star in his graduate creative-writing program, winner of two of its prizes, waiting only for his moment. You could see it in the triumphant curl of his thick black hair, the cool confiding smile, the rivetting dark eyes always on a vision of himself as special, called. In the English Ph.D. program, we liked to make fun of the writers and poets doing M.F.A.s, deriding their clothes, their egotism, their romantic chaos, as if they had no claim at all to the peaks of literature we had climbed and planted our little flags on. But even there, Bill was admired, and people went to his readings.

"He's a diamond," an English professor told me once at a department party in an *Architectural Digest* sort of house where the hors d'oeuvres were arranged to look like a Mondrian. "A diamond," he repeated, drunk, confident, as if he were a refugee who had smuggled that gem in his coat lining across an impassable border. I felt momentarily jealous not to have thought of the term myself.

But Bill's gleam of expectation could not withstand the hundreds of rejections, even the kinder "Send us more" or "Try us again" type. It was no longer almost funny, no longer a fantasy of "Won't *they* be sorry they rejected you when—" There wasn't any "when." Each manila envelope, each typed label, each trip to the post office was like the part of a painful, empty-handed ritual. The man I loved was a prisoner of his dreams.

And I was doing well. My parents had warned me not to go to graduate school in English, because there were no jobs, but I couldn't imagine a more satisfying life than teaching. So, here I was, enjoying my classes, with half a dozen scholarly articles published or forthcoming, and a contract to do a bibliography of James Baldwin's writing. My chairman said that tenure was assured.

I felt almost guilty; Bill's failure had become like a curse in a fairy tale, a sentence we had no hope of escaping.

While Bill was out, I put everything away, turned on the dishwasher, and settled into the enormous ball-footed leather armchair he'd gotten me for our fifth anniversary, to read the draft of a colleague's article on Edith Wharton. In an hour, Bill stood opposite me, red-cheeked, solemn, coat still on.

"I hate it when you're sympathetic," he said.

"Should I make fun of you? Be mean?"

Bill peeled away his coat and came to sit on the wide chair arm. "In the movies, you always see the writer typing, crumbling up the paper, agony, pacing, more typing, a sandwich. Part One. Part Two is the *letter*, the phone call, success. We're still stuck in the agony."

His sadness reminded me of a war memorial we'd seen in Canada somewhere last summer, a robed woman, head down, shoulders tragically slumped, battered sword at her feet, loss, terrible loss in every line of her face, her robes.

I suggested Bill go to bed.

"Am I tired?"

While he showered, I thought about his work, which he hardly showed me anymore. When he did, it was impossible for me to read anything of his without feeling for the hours he'd sat hunched over his desk, rocking as if to catch a troubling melody, face dark, fingers touching his shoulders, hair, his throat. The nights he worked hardest, I wandered through the house, restless, straightening pictures, shuffling magazines, or stalking the unplanted evergreen-bordered half-acre behind our house, breathing in the silence and the night, hoping. Hoping he had discovered the words I would someday read in print.

I couldn't *make* it happen. I could fill the house with white lilacs in May for our anniversary, surprise him with newly published novels he'd forgotten he said he wanted to read, hide jokey little cards under his pillow, cook Julia Child dinners and wear my tux, call him from campus or the mall just to say hi, but I couldn't fill the emptiness of all those unpublished years.

Bill was asleep as soon as he got to bed. I put some dishes away, cleaned up in the living room, and then found myself watering plants that weren't dry. I was nervous. I felt drawn to his study, which I never entered when he wasn't home.

I slipped down the hall and into the study, turning on the light after I closed the door. It was a small room, painted a glossy forest green, full of file cabinets and books, but not even the peeling library table revealed anything about him. This room without decoration, pictures, and mementos disturbed me for the first time. What was he shutting out besides distraction?

I settled onto the dull green carpeting and slowly pulled open the nearest file drawer. His stories were filed alphabetically by year, and each folder spilled out rejection slips, sometimes dozens. I read those along with ten or so stories, and it all began to seem anonymous—the stories no different from the Xeroxed rejection slips.

I had never read so much of his work at one time, and I didn't like it. While I may have enjoyed individual lines, or scenes, or even characters, reading so many stories in a row, I was disappointed. His work was clever, I guess, but empty, and I found myself thinking of our favorite movie, *Dark Victory*, of the scene where Bette Davis discovers her medical file in George Brent's office and asks the nurse what the words *prognosis negative* mean. How had I missed this?

I cleaned up, checked the bedroom to see if he was still asleep, and sat at the kitchen table with a shot of Seagram's, like my father did when he got bad news—the one drink saying he needed not to forget but to be strong. I was struck by how bland Bill's people were, and how none were even demonstrably gay. Why? Being gay wasn't the center of our lives, exactly, but we'd never hidden it from our friends, employers, or family. *His* parents had pretty much disowned him when they found out he was gay, and had never expressed an interest in meeting me, but was that enough to wipe it from his stories? And none of his characters were really Jewish, either, which made even less sense: I didn't think we were Jewish enough to feel any kind of conflict between faith and sexuality. Besides, even though Bill didn't get much out of the holidays or attending services, we had been lucky to find a very liberal congregation in town with a woman rabbi and a few gay and lesbian couples. When we did attend or get involved, there was no sense of exclusion or embarrassment.

Bill's mother had been in a concentration camp, and I was most deeply struck by the absence of any reference to the Holocaust in his fiction. We had certainly talked about it. Just that year, we had watched newly discovered British film of the liberation of Bergen-Belsen. In it, British soldiers forced the SS guards to lift and carry corpses, drop, slide, stack them into four or five pits, "as punishment." The film was silent; there was no creak of carts, no engines stirring into life, no shouted commands—just seven days reduced to black and white minutes on film. The civilized-sounding narrator talked of "graves"—which got Bill furious. "They're garbage dumps!" I couldn't believe the SS felt any differently, felt repentant dropping bodies like a gigolo flicking away the useless stump of a cigarette.

"My mother was there," Bill reminded me. "But she won't tell me." And I tried to imagine the dazed and starved survivor wandering somewhere out of camera range.

I woke up late that night, could feel Bill wasn't sleeping.

"They should have thrown the guards in," he said in the dark. "Buried them alive."

"Yes," I said. "I know."

But there was absolutely no trace of Bill's anger or pain in his stories. Why had he cut all that out of his writing?

A motorcycle tore by outside, and I wished then for a galumphing puppy I could scratch and rub and talk to. In all the years Bill had suffered rejection, I had never doubted his work.

"It's late," Bill said at the kitchen door, squinting at my drink. His face was creased and red with sleep, his hair flattened. He rubbed his eyes, pulled his robe together, and came to sit by me. "What's wrong?"

"I was reading. In your study."

I expected him to blast me, but he just nodded, leaning back in the captain's chair.

He said, "It's no good."

We had been at this place before, I dousing the flames of his depression with torrents of praise—reminding him of Amherst, his successful fiction readings, the two prizes there—like a court chamberlain comforting his monarch-in-exile. But tonight I couldn't offer anything; there was only silence timidly filled by the humming fridge and vague grunts from the sink pipes. I felt we had come to the end of something and I was afraid. Our first years fragrant with discovery, the trips to Mexico, Spain, Japan, buying and decorating this house, all of that seemed one-dimensional now, remote.

Bill reached for my glass and the bottle, poured himself a shot and downed it.

"You never wanted to see," he said.

"What?"

"To see my work." He looked down. "You wanted me to be, I don't know, famous, *wonderful*."

"But isn't that what you want?"

"Not now, now I just want to write something honest. Something real." He stroked my hands. "It's not your fault, it's nobody's fault."

I'm not one of those people who's always being confided in, surprised by friends suddenly announcing "There's something you should know," so I wasn't sure what I was supposed to say or do. I pulled open the fridge and found some leftover veal stew and half a cherry pie to heat up. Fussing at the sink and the stove, I was unable to look at him. Bill came up behind me, gave me a lingering, pleading hug, as if we'd just had some kind of fight.

"I don't have the courage to write about anything that hurts —my mom, being gay . . ." he said to my back.

I felt ashamed then of all the times I'd raved about his writing, gone on and on thinking that I was being helpful, when I was just showing I loved him. It was a subtle form of contempt—I had not treated him as an equal, as an adult, but as a glamorous, talented, demanding child.

"I never have," he said, "except once. It was something I wrote about my mom, her past, her secrets, my secrets. She found it . . . well, I left it out where she could. She went nuts. She said I was sick, I was crazy." He held me tighter, still talking to the back of my head.

"What happened to the story?"

"She threw it out." He broke away. "Wait, I want to show you something." He went off to his study and returned with a deeply creased single sheet of pale blue stationery that had been crumpled up and then straightened more than once, I thought.

"She sent this to me at Amherst. Remember that weekend I drove to Boston by myself and you wondered why? It was because of this."

I read the typed, undated note.

When we were married your father said we had to have children because of all the lives lost in the war. I didn't want to have any. Now I know I was right.

"She sent this to you? What did you *say?*"

Bill shrugged.

Feeling suddenly brisk and sensible, I stood up and went to the utility drawer. "Isn't it time for a reply?"

He frowned, not following.

I took the letter and a book of matches to the sink. "Come on."

I held out the matches. Bill hesitated, came over, took one, lit it slowly as I nodded, and set it to the corner of the letter, dropping it into the sink when it started to flame. Little black specks floated up above us as the letter twisted in on itself, crackling, vanishing into black powder and dust.

Bill put his hands down in the sink and rubbed them in the ashes, turned on the tap, washing his hands clean.

"Would it change things?" he finally asked, pale now, drying his hands.

He had the look of a desperate client, hoping the lawyer will say, "Yes, you've got a case."

"If you wrote the truth?"

He nodded.

Little things in the kitchen suddenly seemed very clear to me: the Boston fern hanging over the sink, the brass cabinet knobs, the Sierra Club calendar near the stove. "I don't know."

He smiled. "Well," he said, "it wouldn't mean I got published, but I'd be honest. Isn't that a start?"

I thought then of my favorite lines from James Baldwin's *Another Country*; " 'You've got to be truthful about the life you *have*. Otherwise there's no possibility of achieving the life you *want*.' "

I said that yes, it would be a start.

Abominations

At eight in the morning, it was cool and misty on campus as Brenda headed across the wide concrete bridge to the low and spreading library fronted with broad, shallow beds of scarlet, mauve, and white tulips. This bridge across the tiny Red Cedar River was one of her favorite spots at Michigan State; the aged weeping willows here were so dense and hung so low (like flowering trees after a downpour) that looking off either side of the bridge, you couldn't see any buildings at all. Especially in the morning, you could easily think you were isolated, alone—not surrounded by thousands of students.

Halfway across, she was stopped by white scrawling letters chalked inside jagged circles: KILL ALL FAGS, DEATH TO HOMO QUEERS, STOP FAG DAY, FAGGOTS MUST DIE, GAY? GOT AIDS YET?

She stopped. The crude white letters grew larger, pushing her slowly back against the round steel railing. She could feel herself unable to breathe.

She heard laughter.

Two handsome runners in fraternity T-shirts came loping across the bridge, the incarnation of power and ease. "Awright!" one shouted. "It's about time." The other laughed. "Man, I *hate* fags," he said, and their pounding effort drew them away.

I have to do something, she thought, trying to feel resolute and strong.

But someone had beaten her to it, perhaps. A skinny kid with masses of thick black hair streaked lime green was crouching at the other end of the bridge, taking pictures. He kept saying "Oh wow!" Behind him, a campus police car crept along one of the paths to the bridge, lumbering and out of place.

"Hey," the kid called to her, "I'm with *The State News*. Can I interview you?" His voice was heavy with the nasal twang of western Michigan.

She wanted to run, but he was over in front of her, armed with a pad and a wide-eyed look of attentiveness he might have bought at the campus bookstore along with his journalism course materials.

"My name's Jim. Can I ask you some questions?"

He was already writing in his pad, as if he knew her answers. She wanted to shake up this kid so fashionably dressed in black T-shirt, jeans, and high-tops.

"It's like Selma," she started.

"Wait—" He squinted at her. "*Who?* I don't get it."

"Like Alabama, the bigots. The lynchings. It's *sick*. Whoever did it should be arrested and expelled."

He chuckled as if pleased by her intensity, made notes, and then asked for her name and major. He grinned when she said she was a former graduate student and now a temporary assistant professor in history. People on the way to morning classes were stopping on the bridge, pointing.

Off behind the little reporter, two campus policemen with barely concealed smiles were examining the scrawls.

Brenda rushed over to them. "You have to find these morons." She realized she was being loud—and at MSU, any raised voice except at a sports event, or if you were drunk, was the source of instant contempt, people turning, staring, appalled at your rudeness: where could you be *from*, for God's sake, New *York*?

"They're *dangerous*."

The two handsome policemen, who looked like ex-jocks—thick-necked, wide-shouldered bodies straining at their blue uniforms—nodded, eyeing her a bit suspiciously, as if *she* had done it.

Desperate for some kind of response, she blurted, "My *brother's* gay."

They glanced at each other. "Too bad," one brought out.

*   *   *

Back at her apartment, she was shocked at how nothing around her reflected the uproar she felt—not even the mirror. She just looked tired, flushed.

She found herself remembering how years ago her mother had woken her up at three in the morning to say, "Come kiss Silky goodbye." And she stumbled downstairs after her mother, pulling on a robe, to find their miniature collie lying on his side in the basket near the front door, eyes wide and blank, body slack. The vet had been very negative about Silky's chances of surviving a cancer operation, but the day, oh the day had started out beautifully even though Silky was too old and sick. That morning, looking out the kitchen windows to the backyard, washing her breakfast dishes, Brenda had been unable to turn from the sassafras trees, their large oval leaves blushing like peaches—creamy red and yellow, as if sprayed with fall. So rich, so captivating—surely the whole day would be as soothing.

But her father and Nat were getting dressed upstairs for the ride to the vet clinic, and Brenda and her mother crouched by the basket, weeping, trying to hold Silky; the collie was beyond being comforted or even touched—lost in pain, too stunned by it to even whimper.

That's how *she* felt now. She sat in a stupor for an hour or more, with those vicious slogans from the bridge whirling around as if she were being attacked in *The Birds*.

Finally, though, it was time for her to get back to campus, to teach her afternoon sections of Women in America. And she recalled her mentor at the University of Michigan (where she had done her M.A.) revealing after Brenda graduated that *she* had taught a class the morning her mother died: "I had to. I had to hold myself together. It was like falling from a plane, with no parachute. But I never hit the ground. . . ."

Hurrying on campus, Brenda felt unavoidably pulled from her sense of outrage and disgust, eyes drawn always outward—to trees and shrubs finally blooming after an ugly, dry winter: lush forsythia and lilacs, exquisite hawthorns; to former students she smiled at; to the bicyclists snaking through crowds of students in jeans and Florida suntans.

At her grim department office in one of State's oldest, dirtiest buildings, she heard other faculty members talking about the bridge.

"Well, it's ugly," one said. "But you have to admit that those homosexuals are getting too pushy."

She turned. It was Jack Callahan, the fat, greasy, red-nosed expert in Soviet history who looked like an English Toby mug. His office was near hers and she had once heard him telling someone that he thought *enough* had been written about the Holocaust.

His colleague, Sandra Sparrow, almost as plain as her last name, nodded, adding as if parlaying gossip, "And they want to be able to go to charity dances on campus and *dance* together!"

Brenda snatched up her mail and fled the office.

Five minutes away, in Berkey Hall, she found her class of thirty was embroiled in an argument she could hear in the hallway.

Brenda stopped at the door.

"Those fags make me sick," Lynne was saying. "They are *all over.*"

"How can you say that!" Teresa shot back. Small, squinting, incredibly shy, she produced papers that surprised Brenda and everyone in class with the power of her writing. But in class, she was almost always silent. And people were smiling at this outburst—some nervously, others as if they were thinking, Finally. . . .

"How can you say that? You should drop this class. You think it's cool to complain about men treating you like you have no brain, like you're not even a person because you're so pretty but it's okay for you to dump on gays, right?"

"It's perverted," Lynne dropped, primly.

No one had turned to Brenda, who had quietly joined the circle of chairs; they already were used to her not riding herd on every discussion as they read each other's papers written in response to the assigned readings, in small and large groups.

Teresa went on: "You want everybody to be like *you?*"

Lynne tossed her head, blushing.

Two of the half dozen guys in the class were muttering to each other. One—a Tom Cruise look-alike—had practically cried in Brenda's office last week about how hard it was doing his two-page response to an article on homosexuality, because of how he felt "so close" to his roommate, and he wasn't sure what that meant. But now he was sneering. The other guys looked bored and blank. They had not signed up for this course but had been bumped into it by a computer error, and Brenda felt relieved that they liked the class enough to declare a truce of sorts: they would not hassle her if she didn't force them to talk.

"You wouldn't say that if they'd written stuff about blacks, would you?" Andrena chimed in, pointing a pen at Lynne. "But it's acceptable for you to hate gays, you can say it and not be ashamed. Well, girl, you *should* be ashamed."

"Listen." That was Paul, the psychology major who Brenda suspected was either dyslexic or had learning disabilities. (How had no one noticed?) "Listen. The Bible says—"

Half of the class rolled their eyes, looked away, or started leafing through their essay books, shut off from what Brenda knew they thought would be another tirade like those delivered near the campus bridges in the spring by all sorts of Christians, inveighing against sin and degradation, which they saw everywhere around them. Their ferocity could make you think Michigan State University was a thundering pit of evil, like New York or Los Angeles.

"Enough," she said. "Let's leave the Bible out of this. Let's forget about the damned bridge and get to work."

In the silence, she could hear the humming of the banks of neon lighting.

"Are you okay?" Teresa asked after class, Andrena and a few others lingering by the door, close enough to hear. Brenda had explained her first day how important it was to her to have a feminist classroom, in which she was not the sole authority. "You never pull rank like that. . . ."

Brenda wanted to scream at her, at someone, anyone, but she could only shrug and head for her next class.

It was as awful as last summer, when her brother Nat had been kicked out of the Orthodox congregation here in town because someone had seen him—and his lover, Mark—leaving a gay bar in Lansing. She had felt assaulted then, helpless, exposed. She kept waiting for a phone call from her mother or father in Southfield; surely they would've found out, but Nat insisted they wouldn't.

"No one in the *minyan* will say anything. That's *gossip*."

And she thought of the Hebrew term for gossip—*lashan harah*, evil talk. It was one of the things you confessed during the High

Holy Days, several times, perhaps because it was one of the easiest sins to commit.

"Besides, it would be bad for *them*," Mark pointed out with a cynical smile, "because you're supposed to protect the honor of the community."

Still, though her parents didn't seem to have heard of the incident, and none of her Jewish friends in town brought it up anymore, she did not like the idea of the three of them driving down to Southfield that fall for Kol Nidre services on the eve of Yom Kippur.

As they drove down that Monday morning in September, Nat thrashing around in the front to talk to Mark, who was quieter than usual in the back, she felt party to a lie. Introducing Mark as a friend, or even Nat's friend, when she knew what he really was, made her feel like a child anxiously watching waves lick closer to the sand castle built with hours of fantasy and concentration.

It was sad driving up the curving street to their ranch house —all the crab apple trees in front had lost more than half of their leaves, and fall that day seemed melancholy and not beautiful. Her mother opened the door with such a Loretta Young sweep of her arms, Brenda expected one of those breathtakingly vapid greetings like "I've heard so much about you," but she only said, "I was tired of waiting." And smiled.

"Are we late?" Nat asked while his mother said hello to Mark, who introduced himself.

Her father was showering, and they had coffee and fresh marble cake in the long, gleaming kitchen, Mark sitting so impassively, saying so little even for him, that Brenda felt sure he was willing himself not to seem "obvious" in any way, though she doubted anyone in her family would guess someone so masculine and attractive could be gay. Mark made no request for a tour or even a look at photos, no interest in favorite *tchatchkehs*. He was being very cool.

When Nat led Mark off with their clothing bags to change, Brenda's mother said, "He's so attractive. Where did you meet him? At *services*?" She smiled as if picturing herself victorious on the phone: to meet a Jewish man at services—!

Brenda didn't correct the misapprehension, and they chatted about the job she had gotten right after finishing her Ph.D. at MSU.

Even though it was only temporary, her parents kept telling her that they bragged about their "Professor."

Nat was smiling when he came back in a gray three-piece suit that made him look like an uncertain law student. Mark wore a charcoal gray blazer, black slacks, white shirt, soft-striped tie and seemed almost embarrassed at the silence in the room, which was obvious appraisal on her mother's part, stifled reverence in Nat, and something indefinable on hers. Mark looked more than ever like a tall, bearded Robert De Niro. She wanted to think of him as an intruder, a fraud, a pervert. But there he was, ready to go to services, to be part of their world in a profound, historical way.

Her mother had always set a magnificent table for holiday dinners, with French china and crystal, and silver so heavy that each movement of your hand seemed to mark the importance of the meal. In the gold and white dining room, Nat kept saying how wonderful everything was (Mark's praise was more judicious), but Brenda was lost in imagining the future. Would Mark be having more family dinners with them, coming to shul and bar mitzvahs, or would he be banned from their house, along with Nat? Would their relatives smirk and hold back, or be unpleasantly kind and attentive, as if talking to someone whose cancer left them only months to live?

Her mother told several of her long stories about the children of friends of theirs who were in debt, divorced, having trouble with finding a job. These always sounded like oblique warnings to Brenda.

Her father, red-eyed, crumpled in his blue suit, asked them how the traffic had been, and if Brenda was maintaining the Chevette, a birthday present now three years old. He did not seem to like Mark. It was, Brenda thought on the way to services in the family Delta 88, the average man's suspicion and envy of any man whose excessive good looks invited contemplation for themselves alone. Only women were supposed to be that striking.

There were so many temples in Southfield with Beth in their names (Hebrew for *house*), like Beth Shalom and Beth Israel, that Nat had always called their temple Beth Greenberg, after a girl he'd had a crush on in fourth grade. No one ever laughed at his joke, but Mark did as they pulled into the jammed temple lot, and her father turned around, frowning.

Inside the round, high, gleaming pine sanctuary, she sank into a seat by her mother, Mark at her right, Nat beyond. Leafing through the holiday prayer book, she read notes about the shofar, the ram's horn, "whose purpose it is to rouse the purely Divine in man. . . ." It had to be naturally hollow because attaining God was impossible by artificial means: "no sound which charms the senses, but does not appeal to man's better self, can raise you to God—indeed, you might surrender yourself again to your low, base way of living."

Low, base. The simple words were suddenly more awful to her than the translated doom of Torah: this was a modern voice, and she was condemned along with Nat and Mark.

She felt the peck and jab of glances and unheard remarks from neighbors and old friends, and when the service began, she was unable to respond with anything more than the memory of previous feelings in previous years. Nat kept grinning at her like a jewel thief positive of diamonds and pearls just an evening's work away.

Afterwards, in the showcase-ridden lobby (photos of the congregation's history, a shofar display, gifts), nodding, smiling, clasping hands and kissing friendly cheeks, she wished the admiring glances were *honestly* hers, that she were dating Mark and could truly hug the woman who took her aside for a kiss and "Such pleasure to see a beautiful boy and girl!"

Two white-haired cousins, the Feingolds, as lined and creased as a blanket cold with neglect, crept up to her, dim eyes more focused than usual. Slim Mrs. Feingold, from pre-War Poland, always seemed defeated by her efforts to understand the logic of her expensive, too-stylish clothes.

"So?" she asked. That meant Mark, of course, who was off across the chattering lobby, talking to a couple Brenda didn't recognize. "How long you know him?"

"A few months."

"Get married."

Brenda laughed.

"You'll work, he'll work, it will be okay."

Expressionless, Mr. Feingold said, "Wait."

"What wait?" his wife snapped, not turning to him.

"When I get married," Brenda said warmly, "you'll know."

"Good." Mrs. Feingold stretched up to kiss at Brenda's cheek and moved away.

"Wait," her husband told Brenda, as flatly as someone in a bakery ordering a loaf of bread.

In a few blurred hours, she was in Nat's room, already wishing she didn't have to fast through tomorrow night. Mark was down in the basement guest room, maybe already asleep.

"I loved it!" Nat whispered, pushing both hands through his hair.

"It's not a game. People take it seriously. They thought he was my date. Mom did, or she wants to."

"So did Dad, but he doesn't like Mark." Nat smiled at having reached their father once again by annoying him, even indirectly. It was, Brenda knew, his surest and sometimes only way of making an impact.

She wanted to say, "No more. I don't want to hear about it, I don't want to get involved." But she *was* involved.

She couldn't sleep later and wished she was one of those people who had elaborate strategies for conquering insomnia—like meditation, or a bath, followed by a potent weird drink—or for submitting to it. She felt helpless, afraid in her room. The dolls and stuffed animals, the Nancy Drew books, the old Beatles posters, all struck her as emblems of a past she had betrayed.

She took down the leather-bound Holy Scriptures their congregation had given her at her bat mitzvah and leafed through the thin gold-edged pages, found at last *Vayikra*, Leviticus, and looked at what she had read before with no comprehension but much embarrassment: "Thou shalt not lie with mankind as with womankind, it is an abomination." Coming after the terrible crescendo of forbidden sexual unions in those pages, and before a prohibition against bestiality, it seemed uglier, more perverse.

Her brother was an abomination. And Mark. And she did not protest or understand—it was impossible to picture them.

She felt unbearably *hungry*. Brenda went out softly to the living room and found her mother there, reading a mystery with only one lamp on.

"The New Year—and fasting!—makes me a little restless, and a mystery helps . . . you know everything works out very nicely."

Brenda joined her.

Setting down the book, her mother asked, "Mark is how old?"

"Thirty-five."

"Not bad, five years. I know, I know. I'm not talking about marriage, but even dating."

"He's just a friend."

"The age can make a difference," her mother went on, "he's getting older. It changes you sometimes. Life isn't so open anymore. You can get angry, or scared, maybe. But he doesn't look like that. He's happy. That's good."

It was a rare moment of listening for Brenda; usually, she tuned her mother out or ended up snapping at insults she half-imagined.

"We won't date, Mom."

"Why not? He has somebody?"

"He's divorced."

"So? One mistake doesn't mean you retire."

"Do you like him?"

Her mother nodded. "Except, he should be in a movie, not in my house. He's too good-looking."

They drifted off to talking about the service, and soon Brenda was kissing her good night, and as always, her mother did not object but did not really respond.

The fatigue and hunger of the next day, and her exhaustion by the time services were over and they were breaking the fast at the temple the next night, kept her from thinking about Nat and Mark too much.

Her mother had stopped nagging about Brenda's romantic life ever since the time she had said she was dating a Dutch Reformed teacher from Grand Rapids. Her mother was clever enough not to push and create a crisis by lamenting Brenda's choice. And true to form, her mother was cautious in mentioning Mark's name after Yom Kippur, but every time it came up, Brenda hated herself for lying, and hated Nat.

The day after Brenda discovered the slogans on the bridge, the campus newspaper downplayed the graffiti incident, keeping it off the front page, and making sure it was "evenhanded," Brenda guessed, by quoting students who were against the upcoming Gay Pride Day, calling it sick, perverted, and un-American (the reaction this year was worse than ever before, perhaps because of Reagan's second victory). Since those vicious comments were put in a sidebar, the article was really an editorial in disguise, damning MSU's gays and gays everywhere.

She had been afraid to call Nat because she could hear him saying, See? That's what I have to live with, and she would feel implicated, part of the world that had spit out those ugly white scrawls.

Mark phoned. "Is Natty there?"

"Why?"

"He's not in his dorm, didn't leave any message, nothing, and we were supposed to go out for dinner. Now that you're in *The State News*, though—"

"What do you mean?"

"He must've freaked when he saw what you said in the article."

"About Nat? I didn't say anything about Nat." She grabbed up the paper, trying to keep the phone to her ear, and forced herself to read more slowly than she had before. And then she found it, the phrase: "My brother's gay!" That punk green-haired reporter had heard her, had written it down. . . .

"Oh my God. I was so upset, I—"

"Nat didn't want to come out, but you did it for him."

Mark sounded so measured and calm, she asked him to drive over, quickly, as if he could somehow save her from her own guilt and shock. She felt suddenly stiff with fear: what if something had happened to Nat, someone had beaten him up, pushed him off one of the bridges, run him down? It happened, she knew it happened all the time—just not here at MSU, not yet.

When Mark walked in fifteen minutes later, she hugged him, held on as if *he* were her brother, an older brother who could speak soothing platitudes that would tranquilize *any* pain.

"You should sit down." Mark sat by her, held her hand.

"There's nothing terrible you can say to me I haven't said since I hung up." She slapped both hands to her forehead, covering her eyes, starting to rock and cry, able to let go now that she was no longer alone. Waiting for him, she had felt like a traitor, branded by her own shame.

Mark slipped an arm around her.

"He won't hate you, you know. He might even be glad."

"But it wasn't mine to tell," she said.

"Some people might hassle him at the dorm, but he isn't over there that much, and he's got a single." He shrugged. "You know, the janitor at my apartment complex figured us out real quick, and once when we were leaving the apartment, I heard him down the hall say something to another workman about hating faggots near him."

"Nat didn't tell me!"

Mark smiled. "He probably didn't think you would listen."

"What happened?"

Mark leaned back with the ease of someone in a mammoth dark library in an English country house, twirling brandy in a snifter, wreathed in cigar smoke. "I said, real loud, 'Don't worry, you'll be fine, most gays don't like effeminate men.' "

Brenda laughed like a delighted child discovering a present under her pillow, clapping her hands. "Wasn't he furious?"

"Sure—but he was such a scrawny sonofabitch, so was his buddy. What could they do to me, *or* Nat?" He was right, she knew. Nat had taken to working out with Mark so seriously in the last six months that he already had a different body, more imposing—broad-shouldered, with a firm, hard chest. His whole outline and presence had shifted.

The doorbell shot Brenda from the couch and she sprang to open the door.

Nat was standing there, smiling. "Since when did you take on public relations?"

And he hugged her, ruffled her hair. They all sat on the couch like spies who'd escaped some dangerous and unexpected blockade of a civil war by pretending to be tourists: smug, delighted with themselves, but suitably rueful. Nat had to tell her three times where he was when he read the paper, and then, how many people knew his sister taught history, and how he'd just driven around for hours that evening, unable to cry, but thinking perhaps he should, now that the secret was out, "And with a bang, *Jesus*, Bren—"

Mark went out to get a bottle of champagne. "Let's turn it into a celebration," he said, and they drank toasts to each other. She watched him as Nat might, not just someone handsome—those blue eyes!—but the center of his life now. And Nat, grinning, a little drunk, was invested with a kind of grace. She had to admit

that he was no longer so tense, so watchful, but sat with his body
open and sprawling. His face was smoothed out, relaxed, as if before
he had always been on the edge of a migraine, and she saw that he
had never really been as plain and unattractive as she believed—
merely downcast, lonely, and even unformed. He was becoming a
man, and would be quite interesting at Mark's age, she thought.

"What're you staring at?"

"You," she said. "Just you."

Mark sat on the floor, back against her couch, one arm tight
around Nat, who lay back against him, reaching up now and then
to stroke Mark's face.

As always, she couldn't help thinking how their parents would
react seeing this simple closeness, it would disgust and shame them.
Jews don't do that, they'd think. But just this past Chanukah, her
mother had told her that she finally had figured out why a friend's
daughter had moved to Argentina to teach English, deeply upsetting
her family. "She's a lesbian, Brenda," and the word sounded almost
quaint coming from her elegant mother—as old-fashioned and un-
common as *sodomite.* "She must be, remember how she never dated
much, and how her mother would always say Laura was 'different.' "
Brenda had said nothing, waiting for a judgment, a comment, but
all her mother added, while putting on her earrings, was a cool
sigh: "The world is changing."

Brenda told Mark and Nat about her first class yesterday afternoon.

"But it's not just gays," Nat said. "That black girl you told us
about, Andrena? She was wrong. I mean, maybe people wouldn't
say it in class, but you should hear guys at the dorm talk about
'niggers' and 'kikes.' This black guy on my floor told me how he
got beat up in an elevator once, it happens all the time." He looked
up at Mark. "Glad you moved here from the East Coast?"

She made them each drink several glasses of water before she
let them drive back to Mark's apartment. In the year she had known
Mark, and known about him and Nat, finally watching Nat let
himself be gay, she had relaxed a little, no longer feeling like their
bond was some ugly and mysterious blight withering a lovely spring
garden, or that she was the owner of a flawless lawn, driven wild
by discovering a network of mole tunnels one morning. Yet she

still wished that Nat and Mark hadn't been kicked out of the Orthodox *minyan* in town when people found out they were gay, wished that everything could be smoother—on the surface, anyway.

Getting ready for bed, she heard a far-off fire engine's blare, so different from the usual late-night hooting trains, and thought it would be like that for her parents when they finally found out about Nat—a crisis, an emergency in which they would probably panic, but might, just might, she was beginning to hope, rally and find some strength. Maybe they would be glad it wasn't AIDS, and even relieved that Mark was Jewish. And *such* a Jew, she said aloud, shaking her head in the bathroom mirror with a satisfied grin— *Orthodox*, even!

She was pulled from sleep by her insistent doorbell and she glared at her alarm clock as if it should have protected her from this intrusion. She shoved it off the night table, found her robe on the floor, and hurried out to the door, rubbing at her eyes.

It was Nat, sickly pale, eyes down, hands cold when she grabbed them to pull him inside. He smelled strange to her.

"It's gone," he said, drifting to her kitchen, mechanically filling the fat black teakettle with water, setting it on a burner.

His car's been stolen, she thought—or vandalized. She saw white letters of hate—and then wondered if it wouldn't happen to *her* car, too. . . .

"It's all gone. My dorm room."

She sank into a chair at the table as if his words were heavy hands weighing down her shoulders.

"I went back to get some stuff for my eight o'clock class. And from the parking lot across the street, I could see this big black hole on the first floor of the dorm. Fire, I thought, and then I saw all these puddles of sooty water and you could smell plastic, burned plastic. It was my room. Everything's gone, my clothes, the books, even the phone . . . it's melted. I found the RA, Dave, he said it happened at night—it looks like someone broke in and torched the place—and they were lucky it wasn't worse. Lucky? Someone called the fire department before the smoke alarm even went off. The marshal said it looked like arson to him, but he wasn't sure."

She realized that Nat smelled of smoke, as if he'd been in a bar all night. "Everything's gone?" She was suddenly flooded by all the terrible films she'd seen of Germany in the Thirties, with *JUDEN RAUS* ("Out with the Jews") whitewashed across Jewish-owned storefronts, synagogues collapsing in flame, religious Jews beaten, bloody, dead.

He looked at her, eyes heavy, grim. "Except this." Nat reached into his jeans pocket and tossed a two-inch black button onto the table. It had one of those Gay Liberation pink triangles she had argued with Mark about. "But you're Jewish, too!" she had said. "Don't you hate that they use something from the camps? You never see Jews wearing yellow stars in a parade!" Mark had tried to convince her that the triangle's origin was precisely the point: shocking people, reminding everyone of the worst that could happen, that *did* happen.

Now, the pink and black button glared up at her like a baleful witch in a fairy tale, gloating over the princess's crucial mistake, which was about to plunge her into darkness and slavery. Nat was telling her about the campus police, how aloof and matter-of-fact they were, even wanting to know where he had been all night, how much insurance he had, if any—and how everyone on his floor said they had no idea what had happened, hadn't heard or seen anything. Nobody would look at Nat—as if it was *his* fault, as if *he* had humiliated everyone in the dorm by not only being gay but also the victim of an attack.

"I called Mark . . . I asked him to meet me here. Okay? Is that okay?"

The teakettle—*tchynick* in Yiddish—started whistling and Brenda said in her father's Yiddish, "*Hock mir nisht kein tchynick*"—don't make such a fuss. It was stupid, not at all funny, but Nat smiled a little as he made some instant Folger's, stirred in three teaspoons of sugar, which she knew he'd given up years ago. It was as if he were retreating to the year he had begun drinking coffee—when he was fifteen, a year safe from all this.

"Nat, what can I do?"

"Just sit," he said, sipping his coffee. "Listen." And then he went through a terrible inventory of everything he'd checked and looked for in his room. She couldn't stop thinking of all the Jewish homes and apartments throughout Europe that had been looted, burned, destroyed, trainloads of plundered bloody goods snaking back to the Fatherland: mattresses, pianos, candelabras, coats.

Mark rang sharply, and pushed past her, flushed, rumpled, smelling of sleep and sweat. At first, Mark and Nat held each other's arms without hugging, peering at each other like relations meeting at an airport after forty years, not quite sure they had the right person. Then Mark embraced him, looking fierce and defiant, like a king sending off his armies to avenge his honor.

"I've been making lists of phone numbers. We're calling all the papers, the ACLU, the FBI, because it's arson. You need a lawyer."

Nat moved to the couch, sat. "I need a room."

"Couldn't we leave?" Brenda asked, arms out like an opera singer imploring the tyrant for her lover's release. "Just today—go home and get out of this place? I'll cancel my office hours. I want to go home."

Mark shook his head. "I'm staying. We've got lots to do."

"No." Nat stood up. "Brenda's right. Not today. I want you to come down to Southfield with us, so we can *all* tell them what happened before they hear about it on the news, in the paper—"

"Or in the supermarket," Brenda put in. "From a neighbor."

Mark and Nat grimaced. They decided to go back to Mark's, shower and change, and Brenda would meet them there in an hour.

Washing her hair, she thought of Scarlett O'Hara, dirty, desperate, fleeing the flames of Atlanta for her beloved Tara. For the first time she understood the longing to be released from fear by simply being someplace you loved.

She fondly pictured their enormous backyard, a full acre, blooming now thanks to the unusually warm spring. Putting on the blue silk dress that her mother said made her look like an actress, Brenda saw them all sitting out in the lacy high-peaked gazebo Nat had always dreamed about and finally gotten this last year with money he earned as a waiter. They would sit in the deep cool shade, admiring the crocuses and tulips springing up at the back of the house, and breathe in the rich sweet smell of the thirty white lilac bushes her parents had planted themselves on their thirtieth wedding anniversary. The stench of burnt clothes would be banished.

Her parents would *have* to be on Nat's side—the fire would be too familiar and threatening, like synagogue bombings, cemetery desecrations.

She slipped Nat's triangle button into her purse before she left.

She would have to ask Nat the date of Gay Pride Day, and where people would be marching and what time.

In her car, before putting her key in the ignition, she remembered how the king of Denmark had worn a yellow star when the occupying Nazis started persecuting Danish Jews.

She took out Nat's button and used the rearview mirror to help pin it to her dress.